— STORIES BY —

STORIES BY

Gao Yang

"REKINDLED LOVE"
AND
"PURPLE JADE HAIRPIN"

TRANSLATED BY CHAN SIN-WAI

The Chinese University Press

ISBN 962–201–446–1

THE CHINESE UNIVERSITY PRESS
The Chinese University of Hong Kong
SHATIN, N. T., HONG KONG

Cover: *Lady* (detail), round fan, dated 1877,
by Ju Lian (1828–1904). Courtesy of the Art Gallery,
The Chinese University of Hong Kong.

Printed in Hong Kong by Ko's Arts Printing Co., Ltd.

To
My Mother

Contents

Contents

Introduction

Xu Anping 許晏駢 (Hsü An-p'ing), better known by his pen-name Gao Yang 高陽 (Kao Yang), is one of the most prolific and respected writers in Taiwan today. Born in Hengzhou (Hangchou) and educated in Taiwan, he later served for many years as the chief editor of *Zhonghua ribao* 中華日報 (Chung-hua Daily). A firm believer in the inseparable relationship between history and literature, he has published more than fifty books that fully manifest his profound knowledge of Chinese history and his excellent mastery of the Chinese language. Broadly speaking, his works fall into three areas: fictions based on accounts of famous personalities; historical novels in late Qing settings; and studies on the *Dream of the Red Chamber*; thus making him at once an author, a historian, and a Redologist. An eminently successful author with a worldwide following, particularly in Taiwan, Mainland China, Hong Kong and in many overseas Chinese communities, he is surely one of the very few outstanding Chinese writers whose works truly deserve to be introduced to the English-reading public. The two stories translated here, "Rekindled Love" (藕絲蓮心) and "Purple Jade Hairpin" (紫玉釵), are taken from his book entitled *Purple Jade Hairpin* in which four stories, each one dealing with romantic anecdotes of famous Chinese writers, are included.

"Rekindled Love" is the story of Zheng Banqiao 鄭板橋 (Cheng Pan-ch'iao, 1693–1765) and his childhood lover Wang Yijie 王一姐 (Wang Yi-chieh). Zheng was one of the "Eight Eccentrics" of the Qing dynasty who excelled in poem-writing, calligraphy, and painting. The story begins with the unexpected reunion of Zheng and Wang after a lapse of seventeen years. Zheng was travelling through Yangzhou on his way to take part in the civil service examination when a piece of his ink painting bought by her husband Yu Shaotang 于少棠 (Yü Shao-t'ang) revealed his whereabouts to Yijie. Yijie and her husband decided that Banqiao, who was actually her cousin, should stay with them while preparing for his examination. His stay brought back many vivid memories of the past when he and Yijie were young sweethearts. Two lines in Zheng's poem reveal his feelings:

> Today, we meet again in this secluded courtyard,
> And there is a kind of tenderness as of old.
> 今日重逢深院裏，
> 一種溫存猶昔。

But his affection for Yijie was far more than that. On a sleepless night, Banqiao poured out his lovesickness in verse:

> I never ceased thinking of you;
> Through trials and tribulations dimly apprehended.
> The heart of a lotus is bitter
> When threads of its fibre resist severance.
> Though I know only too well that my soul will be crippled
>   when I see you,
> Yet my fear is that this opportunity will not be granted me.
> 顛倒思量，
> 朦朧劫數，
> 藕絲不斷蓮心苦！
> 分明一見怕魂消，
> 卻愁不到魂消處。

Banqiao knew very well that since he had his own wife, he would have to avoid rekindling his love for Yijie and would therefore have to decline their hospitality and leave as soon as he could. However, this did not work out as he had planned. Yijie was eager to have him stay. Though very little was said between the two, a strong feeling of mutual affection persisted. As Banqiao wrote in one of his poems:

> *When we are separated, I am sick with love;*
> *When we meet, I am sick with love;*
> *By myself, I feel a thousand strands of love,*
> *But when we meet among the flowers,*
> *I am unable to come out with a single word.*
>
> 不見也相思苦，
> 便見也相思苦！
> 分明背地情千縷，
> 奈花間，
> 半句也何曾吐？

On a chilly rainy autumn evening, when Yu Shaotang was away on business, Yijie and Banqiao almost lost control. Yijie confessed she couldn't live without him, and Banqiao, on the other hand, felt apologetic towards her for not taking the opportunity to marry her. They were on the point of making intimate contacts when a clap of thunder suddenly crashed around them and reminded them that those who did things against their conscience would not succeed in the examination. They held back and suppressed their impulses. In an unrelenting mood, Banqiao wrote down his feelings in these lines:

> *I watch the autumn grass grow behind my humble door,*
> *Year after year, the lane becomes more run down.*
> *A fine rain falls before the scanty window*
> *Night after night, I sit beside the solitary lamp.*

Why do the gods still stifle my plaintive words,
And prevent me from heaving a few long sighs?
Driven frantic,
I take out a hundred pieces of silk paper,
On which to write out
All the sorrows that have befallen me.

看蓬門秋草，
年年破巷，
疏窗細雨，
夜夜孤燈。
難道天公，
還箝恨口，
不許長吁一兩聲！
顛狂甚，
取烏絲百幅，
細寫淒清！

The second is the intriguing love story between a famous Tang (T'ang) poet Li Yi 李益 (748–827) and a well-known courtesan Huo Xiaoyu 霍小玉 (Huo Hsiao-yü), a granddaughter of King Huo. Attracted by her beauty and through the arrangement of match-maker Eleventh Lady Bao 鮑十一娘, Li Yi made a verbal promise to Xiaoyu that after he had passed the civil service examination he would marry her; and if he didn't, he swore to be "deserted by gods and men, and die willingly by being struck on the head by fierce ghosts". To make her feel happy and safe, he quoted Meng Jiao's 孟郊 (Meng Chiao) poem to express his love:

Your heart and my heart,
Our hearts are closely linked.
Sitting or walking,
Our hearts are closely linked;
Linked together,
For as long as a hundred years.

心心復心心，
結愛務在深。
坐結行亦結，
結盡百歲月。

But when Li Yi passed his examination, he didn't keep his promise to marry Xiaoyu. He followed the advice of his mother, who didn't know of his relationship with Xiaoyu, and began to court his cousin Lu Yuxiang 盧鬱香 (Lu Yü-hsiang). In order to get the one million cash betrothal gift to marry Yuxiang, in addition to using his own corrupt means, he sought the help of his uncle Li Kui 李揆 (Li K'uei), an exiled Prime Minister. Xiaoyu was kept in the dark and longed for the day when Li Yi would marry her. Eventually she had to sell her family heirloom — a purple jade hairpin — to keep the family going. A stranger in yellow came into the picture when he heard the sad story of Xiaoyu from her maid Huansha 浣紗 (Huan-sha). He "kidnapped" Li Yi when he came to Luoyang to marry Yuxiang, and forced him to take Xiaoyu as his wife. But Li Yi remained unmoved, and would not keep his promise made to Xiaoyu. In despair, Xiaoyu died of heartbreak in front of him. From that moment onwards, Li Yi always had the feeling of being struck on the head by a fierce ghost! In short, it is a story of an infatuated girl being deserted by a heartless man. And the heartless Li Yi was later known more for his jealousy than for his poetic talents.

In translating these two stories into English, I have received enormous help from Professor D. C. Lau of The Chinese University of Hong Kong who not only introduced me to the works of Gao Yang and suggested translating some of his stories, but also meticulously polished my translation of the first story. Due credit should also be given to Mr Stephen Soong, who made many useful suggestions in reviewing the manuscript; to Professor Roger Ames of Hawaii University, who went over part of my translation; and to Dr Mayching Kao, Curator of the Art Gallery, who provided the illustration for the cover of the book. Special thanks are due to the author Gao Yang, who kindly allowed me to print the original text and gave me the right to translate his two stories. Lastly, I owe a debt of gratitude to Mr T. L. Tsim, Director of The Chinese University Press, and his colleagues for their excellent efforts on the production of this book.

Chan Sin-wai

REKINDLED LOVE

藕絲蓮心

展開一幅畫，是墨竹，枝葉披離，佔了大半張紙；右上角一塊空白題着字，——題詞是一篇小品，寫得篇幅不夠了，就寫向枝葉間的空隙。一眼望去，滿紙糊塗，王一姐就懶得多看了。

『畫得眞不壞，字也別成一格，好，好！』

揚州人略堪溫飽，便要附庸風雅；于少棠的境況很不壞，脾氣又隨和，經常有人拿些假字畫、假古董上門，左一句『你于大爺大行家』，右一句『瞞不過你于大爺法眼』，把他捧得飄飄然忘掉了自己的身份，就不會敎人空手而回。一姐最恨她丈夫這易於受欺的性格，所以這時便故意掃他的興！

『哼！』她冷笑一聲，『你的眼力越來越高明了！你看你買回來的甚麼東西？畫不是畫，字不是字，字畫不分，還說好！有那種不懂章法行款的畫家，就有你這種「醉雷公胡劈」的「行家」。眞正叫「武大郎玩夜貓子，甚麼人玩甚麼鳥」！』

于少棠懼內，聽一姐這頓尖刻的排揎，脹紅了臉分辯：『大家都說好！這密密麻麻的字，寫得滿紙都是，好像怪，實在是新，新

Unrolled, it was an ink painting of bamboo, with branches and leaves spreading out in all directions, occupying more than half of the entire sheet of paper. At the upper righthand corner was an empty space where a poem was written. There not being enough room, the inscription was continued into the gaps between the branches and leaves. Wang Yijie on a first glance found the painting such a mess that she was inclined not to give it a second glance.

"This painting is not bad at all. And the calligraphy has a style of its own as well. It's good, really quite good!"

People of Yangzhou, when they had no problem feeding and clothing themselves, liked to pose as connoisseurs. Yu Shaotang's circumstances were comfortable, and he was an easy man to get on with. That is why people would often bring him forgeries in calligraphy and antiques, showering him with flattery such as "Mister Yu, you are a great connoisseur," "Mister Yu, one cannot pull wool over your eyes." This would go to his head and make him forget himself and these people would not be allowed to go away empty-handed. What infuriated Yijie most was her husband's gullibility, so this time she had every intention of throwing cold water over his enthusiasm.

"Humph!" she sneered. "Your eye for what is good in art is really getting sharper and sharper! Just look! What on earth is this thing that you have bought this time! It's neither painting nor calligraphy; the painting is indistinguishable from the calligraphy. And you still say it's good! When there are artists who know nothing of composition and style, then there will have to be connoisseurs like you who, like 'the drunken God of Thunder, strikes blindly with his thunderbolts.' It truly illustrates the saying, 'It's like Wu the Elder finding sport with the night owl — there is a bird to suit every kind of person.'"

Scolded by his wife with such biting sarcasm, the henpecked Yu Shaotang turned crimson but, nevertheless, defended himself, "Everybody says he is good! The characters peppering the painting

就好。這個姓鄭的畫家，架子大得很；不高興畫，再大的面子，再多的潤筆也不行。』說到這裏，他忽然覺得委屈，『我好不容易才弄了一張來，妳就說兩句好的，讓我高興高興吶！偏偏就是兜頭一盆冷水！』

平日相處，一姐雖佔慣了上風，卻不是蠻不講理的悍潑婦人，聽丈夫這樣訴苦，不免生出歉意；同時覺得這姓鄭的畫家，人品似乎很高。便攏着鬢髮笑道：『你說得他這麼好，我倒不相信——只怪你上的當太多了！』

『吃虧就是便宜，上的當多，無意中才有好東西到手。這姓鄭的畫家，跟妳是同鄉，現在紅得很。』

一姐突然心中一動，姓鄭、同鄉、會畫畫、脾氣又怪！『嗨，』她問，『這姓鄭的叫甚麼名字？』

『叫鄭板橋。』

這就不對了！一姐仔細去看畫上的下款，找了半天才在竹根縫裏找到，題的是『板橋道人』四個字；字也不像。

『鄭板橋是秀才！這篇題詞就不壞。』于少棠因爲一姐的詞色，興致又好了；琅琅然唸着題詞，居然沒有讀成破句。

余家有茆屋二間，南面種竹，夏日新篁初放，綠陰照人，置

may look odd, but they are novel in style. And novelty is good. This painter Zheng has a high opinion of himself. If he is not in the mood, he won't paint for you however influential you are and however much you pay him." At this, he suddenly felt trampled upon. "You should have seen the difficulties I was up against in trying to get a painting of his. It would not have hurt you to say a nice thing or two to make me feel happy, but you would have to pour cold water on me!"

Though Yijie was used to getting the upper hand over her husband, she was not a shrew who would not listen to reason. On hearing the plaintive tone of her husband, she felt a bit guilty. Moreover, she got the impression that this painter Zheng was a man of integrity. So she passed her hand over her hair and said with a smile, "You've made him out to be so good that it is difficult to believe it — it is because you've been cheated so often that I am sceptical."

"To be taken in is in itself an advantage. You have to be cheated many times before something good will come your way. This painter Zheng comes from your native place. He is very much sought after."

Suddenly a chord was struck — Zheng by name, from my native place, a painter, and an eccentric.

"Hey, what is Zheng's first name?" she asked.

"His name is Zheng Banqiao."

That wasn't right. Yijie searched for the signature on the painting, and it was some time before she could make out in the space between the roots of the bamboo the four characters: Banqiao the Taoist. The calligraphy didn't look like Zheng's either.

"Zheng Banqiao is a *xiucai*! This inscription is not a bad piece of composition at all."

Yu Shaotang perked up at the slightest show of consideration on Yijie's part. He intoned the inscription out loud, and, quite incredibly, read it through without making any wrong pauses:

At home I have two thatched cottages. To the south are

一小榻其中，甚涼適也。秋冬之際，取圍屏骨子，斷去兩頭，橫安以爲窗櫺。用勻薄潔白之紙糊之，風和日暖，凍蠅觸窗紙上，鼕鼕作小鼓聲。於時一片竹影零亂，豈非天然圖畫乎？凡吾畫竹，無所師承，多得于紅窗粉壁，日光月影中耳！

『怪不得！這是竹影。一姐——！』于少棠回頭看到妻子，頗爲詫異，『妳怎麼了？是不是不舒服？人在發燒，眼睛發定。』

從沉思中驚醒的一姐，由她丈夫的話中，才意識到自己在這片刻間，心底已經掀起萬丈波瀾。定神想一想，決無瞞着丈夫的道理；而要說也就在此時了。

『你倒去打聽看，這鄭板橋單名是不是一個燮字？燮理陰陽的燮；號叫克柔。』

于少棠越發詫異，『妳曉得這鄭板橋？』他問，『你們認識？』

『現在還不曉得。大概不錯；他家是幾間茆屋，前面種好些竹子。』

『那是認識的囉？』

『如果是他，就是我的表兄。』

planted bamboo. In summer, when the new clumps of bamboo first appeared, they cast a lush shade under which one can take refuge. A small chez-lounge placed in the grove would be so cool and comfortable. At the end of autumn, one takes the frames from the folding screens, cuts them off at either end, and places them horizontally to serve as window frames for the cottages. One pastes thin white paper of even thickness over them. In the breeze under a warm sun, the near frozen flies would strike against the window paper, making a sound like the beating of a drum. At such a time, there would be a mass of confused bamboo shadows. Would this not make a natural picture? When I paint bamboo, I don't follow any master, but draw great inspiration from light and shadow cast by sun and moon on red windows and painted walls.

"No wonder! ... these are the *shadows* of bamboo! Yijie ..." Yu Shaotang, seeing his wife on turning round, was rather taken aback. "What is the matter? Are you unwell? You seem feverish with staring eyes."

Yijie was awakened from her reverie. Only with the words of her husband was she aware that in the brief interval a tempest had raged in her heart. She composed herself and, after a brief moment of reflection, came to the conclusion that there was no cause for secrecy and this was the right moment to speak out.

"Go and ask around and see if this man Zheng Banqiao has a single-character given-name, Xue, meaning 'Harmony', as in 'harmonizing the *yin* and *yang*, and see if his style-name is not Kerou: 'Overcoming the pliable?'"

Yu Shaotang was getting more and more perplexed. "You know this man Zheng Banqiao?" He asked. "You two know each other?"

"I am not sure yet. I am unlikely to be mistaken. Where he lived, there were several thatched cottages, in front of which there was a lot of bamboo."

"In that case you must be acquainted?"

"If it is him, he is my cousin and is older than me."

　　『表兄！』于少棠目炯炯地望着，『這不曾聽妳說過，有這麼一個親戚？』

　　『我的親戚多了！』一姐嫌他多問，嗓子不由得就高了，『那能都說給你聽，況且又是遠房的表親！』

　　于少棠的性情最溫和不過，陪着笑說：『何必又發脾氣？妳有這麼一位表兄，連我也有面子。我馬上去打聽。奶奶，我請妳的示，打聽確實了，怎麼說？是不是把他請到家來？』

　　『那還用說？親戚難道不認！』

　　『妳沒有弄明白我的意思。我是說，把他請到家來住。』

　　『也還不知道人家的意思怎麼樣？』一姐用裁決的語氣說，『這都再談！此刻不忙。你先去打聽了來！』

　　應南闈鄉試，路過揚州的鄭板橋，怎麼也沒有想到跟王一姐還有重見的日子。

　　引入曲曲的深院，在燁燁的紅燭照耀之下，他無論如何不能相信，眼前這位豐腴的盛裝麗人，就是當年胭脂點額，慣作男孩兒裝束的遠房表妹。視線所及，沒有一樣略微熟悉的東西，可以為他喚起比較生動清晰的回憶。朦朧的不僅是往日，也是此刻！

　　『表哥！』

"Cousin!" Yu Shaotang gazed at his wife in amazement. "How is it you've never said anything about having such a relative?"

"I've got lots and lots of relatives." Yijie, annoyed with his questioning, raised her voice. "How can I tell you about all of them? And anyway, this one is only a remote cousin."

Yu Shaotang was a man of the gentlest disposition, so smiling apologetically he said, "There is nothing to be upset about.That you have such an illustrious cousin reflects credit on me as well. I'll ask around immediately. Madam, what is your pleasure? If it turns out to be true, what am I to do? Do you want to invite him here?"

"Of course! How could we do otherwise with a relative!"

"You haven't got my meaning. I mean, do we invite him for a stay with us?"

"We don't even know how he feels." Yijie said with decision. "All this we can discuss later on. There is no rush. First go and find out whether it is him or not."

 It never occurred to Zheng Banqiao who was passing by Yangzhou on his way to participate in the provincial civil service examination in the south that he would again see Wang Yijie.

Led into a quiet winding hall, Zheng Banqiao, under the light of the radiant red candles, simply could not believe that this plump and regally attired elegant lady with the full figure standing before his eyes was the same distant cousin who, in the old days, used to put rouge on her forehead and dress like a boy. Nothing within sight had even the most remote familiarity to summon up a vivid memory of the past. But not only were those past days in a haze, so was the present moment.

"Cousin."

終於有了熟悉的東西！叫『表哥』的聲音是顯得莊重了，但第一個字重，第二個字促，依然是當年把他呼來喚去的語氣。

『一姐！』他仍舊不改稱呼，『認不得妳了。妳完全改了樣子。十六年不見——。』

『十七年。』一姐糾正他說，『十七年不見，想不到從畫上訪着了你。請坐！秋兒，快泡茶，端果盤來！』

看得出她也不免有陌生之感，而且有意矜持；除卻盈盈欲流，時時關注的眼波，鄭板橋所看到的，只是一位日子過得很稱心的能幹主婦。她在指揮婢僕款客的同時，問訊鄭家上下，正是那種至親久別重逢所應該有的周旋。

于少棠插不進話去，一姐似乎也忘卻了丈夫在座；但這樣反倒是他求之不得的事；從他們表兄妹絮絮不斷的敘舊中，他對他的妻子有了較多的了解——十幾年夫婦相處，不如此一刻作為旁觀者所得到的多！窗前枕上，問起她的過去，她總搖搖頭，表示沒有甚麼可談的。這是為甚麼？為了她對她父親的抗議，以不談過去作為對娘家恩斷義絕的表示？

早幾年，于少棠常常這樣在想；而每一想到，總覺得對死去的岳父，懷着無可彌補的歉意。在一姐看，甚至在旁人看，做父親的

At last, something familiar. The voice that called out "cousin" sounded somehow more dignified, but the stressed first syllable with the clipped second was unchanged from the way she used to summon and dismiss him in the old days.

"Yijie!" He too kept unchanged his manner of addressing her. "I couldn't recognize you. You've changed completely. It's been sixteen years ..."

"Seventeen," corrected Yijie. "It's been seventeen years, and who would have thought that it was a painting that led me on to you. Please, sit down! Qiu'er, go and make us some tea and bring some nuts."

He could see that she too was overcome by this sense of being strangers but that she was deliberately keeping her composure. Apart from a glance of concern every now and then from eyes that were ever expressive, what Zheng Banqiao saw was simply a competent housewife in comfortable circumstances. The way she gave orders to the maids to make her guest comfortable while asking after other members of the Zheng family was precisely the ways relatives would greet each other meeting for the first time after a long lapse of time.

Yu Shaotang could not get a word in, and Yijie seemed to have completely forgotten his presence. But this surprisingly was just what he wanted. From the seemingly endless reminiscences of these two cousins, he gained a clearer understanding of his wife. He got more by playing the onlooker in these brief moments than he had from the dozen years they had lived together as husband and wife. Whenever in their more intimate moments he had asked her about her past, she invariably dismissed the subject by a shake of the head and said there was nothing worth talking about. Why was this? Was it a protest against her father? Was her unwillingness to talk about the past a symbol of her break with her family?

Several years ago, Yu Shaotang had frequently thought that was the case. And every time he thought about it, he inevitably felt he owned his late father-in-law a debt of conscience he could never

不是個好父親；而唯獨自己，不但要感激，也還該佩服，永遠記着
岳父是個信義君子，不肯賴賭帳的硬漢──。

　　『少棠！我欠得你多了；你雖不說，我心裏拋不開。我的女兒
你見過的，我把她許了給你；嫁粧、聘金，彼此兩免。』

　　就這麼片言之下，了掉了一姐的終身大事。雖然是明媒正娶，
而且于少棠也從未有過花錢買了個老婆的想法；但他知道，一姐總
覺得是她老子賣了女兒！娘家絕情，她也斷義；事實上從他岳父在
運河船上，半夜裏起身到船頭上小解，失足落水而死以後，她似乎
也沒有甚麼娘家人了。

　　如今方知不然！她還有娘家的表兄；而且她似乎也不恨娘家──
也許，于少棠在想，是表兄的緣故。如果是她的同胞手足，反容易
讓她記起恨事。

『表哥！』一姐有些酒意了，偏着紅馥馥的臉，大聲說
道：『你的人跟你的字一樣，都變過了！』

　　『我的字變過了，我知道。我不知道我這個人怎麼
變了？二十年來，依然故我。』

repay. To Yijie, and even to a bystander outside, her father could hardly be called a good father. But to him alone, his father-in-law was not only deserving of his full gratitude, but also of his admiration. He always remembered him as a gentleman of his word, as a strong character who would not renege on a gambling debt.

"Shaotang! I am too much in your debt. You don't say anything, but I cannot put it out of my mind. You've met my daughter; I'll give her to you. No dowry, no bethrothal gifts. Neither of us owes the other anything any more."

It was these few brief words that sealed the fate of Yijie's future. It was a proper marriage arranged by a go-between with all the ceremonials observed, and it never entered Yu Shaotang's head that he had bought his wife with money. But he knew that Yijie always felt that her father had sold his daughter. If her family was so heartless, why should she not repudiate them? In fact, ever since the night that his father-in-law, going to the front of the boat to urinate, had lost his footing and his life, she seemed to have no relatives at all.

Only now did he realize that this was not the case! She still had this cousin, and she didn't seem to hate her family. Perhaps, thought Yu Shaotang, it's because he was a cousin. If he had been a brother, her resentment might have been easier to stir up.

3   "Cousin," Yijie, a bit tipsy and tilting her blushing face to one side, said in a rather loud voice, "You and your calligraphy are the same — both have changed."

"I know my calligraphy has changed. But I don't know that I myself have changed that much. I am very much my old self in the last twenty years."

『從前——，』一姐凝視着他，『我總覺得你心裏有話不肯說，拘拘謹謹的；不比現在，有點兒——，有點兒狂態！』

『狂態？』鄭板橋笑了，『妳不曉得讀過兩句書的人，到了揚州，不狂也要狂了。』

『嗯，嗯！』于少棠大爲點頭，『表哥這句話有點意思。』

『我倒不懂！』一姐問道：『甚麼意思？』

『揚州人多的是銅臭，少的是書香。物稀爲貴，自然要狂，也應該要狂！』

出語倒不俗！鄭板橋心裏在想，爲何一姐神色之間，總有才女嫁了市儈的那種委屈？

『表哥，你莫聽他的，他是個「名士迷」。』一姐忽然換了副鄭重的神色，『只有從科場上去巴結，才是正途。試期快到了，你總也要靜下心來，用幾天功才好！』

『原是靜不下心來。再說——。』鄭板橋搖着頭，不肯再說下去。

就不說，一姐和她丈夫也能猜得到，鄭板橋上有祖母，下有妻女，光是靠敎幾個蒙童如何度日？旣然畫出了名，便得賣畫，不賣畫何以爲生；要賣畫又那裏來的功夫讀書？

夫婦倆對看了一眼，取得了默契。一姐便說：『表哥，我有個計較；你搬了我這裏來住——現成的客房，今夜就不必回去了。少棠

"In the past ..." Yijie gazed at him, "I always had the feeling that you kept things to yourself and refused to be out with them. But now you're different. A bit ... a little wild!"

"Wild!" laughed Zheng Banqiao. "Don't you know that anyone who can read at all will be wild when he finds himself in Yangzhou!"

"Mh-hmh!" nodded Yu Shaotang approvingly. "You have got a point."

"But I don't follow," said Yijie. "What is the point?"

"What the people in Yangzhou have in plenty is the stench of money, but what they lack is the fragrance of books. Rarity adds to the value of things. One is naturally wild and justifiably wild here."

His sentiments were those of a cultured man. Zheng Banqiao was wondering why in her countenance Yijie wore the frustration of a blue stocking who had been given in marriage to a tradesman.

"Cousin, don't listen to him. He is Bohemian-crazy." Yijie suddenly put on a solemn countenance. "The only proper path to advancement lies in the halls of the civil service examination. It will soon be examination time. You ought to settle down for a few days' study."

"The problem is I can't get settled. Moreover,..." Zheng Banqiao shook his head and would not say anything more .

Even with his silence, Yijie and her husband could guess what the reason was. Zheng Banqiao had a grandmother, a wife and a daughter to look after. How could he get by on the tuition fees he received from the few prep school pupils he taught? Since he had made a reputation for his painting, he had to sell his works to earn a living. Having to sell his paintings for a living, where could he find time to study?

The husband and wife exchanged glances and came to a tacit understanding. So Yijie said, "Cousin, I have an idea. You move in here and stay with us. We've a guest room ready; there is no need for you to go back even tonight. Shaotang has a few hundred taels

有幾百兩銀子，是別人寄存的；不要利息的錢，你借了去用。百事不管，好歹在書本兒上「啃」它兩個月，等鄉試過後再說。那怕中個副榜，也教你家那個赤膽忠心的費媽笑一笑！』

提起費媽，鄭板橋的眼圈便紅了。

費媽是他祖母的陪房丫頭，也是他的乳母。

鄭板橋四歲喪母，就靠費媽撫養。那兩年鬧災荒，鄭板橋的父親又宦遊在外，不能按時接濟家用；費媽和她丈夫，在外面做工餬口，到晚來回鄭家操持家務。每天一早揹着鄭板橋出門，先用一文錢買個燒餅放在他手裏，找個安靜地方把他安頓好了，才去做自己的事。她自己也有個兒子，比鄭板橋大着好幾歲；但凡有食物，不論精粗，總是先餵鄭板橋。這樣四、五年下來，費媽的丈夫看看不是路數，決定帶着妻兒去另覓生計。費媽不肯；夫婦倆回到鄭家來不作聲，在外面天天吵架。

of silver some people deposited with him for safe keeping. It is interest-free money. You can have it on loan. Put aside everything. Just bury yourself in your books for a couple of months, and leave everything till after the provincial examination. Even if you only make the supplementary list, it will still bring a smile to the lips of Mother Fei who has been such a loyal servant to your family."

Zheng Banqiao was on the verge of tears at the mention of Mother Fei.

Mother Fei was the maid his grandmother brought with her when she married into the Zheng family, and was also his wet nurse.

Zheng Banqiao had lost his mother when he was four, and it was Mother Fei who took on his upbringing. There were those two years of famine. Zheng Banqiao's father was away wherever his official duties took him, and could not always get money to them at regular intervals. Mother Fei and her husband found work outside to help make ends meet, and returning in the evening they would attend to the household responsibilities. Every day early in the morning, with Zheng Banqiao on her back Mother Fei went out to work. She would first buy a sesame-seed cake for one cash and putting it in his hand, she would then settle him in a quiet spot before going off to her own work. She also had a son who was quite a few years older than Zheng. But whenever there was anything to eat, good or bad, she would always feed Zheng first. After four or five years, her husband, feeling that they simply couldn't go on in this way any longer, decided to look elsewhere for a livelihood with his wife and son. Mother Fei wouldn't have it. The couple would stay quiet when in the house, but quarrelled about it incessantly outside.

鄭板橋不知道他們吵些甚麼？只見費媽無緣無故流淚不止，每天找出他祖母的舊衣服來，補的補、洗的洗；廚房中水缸裏的水，總是汲得滿滿地；灶下也突然堆了幾十把柴。然後有一天清早，鄭板橋發現費媽不見了！她住的那間屋中，除了一副床板，兩樣破舊家具以外，空空如也；而灶灰猶溫，揭開鍋蓋來看，裏面一小缽飯，一碗小鹹魚煮豆腐，正是他每天吃慣了的早飯。

鄭板橋放聲大哭！平生第一遭識得一個悲字！

不過三年功夫，竟想不到地，費媽又回到了鄭家，她說她的兒子已經中了武舉，娶了妻子，可以自立；因爲不放心十二歲的鄭板橋和六十多歲的老主母，所以回鄭家來住。第二年，她的兒子做了江南水師提督衙門駐京的『提塘官』，幾次奉迎她去享福，她始終不肯；至今整整二十年，已是白髮盈顛了。

他知道白髮乳母一生的志願是甚麼？爲了她，他覺得也不能不聽從一姐的勸告。

『表哥！』于少棠很懇切地說：『今年秋天得意，自然是北上趕明年的會試，一舉成名天下知！前前後後，沒有五百兩銀子過不了門；家用總也要百把兩銀子。這樣，我借六百兩銀子給你，等你得

Zheng Banqiao had no idea what they were quarrelling about. What he could see was that Mother Fei was constantly in tears for no apparent reason. Day after day she took out his grandmother's old clothes, and mended those that needed mending and washed those that needed washing. The water crock in the kitchen was always filled to the brim, and scores of firewood bundles suddenly appeared under the kitchen range. One morning, bright and early, Zheng Banqiao discovered that Mother Fei was nowhere to be seen. In the room where she had lived, apart from an empty bed and two items of old furniture, there was nothing. But the ashes in the kitchen range were still warm. And when he lifted the lid of the pot, there was a small bowl of rice, a bowl of small salted fish cooked with bean curds — his usual breakfast, in fact.

Zheng Banqiao howled without abandon. This was the first time in his life he tasted the bile of sorrow.

After less than three years, Mother Fei unexpectedly came back to the Zheng family. She said that her son had already passed the military examination and had taken himself a wife, so he could stand on his own feet. Being anxious about the twelve-year-old Zheng Banqiao and his sexagenarian grandmother, she had come back to be with them. The following year, her son was made a liaison officer of the Jiangnan Admiral's Office stationed in the capital. He several times asked her to go and lead a life of ease and plenty, but she steadily refused. These twenty years have elapsed and she has become hoary-headed.

He knew what his hoary-headed wet nurse's lifelong wish was. For her sake alone, he felt obliged to listen to the advice of Yijie.

"Cousin!" Yu Shaotang said in great earnestness, "If you are successful at the examination this autumn, needless to say, you'll go north to take part in the metropolitan examination next year, and at one stroke, you'll be known to the world over. All in all, you can't manage on less than five hundred taels of silver. And you will also need a hundred taels of silver or so for household expenses. Now, I can lend you the six hundred taels of silver, and you can

意了再還我。』

　　六百兩銀子在鄭板橋看，不是一個小數。果然鄉試中舉，會試
聯捷，自有親戚故舊幫忙；但『場中莫論文』，功名遲早，誰也沒有
把握，『落第歸來，卻又拿甚麼來還債？』他問。

　　『那也不要緊。』于少棠笑道：『「閒來寫幅丹青賣，不使人間
造孽錢」，你畫畫還我！』

　　『對了！』一姐不待他開口，便替他作了決定，『就是這樣子
辦！』說着，她自己先滿意地笑了，深深的一個酒渦，猶見當年的
嬌態。

　　　　　　　等一個人靜下來，鄭板橋發覺記憶中的一姐，比當面眼
　　　　　　　見更來得清晰，『今日重逢深院裏，一種溫存猶昔！』脫
　　　　　　　口吟出這兩句，隨之便湧現一番詞的境界，趁着酒興，
　　　　　　　剔亮了油燈，取張花箋，打開墨盒，抽出枝筆試了試，
也還趁手，興致就越發好了。

pay me back when you passed the examination."

To Zheng Banqiao, six hundred taels of silver was no small sum of money. If in fact he were to be successful in the provincial and metropolitan examinations, many a relative and old friend would be too glad to help him out. However, "facility in writing is not the only thing that counts in the examination hall," and no one could be sure when his ship would come in. "How would I repay you if I failed in the examination?" he asked.

"That's not important." Yu Shaotang said with a smile. "As the saying goes, 'Selling a scroll painted in an idle moment, one can afford to thumb one's nose at ill-forgotten wealth in this sordid world.' Pay me back with your paintings."

"That's right!" Before he could open his mouth, Yijie had already made the decision for him. "That's settled then!" But even before she spoke she was beaming with satisfaction, and in her deeply etched dimple was the graceful beauty of those days gone by.

 When he was alone with his thoughts, Zheng Banqiao discovered that the Yijie of his memory was more vivid than the Yijie right there before his eyes.

"Today, we meet again in this secluded courtyard,
And there is a kind of tenderness as of old."

On blurting out these two lines, a wave of poetic inspiration flooded over him. Taking advantage of the mood created by the wine, he turned up the oil lamp, took out a piece of flower-patterned paper, opened his ink pot, selected a brush that was responsive to his touch and the mood waxed in him. Starting his thoughts

從二十年前想起，句隨意到，很順利地填成了一闋《金縷曲》：

> 竹馬相過日，
> 還記汝雲鬟覆顋，
> 胭脂點額，
> 阿母扶攜翁負背，
> 幻作兒郎粧飾。
> 小則小寸心憐惜，
> 放學歸來猶未晚，
> 向紅樓存問春消息，
> 問我索，
> 畫眉筆。
>
> 廿年湖海長爲客，
> 都付與風吹夢杳，
> 雨荒雲隔。
> 今日重逢深院裏，
> 一種溫存猶昔，
> 添多少周旋形跡。
> 回首當年嬌小態，
> 但片言微忤容顏赤，
> 只此意，
> 最難得！

寫完重讀一遍，自覺近乎隔靴搔癢。凝神細想，這首詞的毛病出在自己隱藏了感情；旣以自遣，何苦如此？於是回憶着從于少棠口中得知芳訊，一直到久別重逢的感想，信手寫下一首《踏莎行》：

from twenty years ago, he wrote down what was dictated by his thoughts. Effortlessly, he composed a song entitled "The Golden Thread":

> In the days when we were children together riding on bamboo sticks,
> I still remember, your flossy hair hiding your neck.
> With a rouge spot upon your forehead,
> You trotted by side of mother,
> And rode piggy back on your father.
> Transformed by being dressed like a boy.
> A little girl you may have been,
> But my heart was filled with tenderness for you.
> On returning home from school it was not yet too late,
> To go to the red tower,
> To see how you were faring.
> And you would demand from me a pencil for your eyebrows.
>
> These twenty years of wandering across lakes and seas,
> Blown away by the wind like a dream,
> And we have been separated like rain and clouds.
> Today we meet again in this secluded courtyard,
> And there is a kind of tenderness as of old.
> Touched by traces of the worldly,
> I remember the petite beauty of those years
> Who would flush angry at the least offending word.
> There was a feeling
> That cannot be recaptured.

When he finished, he read over what he wrote, and felt that he had failed to hit the mark. He concentrated his mind and after long and hard thought discovered that the trouble with this poem was that he was hiding his true feelings. Since he had written it as catharsis, what was the point in such concealment? So recollecting what he felt from the time he learned of her whereabouts from Yu Shaotang to the time he met her after all these years, he dashed off

中表姻親，
詩文情愫，
十年幼小嬌相護。
不須燕子引人行，
畫堂到得重重戶。

顛倒思量，
朦朧劫數，
藕絲不斷蓮心苦！
分明一見怕魂消，
卻愁不到魂消處。

如今是到得『魂消處』了！卻不辨自己是何心情？枕上遐思，飛向畫牆西畔，不知道一姐與于少棠此刻作何光景？是同床異夢，還是顛倒鸞鳳？

怎會想他們『同床異夢』？鄭板橋深深自譴，猜忌無端，其心可鄙！然而想像他們『顛倒鸞鳳』時，心裏決更不是滋味。

忘不掉，推不開，可又想不下去。他深悔失計，不該相見！只今補過不晚，到明朝辭謝諸般好意，即日渡江，到金陵覓一處冷寺讀書，靜等秋闈下場。

another song entitled "Hiking through the Suo Grass":

We were cousins to each other
Our feelings were conveyed in sweet verses.
As a child for ten years
I took you under my protection.
I needed no swallows to lead my way;
Through the main hall, I reached your door.
I never ceased thinking of you;
Through trials and tribulations dimly apprehended.
The heart of a lotus is bitter
When threads of its fibre resist severance.
Though I know only too well that my soul will be crippled
    when I see you,
Yet my fear is that this opportunity will not be granted me .

Now, he had arrived at the point where his soul would melt away! But he couldn't make out his own mood. His thoughts were wild and fanciful as he lay on his pillow and flew over the western boundary of the painted wall. He wondered what Yijie and Shaotang were up to at this very moment. Were they sharing the same bed dreaming different dreams, or were they locked together in the ecstasy of their love-making?

How could he think that they were sharing the same bed and dreaming different dreams? Zheng Banqiao condemned himself for being so contemptible as to indulge in unfounded suspicion. But when he imagined them locked together in ecstatic love-making, jealousy gnawed at his heart.

He couldn't rid himself of the thought, he couldn't put it aside, nor could he go on with it. He regretted bitterly his miscalculation; he should never have come to see her again. It wasn't too late to remedy the situation. Tomorrow morning, he would decline their kindness and hospitality, cross the river at once, go to Nanjing and find a temple in some remote region, pursue his studies there and wait quietly for the autumn examination.

到明朝，醒來，一時想不起身在何處？窗外陰沉沉地，雨聲淅瀝；五月江城，沒個放晴的時候，鄭板橋第一念便是懶得動。但想到是在于家，想到昨夜枕上所作的決定，一顆心往下一沉，强自振作着，一仰身坐了起來，毅然拋開一切雜念，只是想着，洗一把臉就告辭，不再作片刻勾留。

人剛下床，就聽得房門上剝啄聲響，門外有人問道：『鄭大爺起身了？』

『是的！』鄭板橋答應着去開了房門。

門外是秋兒，一照面便含笑說道：『鄭大爺睡得失眽了！奶奶來看過三趟。面湯水冷了，等我去換了來。』

『喔！』鄭板橋望着窗外的炊烟，愧歉地解釋：『只爲換了張床，直到聽見鷄叫才睡着！妳家大爺呢？』

『上鹽棧去了。』秋兒又說：『奶奶在廚房裏，等我去通知她。』

『好！請妳告訴她，說我馬上就要走了。』

『怎麼？』秋兒把長辮子一甩，睜大了一雙稚氣的眼問：『奶奶說，鄭大爺在這裏有兩個月住；今天特爲搭好了案板，要叫裁縫來家替鄭大爺做衣服，怎麼說要走了？』

『是的，要走了。我有要緊事；過些日子再到妳家來作客。』

秋兒困惑地望了望，轉身去換洗臉水；鄭板橋透了口氣坐下來，知道要走還得費一番唇舌，說不定還會鬧得不歡而散。想想實在懊

 The following morning, when Zheng Banqiao woke up, for a moment he couldn't remember where he was. Outside, it was gloomy and the rain was pattering against the window. May in this riverside town was not a time for clear skies. Zheng's first thought was to stay in bed. But when he remembered he was at the home of the Yu's, and that last night he had made a decision while lying there, his heart sank. With a spring, he sat up, and resolutely cast aside all distracting thoughts. His only thought was to make his apologies as soon as he had a wash , and not to linger a moment longer than was necessary.

Just as he got out of bed, he heard a tap on the door and someone ask from outside, "Are you up, Mister Zheng?"

"Yes!" Zheng Banqiao answered as he went to open the door.

Outside was the maid Qiu'er. Upon seeing him, she said with a smile, "Mister Zheng, you overslept! My lady has been here three times. The water in the wash basin has got cold. Let me change it for you."

"My!" Zheng Banqiao looked at the smoke from the kitchen chimney outside his window, and explained apologetically, "It was because of the change of bed. I couldn't get to sleep until I heard the cock crow! Where's your master?"

"He's gone to the godown." Qiu'er added, "Lady is in the kitchen. Let me go and tell her."

"All right. Please tell her that I am leaving immediately."

"What's the matter?"asked Qiu'er, with a swing of her pigtail, and her childlike eyes opened wide. "Lady said that you, sir, were staying here for two months. Today, she specially set up the work bench and has sent for the tailor to make clothes for you. Why is it you say you are leaving?"

"Yes, I have to go. I have some important business to attend to. After a while I shall come again for a longer visit."

Qiu'er gave him a bewildered look, and then turned around to go and change the water. Zheng Banqiao sat down with a breath of relief. He knew that if he wanted to go he had a lot of explaining to

惱，自己恨自己，昨天不該那麼輕率地留了下來。

聽得腳步聲響，他先就把一顆心懸了起來，但出乎意外地，仍是秋兒，並不見一姐趕來留客，這就不明白她是甚麼意思了！想想放不下心，忍不住問一句：『妳跟妳家奶奶說過了，說我馬上要走？』

『說過了。』秋兒答道，『奶奶點點頭，沒有作聲。』

這該怎麼辦呢？鄭板橋深感困擾。洗完了臉，只見秋兒端了一壺茶來；接着匆匆地又轉身入內，容不得他有所發問，而他也不知道自己有甚麼話可說？

『鄭大爺！』再度現身的秋兒來傳話：『奶奶叫我來問，鄭大爺是先吃點心，還是就吃午飯？快放午炮了，飯馬上就開。』

『我兩樣都不吃。我馬上要走；眞的馬上要走！』

秋兒依然不多說一句，回身入內。這一去，便有好些時候不見蹤影。鄭板橋有着上不上，下不下，身子懸在半空中的那種苦惱的感覺。不管怎麼樣，總不能不待主人出現話別，一走了之；那就只好耐着心等。

『鄭大爺，請進去吃飯！』

情勢所迫，秋兒的這句話成了不可抗拒的命令，鄭板橋跟着她『畫堂到得重重戶』，只見一姐面色不愉，淡淡地說道：『就要走也吃了飯走。鄰居談起來，說于家把多年不見的一個親戚得罪了，午飯開上桌都不肯吃！教我跟少棠怎麼再做人？』

聽得這話，鄭板橋惶恐無限，想要解釋，苦於不是一兩句話說

do, and even then the affair might end with some unpleasantness all around. When he thought of it, he became very vexed. He cursed himself for having so readily decided yesterday to accept the invitation to stay.

When he heard the footsteps, his heart was seized with apprehension. But to his surprise, it was only Qiu'er, and Yijie made no appearance to urge him to stay. What did this mean? He couldn't leave this question unanswered. He had to ask, "Have you told your lady that I was leaving immediately?"

"Yes." Qiu'er replied. "Lady nodded and didn't say anything."

What was he to do? Zheng Banqiao was completely at a loss. When he finished washing his face, Qiu'er came with a pot of tea, but left hurriedly, giving him no chance to ask any questions. As a matter of fact, he didn't know what to ask her anyway.

"Mister Zheng!" Qiu'er reappeared to give him a message, "lady instructed me to ask you if you would like to have a snack first or simply have lunch? We hear the sound of the noon salvo soon, and lunch will be served."

"I will have neither. I am leaving immediately. Really, I am."

Still Qiu'er said nothing more and went inside. There was no trace of her for some time. Zheng Banqiao had the unpleasant sensation of being suspended precisely in mid-air, neither above nor below. Surely, he could not leave without bidding farewell to the hostess. There is nothing for him but to wait patiently.

"Mister Zheng, please come inside to have lunch."

Given the circumstances, these words of Qiu'er's became an order that could not but be obeyed. Zheng Banqiao followed her and "through the main hall, he reached her door." He saw displeasure written on Yijie's face. She said coolly, "Even if you must go, you can go after lunch. If our neighbours heard about it, they would say that our family has so offended a long-separated relative that you refused to eat the lunch that was served! How can Shaotang and I have the gall to go on living here?"

Hearing this, Zheng Banqiao felt terrible and wanted to ex-

得清楚的。只是有一點卻很清楚,如果不吃飯就走,那就表示于家真的『把一個多年不見的親戚得罪了』!

於是他坐了下來,同時說道:『一姐,妳誤會了!』

『我沒有甚麼誤會。』一姐轉臉吩咐秋兒和女僕高媽,分別去拿酒端湯,眼看她們走遠了,才放低了聲音說:『只怕是你對我有誤會!故意給我難堪。』

這一說是真的生了誤會。鄭板橋心意一變,決定把無端自惹的一縷情絲,好好掐斷了再走。

有了這樣的打算,此刻不必多說甚麼;心想,且先享用了這一頓午飯,再作道理。於是定神去看桌上的四樣菜,清蒸鰣魚、紅燒獅子頭、炒莧菜,還有一樣鹽魚燒豆腐——她還記得他當年吃慣了的東西!就這一點上,她的念舊之心便十分明顯。鄭板橋百感俱生,心裏酸酸甜甜地,不辨是何滋味?

酒取來了,淡紅的玫瑰露,斟在白瓷酒杯中,色香的誘惑,都叫本來貪杯的鄭板橋無法抗拒;忍不住說了句:『妳也來一杯!』

一姐沒有說甚麼,只叫秋兒再取一個杯子來。

相對飲了一口,一姐為他佈菜;第一匙就是鹽魚燒豆腐。『一

plain, but it was not something that could be explained in a few words. One thing, however, was quite clear: if he left without lunch, this would really show that the Yu family had truly "offended a long-separated relative."

So sitting down he said, "Yijie, there must be some mis-understanding."

"There is not."

Yijie turned around and sent Qiu'er and her maid Mother Gao off to fetch the wine and the soup separately. When she saw that the maids were out of earshot, she lowered her voice and said, "If there is any misunderstanding, I am afraid it is on your part. You deliberately made things difficult for me ."

Her putting things this way showed that misunderstanding had truly arisen. Zheng Banqiao changed his mind, determined to have any thread of love that he might have unintentionally got himself entwined with severe before taking his leave.

Having thus made up his mind, he felt that for the time being, there was no need to say anything more. He thought to himself: let me enjoy this lunch first before trying to sort things out. Composing himself, he looked at the four dishes on the table: steamed hilsa herring, stewed meatballs, fried amaranth, and salted fish fried with bean curds — she had not forgotten the things he used to like in the old days! From this alone, it was patently clear that their former relationship still counted with her. A hundred emotions welled up in Zheng Banqiao's breast — some bitter, some sweet — he could hardly distinguish the different strands!

Wine was brought in. The pale red wine called "rose dew" was poured into white china cups, and the allure of both colour and fragrance was wellnigh irresistible for Zheng Banqiao, who liked his wine. He couldn't help coming out with the words, "Why don't you join me for a cup?"

Yijie didn't say anything, but just told Qiu'er to fetch another cup.

They sipped their wine together. Yijie helped him with the food,

姐！』鄭板橋不由得以感激的聲音說，『妳倒沒有忘掉我的習慣。』

　　『小時候的事，怎麼忘得了？』

　　就這一句話，又掀開了鄭板橋的塵封的記憶之門；望着盛鬋豐容的一姐，想起刻骨銘心的那些日子，悄然吟道：

　　　　杏花深院紅如許，

　　　　一線畫牆攔住，

　　　　嘆人間咫尺千山路……。

　　側耳凝神的一姐，倏然抬眼，迷惘地問道：『怎的不唸下去？』

　　往下就不便唸了。此意只可燈前月下，自己去細辨那苦中的一點雋永之味；一說破便苦而無味，所以他搖搖頭說：『不相干！』

　　『怎叫「不相干」？』一姐微微冷笑：『不曉得你在背後編派我甚麼？「一線畫牆」偏要說成「咫尺千山」，無情人，就有這種無情話！』

　　鄭板橋震動了！『一姐，』他從牙縫中迸出來四個字：『妳寃枉我！』

　　『也不知道誰寃枉誰？』一姐微咬着嘴唇，把臉偏了過去。

　　『是呀！我也不知道誰寃枉了誰？反正我自己知道我自己。』接着便又唸那闋未唸完的詞：

　　　　……不見也相思苦，

　　　　便見也相思苦！

and the first spoonful placed on his plate was the salted fish fried with bean curds. "Yijie," Zheng Banqiao said with some emotion, "You haven't forgotten what I used to like."

"With children things how can one forget them?"

These words again lifted the dust-laden shutters on Zheng Banqiao's memory. He gazed at the lovely Yijie and thought of the days they spent together that were firmly etched in his mind. He repeated the words:

> The secluded courtyard with apricot flowers in blossom
>   so pink;
> The thin partition of a painted wall baring entry.
> In this world of man,
> A yard is as difficult to traverse
>   As a thousand mountains ...

Yijie, listening attentively with cocked ears, raised her eyes and asked bemusedly, "Why don't you go on?"

What followed was rather unsuitable to be said aloud. It was something whose lingering flavour could only be savoured in the lamplight or under the moon. Once brought into the open it would become insipid. So he shook his head and said, "No matter."

"What do you mean by 'no matter'?" Yijie said with a sneer. "I don't know how you make things up about me behind my back. 'The thin partition of a painted wall,' you unfairly made out to be 'a thousand mountains to cross when separated only by a yard.' Only a man who doesn't care would say such unfeeling things!"

Zheng Banqiao was shaken. "Yijie," he squeezed out the words between his teeth, "You are being unfair."

"I don't know who's being unfair." Yijie bit her lips and turned her face away.

"Well! I don't either. But I know myself." Then he went on to recite the rest of the poem:

> When we are separated, I am sick with love;
> When we meet, I am sick with love;

> 分明背地情千縷，
>
> 奈花間，
>
> 半句也何曾吐？

這下是一姐的臉色大變，一雙眼淚光隱隱，望着他不斷眨動，無限自憐憐人的痛惜怨悔，盡在無聲之中。

『唉！』鄭板橋幽聲長嘆，望了望遠遠侍立，眼神困惑的秋兒，低聲向一姐說道：『這就是我剛才一定要走的原因。談到往事，不堪回首！』

這話似乎提醒了她，微微一驚，臉上恢復了能幹主婦的那番從容穩重的待客的神色，轉臉向秋兒關照：『去換熱的火腿冬瓜湯來！』

等秋兒一走，鄭板橋驚覺到這是個難得的機會，正一正臉色，儘力放出誠懇的聲音說：『一姐，往事都如秋雲，讓它散了去吧！人生這種機遇，只可有一，不可有二；更不可流連癡迷。我吃了飯就走，留着今日不盡的餘味，慢慢咀嚼，豈不甚好？』

一姐沉吟了好一會，『少棠回家，自然要問。』她的聲音顯得很理智，『那該怎麼說？』

這句話把鄭板橋問住了。至親重逢，情好逾恆，形跡上再親密，還是可以解釋的；而正作久住之計，忽然不辭而別，這樣留下來的

By myself, I feel a thousand strands of love,
But when we meet among the flowers,
I am unable to come out with a single word.

At this, Yijie turned pale. Her eyes glistened. Holding back the tears, she stared at him. And in the silence was the profound regret and pain of a person who was sorry for both herself and the other person.

"Ai!" Zheng Banqiao heaved a long, deep sigh and gazed at Qiu'er who stood at a distance in attendance and whose eyes told of total bewilderment. He lowered his voice and said to Yijie, "This is the reason I insisted on leaving just now. The past is something cannot bear looking back!"

This seemed to have alerted her, and though slightly alarmed, she regained her composure and took on the countenance of the capable hostess attending to her guest. She turned round and instructed Qiu'er, "Go and bring us some hot ham and winter melon soup!"

As soon as Qiu'er had left, Zheng Banqiao was quick to realize that this was a rare opportunity. He put on a serious expression, and tried his best to sound sincere, "Yijie, our past is like autumn clouds. Let us allow them to disperse. In life, such a thing can happen only once, it can't happen a second time. We must not abandon ourselves to this madness. I'll go when we've finished lunch. Isn't it best to keep the lingering taste to be savoured in the future?"

Yijie was silent for some time. "When Shaotang comes home, he is certain to ask questions." Her voice sounded very rational. "What should I say?"

Zheng Banqiao had no ready reply. When relatives are reunited after a long time, it is expected that they should have warmer feelings towards one another, so any intimate behaviour is understandable. But for him to leave suddenly without as much as a goodbye when all along it was taken for granted he was staying for quite some time, the questions that this would leave behind would

一個疑問就太嚴重了！不但無法解釋，甚至連解釋的機會都沒有；因爲自己已不在于家了——在于家的是一姐；從此她將在丈夫猜疑的眼光下過一輩子，此是如何難堪而非同小可的一件事？

僅僅爲了一姐；鄭板橋就不得不放棄原意，另作計較。

『都是三十多的人了！難道眞的自己管不住自己？』

一姐的話中帶着些傷感，但聲音倒是平靜的；鄭板橋聽入耳中，愧在心頭，覺得自己還不如一姐有定力。同時他也感到肩頭的壓力輕了，只要一姐有這樣的定力，自己就比較好應付。他自覺如失足落入情海之中，勉力掙扎，可登彼岸；但如一起掉下去的伴侶，拚命拉住自己的辮子不放，那就非同歸於盡不可。如今伴侶既已釋手，就不妨從容自救。

『你還是住在這裏，好好用一用功；可也不必太辛苦，把身子養得好好的。都說舉子入闈，在那間鴿子籠似的「場屋」裏，比在監獄裏還苦；三場下來，身子不好頂不住。那時，再有滿腹經綸，拿不出來，也是枉然。你聽我的話，沒有錯！』

絮絮叮嚀，說又說得在情理上，尤其是那略帶命令的語氣，鄭板橋的感覺中，一姐應該是表姊而不是表妹，不由得就點頭答應。

『少棠是好人，性情豁達大度，我取他的也就是這一點。不過——。』一姐沒有再說下去。

be too grave. Not only was there no way of explaining his departure, there would not even be the opportunity to do so. For he would no longer be there — there would only be Yijie. From now on for the rest of her life, she would live under the questioning eyes of her husband. This would, indeed, be a serious matter.

Simply for the sake of Yijie, Zheng Banqiao had no choice but to abandon his original plan and think up some other plan.

"After all, we are both in our thirties! We should be able to control ourselves."

There is a trace of sadness on Yijie's words, yet her voice, nonetheless, was calm. Zheng Banqiao, on taking this in, felt a twinge of shame, feeling that he was less able to stand fast than Yijie. At the same time, he also felt that a weight had been lifted from his shoulders. As long as Yijie had the strength to stand fast, it would be easier to cope with the situation. He himself felt as though he had lost his footing and fallen headlong into the sea of love; with effort, he had some confidence he could struggle ashore. But if the companion who had fallen with him were to grab hold of his queue and refuse to let go, they would both be doomed. Now that his companion had released her hold, he was left to save himself in his own time.

"You'd best stay on here and study in earnest. On the other hand you needn't work too hard — take good care of yourself. Everybody says that when the candidates enter the examination hall, the pigeon-coop cubicles are worse than a prison cell. After three sessions, the weaklings can't stand up to it. If that happens, no amount of learning will be of any use to you, for you won't be able to show it. Listen to what I'm saying and you won't go wrong."

Her persistent urgings made good sense, especially when spoken with such a tone of authority. It made Zheng Banqiao feel as though she were his elder rather than younger cousin, and all he could do was to nod in assent.

"Shaotang is a good man. He is open-minded and generous. This is what I like about him. But ..." Yijie did not go on.

　　好話之後加一轉語，就要說出不好的來了。鄭板橋不願聽那話；所以她欲言又止，他也不作追問。

　　『喝點熱湯！』一姐舀了一小碗秋兒剛端上來的火腿冬瓜湯，放在鄭板橋面前，『酒也夠了吧？午間少喝些。』

　　『嗯，嗯，好！』

　　吃完飯剛回到客房，跟着便是秋兒送來了一盞清茶；等她轉身出門，鄭板橋還未坐定，又聽得人聲，這次是于少棠，後面跟着一名挑伕，一肩行李，前頭是鋪蓋，後面是個黃竹書箱。

　　鄭板橋認得是自己的東西，心想：這一下是住定了！

　　『華嚴寺的知客和尚好彆扭！』于少棠說：『費了好半天的唇舌，才肯把你的行李給我。也難怪他捨不得他搬走；登門來求你畫的人不少，潤筆之外的一成「墨費」，就少了他好些收入。』

　　『費心，費心！』鄭板橋拱手道謝，『在華嚴寺，還得送些房金——。』

　　『給過了。』于少棠搶着說，『給了寺裏五兩銀子，我想只多不少。』

　　『旣如此，我得奉還。』

　　『擺着，擺着！隨後再算。』于少棠搖一搖手，指揮挑伕將行李堆在屋角，打發他走了，然後問鄭板橋：『昨夜睡得還安穩？』

　　『很好！』

A "but" coming after something good is sure to lead to something bad. Zheng Banqiao didn't want to hear it. So when she hesitated, he didn't press her.

"Have some hot soup!" Yijie ladled out a small bowl of the ham and winter melon soup that Qiu'er had just brought in and placed it in front of Zheng Banqiao. "You have had enough to drink? Better not have too much at lunch time."

"Yes, yes, that's fine."

When he finished lunch and returned to his room, Qiu'er brought in a cup of tea. When she had left, and before he could sit down, he again heard voices. This time it was Yu Shaotang, with a bearer following him, carrying his luggage on a pole of luggage over his shoulders: bedding and blankets hanging from one end, and a yellow bamboo bookcase hanging from the other.

Zheng Banqiao recognized his belongings. He thought to himself: I'm here to stay regardless.

"The monk in charge of reception at the Garland Temple was a real difficult customer!" said Yu Shaotang. "He took a lot of convincing before he would release your belongings. And I can very well understand why he doesn't want you to move. A lot of people come after your paintings. He is going to be done out of his ten per cent 'ink charge' that is added onto your fee."

"You've gone to so much trouble!" Zheng Banqiao thanked him with cupped hands in a bow. "At the Garland Temple, I still have some rent outstanding ..."

"I took care of that." Yu Shaotang interrupted. "I gave the temple five taels of silver. I think that is, if anything, rather on the generous side."

"I'll have to pay you back."

"Leave it, leave it! We'll settle it later." Yu Shaotang held up his hand and went on with directing the bearer to put the lugguage in one corner of the room, and then dismissed him. After that, he asked Zheng Banqiao, "Did you sleep well last night?"

"Very well, indeed!"

這是言不由衷。于少棠自然不會知道他一夜輾轉，數番坐起，只盡他主人的責任，在屋中四處細看，彷彿是檢查有甚麼不適居住的地方，好立即改正似地。

等看到書桌，鄭板橋驀然警覺，桌上的詞稿未收，如果落入于少棠眼中，大為不妥；一急之下，不由得先喊了聲：『少棠！』

聲音很急促，所以于少棠回臉相看時，略有詫異之色。

鄭板橋自己也發覺了，便力持從容，『你喜歡蘭花，還是竹子？』他問，『我畫一幅送你。』

聽得這話，于少棠未語先笑，而又搓着手躊躇，彷彿高興得不知怎麼說才好？好半天才說：『表兄既然賞賜墨寶，倒起了我的貪心，又要蘭花，又要竹子。』

『可以！』說着，鄭板橋已移動腳步，到了書桌前面，一面將詞稿塞入抽斗，一面說道：『此刻就磨墨動手！』

『叫秋兒磨。』于少棠說，『我那裏有大墨海。』

正說着，一姐也來了。重新勻過臉，換過衣裳，粉臉生春，不知是胭脂還是酒暈；在鄭板橋只覺有股迫人的熱氣，烘得他一顆心跳蕩不止，不自覺地退了幾步。

『表哥趁着酒興，要畫畫給我！』于少棠向他妻子笑道：『快叫秋兒磨墨。』

He of course was just saying this. How would Yu Shaotang know that he had tossed and turned all night and got up several times? Yu was simply being the host. He looked around the room carefully as if to see if there was anything not quite right that he could have taken care of immediately.

When he looked toward the desk, Zheng Banqiao was suddenly alarmed, noticing that he had not put his poems away. If Yu Shaotang caught sight of them, it may be awkward. In a panic, he simply called out, "Shaotang!"

His tone was rather peremptory, so Yu Shaotang turned round, somewhat surprised.

Zheng Banqiao also realized this, and made an effort to appear calm, "Which do you like, orchids or bamboos?" he asked. "I want to do a painting for you."

On hearing this, Yu Shaotang burst into a muted laugh, and, rubbing his hands together in hesitation, seemed so delighted that he didn't know what to say. It took him some time to say, "By honouring me with a painting of yours, you bring out the greedy side in me. I would like to have both orchids and bamboos!"

"And so you shall!" Zheng Banqiao had to move before he finished replying. On reaching the desk, he at once stuffed the draft which was lying on top into the drawer while remarking, "Let's get some ink ground this very moment!"

"Let Qiu'er do it for you." Yu Shaotang said. "I have a large ink bowel."

Just as he spoke, Yijie came in. She had redone her makeup, changed to another dress, and there was an air of spring on her beautiful face. It was hard to tell if it was the rouge or the effect of the wine. Zheng Banqiao only felt the warmth pressing in on him, accelerating his heart to a full race. Unconsciously he retreated a few steps.

"Cousin wants to do a painting for me under the inspiration of the wine he has drunk." Yu Shaotang smiled and said to his wife, "Quickly, get Qiu'er to grind some ink."

『你是得其所哉了！』一姐笑道，『秋兒可有了苦差使。只怕她還伺候不來書房，得替表哥買個書僮才好。』

『那容易。明天就找幾個孩子來，讓表哥自己挑。』

『不必，不必！我已經打擾了，如何再添一口人，來替府上添麻煩。』

『添個人來做事，麻煩甚麼？』于少棠說，『這個孩子得要好好找；下個月表哥去應考，秋闈、春闈，一路跟到京裏，不得力的可不行。』

『那只好慢慢再找。』一姐忽然變了口氣，『先不忙！』說着轉身走了；必是去找秋兒磨墨。

『表哥，』于少棠看着一姐的背影，悄然問道，『膝下還沒有男娃娃，倒不曾打算過？』

鄭板橋報以苦笑，『打算也是白打算。』他這樣答說。

于少棠不即回答，把他的話辦一辦味，估量還是家貧親老，功名未成的緣故。既爲至親，不能不勸勸他。

『等秋闈以後，可不能躭誤了。那時要辦事也容易。』

所謂『辦事容易』，是指不難籌措一筆藏嬌的費用；中了舉，自然有人肯放帳，甚至肯贈金，結個後來飛黃騰達的因緣。鄭板橋體

"You're getting your heart's desire," Yijie said with a smile, "but Qiu'er has her work cut out for her. What I am afraid of is that she'll not be able to cope with the job of serving Cousin in the study. We'll have to buy a boy attendant for him."

"No problem. Tomorrow I'll have several boys brought here for Cousin to choose from."

"That's not necessary! Really! I've already put you out enough. To add yet one more person would just be that much more trouble for the household."

"Just one more person to help out. What trouble is there?" Yu Shaotang said. "We must be careful in our choice. Next month Cousin is going to sit for the autumn examination, and then the spring examination, with the metropolitan examination to follow. He would need to be very capable."

"In that case, we'll have to take our time looking for one." Yijie's tone suddenly changed. "There's no hurry for the time being," she turned round and left the room as she spoke, probably to go and fetch Qiu'er to grind the ink.

"Cousin," said Yu Shaotang softly, looking at the receding figure of Yijie. "You have as yet no heir, but have you thought about the matter?"

"There is no point thinking about it. It will just be effort wasted." Zheng Banqiao replied with a bitter smile.

Yu Shaotang didn't respond immediately. He savoured Zheng Banqiao's words. He figured that it was probably because of poverty and the burden of having to support an aged grandparent, and the lack of success at the examinations. Since they were close relatives, he felt obliged to urge him, "No more delays after the autumn examination! It will not be too difficult to manage then."

"Not too difficult" referred, of course, to the fact of raising money for a concubine. When a person passes the civil service examination, there are naturally people willing to make loans and even straight gifts in order to forge a link with burgeoning prosperity. Zheng Banqiao knew this to be the case himself, and so

會得此意，便即笑道：『明朝士林的習氣，中舉以後，有兩句口號：「起個號，娶個小。」我不學那種俗氣。再說，我也錯過了——。』

　　『錯過了！』于少棠極感興趣地搶着問，『必是一段哀感頑豔的故事？』

　　這從何談起呢？有了幾分酒意，而且一夜不曾睡好的鄭板橋，神思昏昏，要他全本大套講那個故事，也不可能，想一想便說：『我唸一首詞你聽吧！』

　　『是！』答了這一聲，于少棠忽又笑道：『索性請表哥寫下來吧！我又得一幅好斗方。』

　　『也好。』

　　於是鄭板橋坐到書桌前面，鋪紙伸毫，寫的是：

　　　　　有　感

　　　綠楊深巷，
　　　人倚朱門，
　　　不是尋常模樣。
　　　旋浣春衫，
　　　薄梳雲鬢，
　　　韻致十分娟朗。
　　　向芳鄰潛訪，
　　　說自小青衣，
　　　人家廝養；
　　　又沒個憐香惜媚，
　　　落在煮鶴燒琴魔障，
　　　代他出脫千思萬想。

　　　究竟人謀空費，
　　　天意從來，
　　　不許名花擅長！

he said with a smile. "It is common for Ming dynasty intellectuals, after passing the civil service examination, to indulge in the saying: 'give yourself a style-name and take yourself a concubine.' I don't go in for such vulgarity. Besides, I've missed the boat ..."

"Missed the boat?" Yu Shaotang fenced with heightened interest. "It must be a very sad and touching story!"

Where does one start? Zheng Banqiao's wits were dulled by the lingering wine and a sleepless night. There was no way he could possibly tell the whole story. So he thought for a while, and then said, "Let me recite you a poem!"

"Good!" Yu Shaotang replied but then suddenly smiling again, said, "You might as well write it down. Then I'll have another piece of your fine calligraphy."

"Not a bad idea."

So Zheng Banqiao sat down at the desk, spread out a piece of paper, picked up his brush, and wrote down the following poem:

> An Occasional Poem
> *A secluded lane flanked by green willows.*
> *A lady leaning on the vermillion gate.*
> *A scene quite apart from the ordinary.*
> *Attired in spring finery,*
> *With a whisp of thinly combed hair gracing her temples,*
> *She has a demeanour so poised and elegant.*
> *On discreetly making inquiries with her neighbours,*
> *I am told that she had been poor through childhood,*
> *And had served as a housemaid.*
> *As there was no one to love or to take pity on her,*
> *She fell into the hands of a vulgar man*
> *   devoid of finer feelings.*
> *This provoked in me a futile sympathy*
> *Making a thousand plans for her liberation.*
> *In the end, the plans of man are for naught.*
> *Providence never had any intention*
> *Of allowing beautiful flowers to shine forth in their beauty.*

屈指千秋，

青袍紅粉，

多以飄零骯髒。

且休論已往，

試看予十載，

醋缽齋盆。

憑寄語雪中蘭蕙，

春將不遠，

人間留得嬌無恙，

明珠未必終塵壤！

（調寄《玉女瑤仙珮》）

　　這首詞，于少棠是看得懂的，借『紅粉』以寫『青袍』，自抒其胸中不平之氣；結局幾句是個好兆，他也代鄭板橋高興，『恭喜，恭喜！』他說，『「明珠未必終塵壤！」就要得意了；「春將不遠」，明年會試高中，也在意中。』

　　看他居然懂得詞意，鄭板橋大為興奮；不覺另眼相看；也因此，等秋兒磨了墨來，便加意揮灑，畫蘭、畫竹、畫石，還很罕見地添了一座茅屋，一個負手閒眺的老者，另外加上一大篇題詞：

　　三間茆屋，十里春風；窗裏幽蘭，窗外修竹，此是何等雅趣！而安享之人不知也。憒憒懂懂，沒沒墨墨，絕不知樂在何處？

When I look back over the centuries and take a tally,
It seems as though most beautiful girls of humble origin
Drift through life soiled and forsaken.
Putting aside the more distant past,
And looking only at the last decade,
I have had to contend with vinegar jars and pickled bottles.
Let me send the following message to the orchids in the snow:
Spring is not far off.
So long as beauty is preserved in this world
A lustrous pearl will not spend the rest of its life on this sordid earth.

This poem was not beyond the grasp of Yu Shaotang's understanding . "Beautiful flowers" was used as a metaphor for young men of letters who had not yet passed the civil service examination, and this was an expression of his pent-up frustrations. The concluding lines were a good omen, and he was happy for Zheng Banqiao. "Congratulations, congratulations!" he said. " 'A lustrous pearl will not spend the rest of its life on this sordid earth' means that you are going to attain success. And 'Spring is not far off' means that you can count on having your name high on the metropolitan examination list next year."

Zheng Banqiao was delighted to see that he was actually able to understand the meaning of the poem, and couldn't help viewing him in a new light. So when Qiu'er came and had finished grinding the ink, he wielded his brush with extra inspiration. He painted orchids, bamboos, rocks, and even put in something rarely seen—a thatched cottage and an old man, with hands clasped behind his back, gazing in a leisurely manner into the distance. He also added a long inscription:

Three thatched cottages; ten miles of spring breezes. Inside the window, orchids; outside, tall bamboos. It is out of this world. But those who enjoy this are unaware of it. They are muddle-headed and benighted, and have no idea wherein happiness lies. Only those who toil or suffer, who are poor or sick, on

惟勞苦貧病之人，忽得十日五日之暇，閉柴扉、掃竹徑、對
芳蘭、啜苦茗，時有微風細雨，潤澤於疏籬仄徑之間，俗客
不來，良朋輒至，亦適適然自驚爲此日之難得也！凡吾畫蘭
畫竹畫石，用以慰天下之勞人，非以供天下之安享人也。

題罷落款，說了聲：『獻醜！』便擱筆避到一邊，好讓于少棠夫
婦欣賞。

『表哥真是賞面子！』于少棠異常滿意，『收藏得表哥這幅大件
精品；花錢買不到，拿出來才夠面子。』

『你就是這麼俗！』王一姐毫不客氣地指出她丈夫的本心，『一
開口就是暴發戶附庸風雅的話，你不細看題詞？真是「絕不知樂在
何處」！』

凡是一姐有所呵責，于少棠總是逆來順受，笑笑不響；但此時
有鄭板橋在，不免臉上訕訕地，有些不大得勁。

一姐卻管自己又說：『表哥替你畫了這麼幅畫，你怎麼謝謝人
家？』

『妳說呢？』于少棠這樣回答他妻子；突然間，出現了詭祕、
好奇而又有些頑皮的神色，『一姐，』他終於說了，『我們替表哥置
個人，妳看，怎麼樣？』

這建議在一姐聽來異常突兀，『好啊！』先這樣順口答了一句，

getting a respite of five or ten days, shut their rough wooden door, sweep the bamboo path, and appreciate the fragrant orchids, and the fine taste of tea. When a faint breeze and drizzle come to moisten the crevices between the sparse bamboo fence and narrow path, and congenial friends instead of the visitors appear from nowhere, they become suddenly aware what a wonderful day it is! When I paint orchids, bamboos, and rocks, I paint them to please those in the world who toil, not for those who are well provided with comfort.

After affixing his signature and seal, he said, "That is the best I can do." He put down his brush and stood to one side so that Yu Shaotang and Yijie could admire the painting.

"Cousin, you have really given us face!" Yu Shaotang was extraordinarily satisfied. "The addition of such an exquisite painting in such an ample dimension from your brush to our collection is something no amount of money can buy, this will indeed give us face!"

"There goes your vulgarity again!" Yijie went on to give a description of her husband's character in the most candid terms. "Whenever you open your mouth the words that come out are those of an upstart trying to appear sophisticated. Why don't you take a close look at the inscription? It's got to be you who has 'no idea of wherein happiness lies.' "

Whenever Yijie berated him, Yu Shaotang always took it in good part, with a smile. But this time it was done in Zheng Banqiao's presence, and he couldn't help being embarassed and a bit upset .

Yijie took no notice of him and added, "Cousin has painted you such a fine painting. How are you going to show your gratitude?"

"What do you think?" was Yu Shaotang's reply to his wife. Suddenly, a strange, mysterious and somewhat mischievous look came to his face. "Yijie," he said at length, "What about getting him a concubine?"

His suggestion was completely out of the blue. "Sure!" she

接着便去看鄭板橋的態度。

『談不到此，談不到此！』他雙手亂搖着，似乎談都不願談。

『這件事要從長計議。』一姐說道，『「若要家不和，娶個小老婆！」』

于少棠深爲懊悔，不該輕發此言；鄭板橋也覺得十分無趣。而一姐卻辨不清自己的感覺，說這句話到底是阻止丈夫起納妾之想，還是不贊成鄭板橋置個偏房？

置偏房，買書僮的話，都不見再提起；『伺候書房』是秋兒和她的主母『當值』。

當然，那不是經常在鄭板橋的左右，爲他磨墨烹茶，添香剪燭；只是間歇地走來照料。到了薄暮時分，便是于少棠走來閒話，然後邀入內廳，一頓酒有個把時辰好吃——鄭板橋自己也奇怪，每到那辰光，如何會有如許的話好談？

半個月的功夫，他跟一姐無日不共晨夕；然後有一天，一早晨不見一姐的影子，到了午間秋兒來送飯時，他畢竟忍不住要探問了。

『喔，奶奶探望親戚去了。是我家大爺的姑太太；一早派人來

replied on the spur of the moment, and then continued to watch for Zheng Banqiao's reaction.

"That is out of the question. That is out of the question." He waved his hands about wildly, and it seemed that he really didn't want to talk about it.

"This kind of thing requires careful consideration." Yijie said, "As the saying goes, 'If you want to banish peace from your household, get yourself a concubine.'"

Yu Shaotang deeply regretted having made such a rash suggestion. Zheng Banqiao also felt put out. But Yijie couldn't be sure what was behind her own remark. Was it to nip any such thought in her husband in the bud or was it to prevent Zheng Banqiao from taking a concubine?

 From then on, the acquisition of a concubine for Zheng Banqiao and the purchase of a boy to wait on him were never again mentioned. Instead, it was Qiu'er and her mistress who took turns to be "on duty" in the study.

Of course, they were not always around to grind ink, boil tea, put in fresh incense, or cut the candle wicks for Zheng Banqiao; they would only come to attend to his needs occasionally. In the evening, it was in fact Yu Shaotang who would come to pass the time with him, and afterwards to invite him into the inner hall to spend a happy couple of hours drinking wine. Zheng Banqiao himself found it a wonder that when the time came round every day he was able to have so much to talk about.

For a fortnight, he was with Yijie most part of the day. Then one morning, however, there was no sign of her. When Qiu'er brought him lunch at noon, he finally could not contain his curiosity.

"Oh, lady has gone to visit a relative — master's aunt. They

通知，得了急病。』秋兒說，『我家大爺是那位姑太太抱大的，跟親娘一樣。』

『那麼，你家大爺呢？也去探望姑太太了？』

『大爺鹽棧裏有公事。』秋兒答道，『還不知道去不去呢？』

如果于家姑太太病勢無礙，于少棠暫時就不去了；這是他自己跟鄭板橋說的，因爲家裏有客。

『少棠！』鄭板橋急忙聲明，『你不必在這裏陪我。說句老實話，我自覺已不是府上的客了。聽說你那位姑太太，視你如己出；你還該去省視一番，莫傷了老人的心！』

于少棠原就懸念着姑母的病，聽他這一說，便拱拱手：『表哥體諒我！既如此，我抽空去看一看；只是失陪不安。』

『你請，你請！我替你看家。』

於是于少棠一再叮囑秋兒盡心照料，留意火燭；然後騎一匹馬，匆匆趕往東鄉。而鄭板橋這一夜便覺悽涼萬狀。

那是忽忽若有所失的感覺，心裏有莫名的煩躁，書看不下去，酒也喝不出味道；草草敷衍了一頓夜飯，回到自己屋裏，兀坐在燈下，彷彿置身於大海孤舟，四面黑茫茫一片，不知自己到明朝是何光景。

『鄭大爺，』秋兒收拾一切，檢點門戶，等諸事已了，走來問道：『可還要甚麼？』

sent someone very early this morning to tell us that she had been taken ill suddenly." Qiu'er said. "It was this lady who brought master up. She is like a mother to him."

"And what about your master then? Has he also gone to visit his aunt?"

"He had some business at the godown." Qiu'er replied. "It is not yet certain whether he can go."

If his aunt's illness turned out to be not so serious, Yu Shaotang wouldn't go for the time being. This was what he had told Zheng Banqiao himself, the reason being that he had a guest at home.

"Shaotang!" Zheng Banqiao hastened to make his position clear. "You don't have to stay behind just to keep me company. To tell the truth, I don't feel I'm a guest here any longer. I hear that this aunt of yours looks on you as a son. You really ought to go and see her — don't make the old lady feel neglected."

In fact, Yu Shaotang was very concerned about his aunt's illness. On hearing this, he bowed with cupped hands and said, "Cousin, thank you for being so understanding. Since that is how you feel, I shall excuse myself and go to see her, although I am still uneasy about leaving you on your own."

"Please! Please! I'll take care of things here for you."

After he had repeatedly impressed on Qiu'er to take good care of the guest and guard against fire risks, Yu Shaotang rode out on horseback in the direction of the East Village. And that evening, Zheng Banqiao felt utterly dejected.

He suddenly felt as though there was something missing. He seemed for no reason to be on tenterhooks — he couldn't read and found no pleasure in his wine. Hastily disposing of dinner, he returned to his room and sat down alone under the lamp. It was as though he was adrift in a solitary boat in a wide ocean, with darkness closing in on him from all sides. He didn't know what was to become of him on the morrow.

"Mister Zheng." When Qiu'er had finished tidying up and locking the doors, she went to him to ask if there was anything else

『喔，甚麼都不要！』鄭板橋想說：只要妳陪我談談。但瓜田李下的嫌疑，不能不避，所以改了這樣一句話：『妳去睡吧！』

『還早！』秋兒這樣說，站着不動。

『那，那妳就坐下來，』他終於說了，『我們談談！』

秋兒原就有意跟他說些閒話，好消磨上床之前這一段無聊的辰光，因而答應一聲：『是！』在靠門的一張小櫈子上坐了下來。

『妳家大爺的脾氣，倒是真好。』

『是啊！』秋兒笑道，『太好了！奶奶反不中意。』

『怎麼呢？』

『奶奶總說大爺欠剛强，不像個男子漢。』

『那麼，也有吵嘴的時候麼？』

『怎麼？』秋兒說，『常是一起床就吵！奶奶也不知摔壞了多少黃楊木梳。』

『妳家大爺呢？』鄭板橋問：『總是讓她！』

『是的，總是不開口；倒像做了甚麼對不起奶奶的事似地！』

于少棠是如何『對不起』一姐？鄭板橋怎麼樣也猜度不出。

『鄭大爺，』秋兒忽然問道，『你跟我家奶奶是從小就在一起的？』

他不知道她問這話有無用意？很謹慎地答道：『原是表兄妹，住得又近；從小便有往來。』

『那──，』秋兒遲疑了一會，終於帶些不安的神情問了出來：『鄭大爺跟我家奶奶，既然是表兄妹，又住得近，當年倒不曾親上加親？』

he wanted. "No, nothing at all." What Zheng Banqiao wanted to say was: I could do with a bit of company and a chat. But, not wanting to put himself in a compromising situation, he changed his mind and said, "You can retire now."

"It's still early." Qiu'er said without stirring.

"Then ... then sit down for a bit," he said at length, "and talk to me."

In fact, what Qiu'er wanted was to chat with Zheng Banqiao to idle away the time before going to bed. So she replied, "All right!" and sat down on a small stool near the door.

"Your master is really a very good-natured gentleman."

"Yes, he is." Qiu'er replied with a smile. "Too good-natured in fact. That is not to the liking of my lady."

"What is the matter?"

"Lady always says that he is weak, not like a man."

"Then, do they quarrel sometimes?"

"Quarrel?" Qiu'er said. "They quarrel almost the moment they get out of bed. Lady has broken I don't know how many boxwood combs!"

"How about you master?" asked Zheng Banqiao. "Is he always submissive?"

"Yes, he says nothing, almost as though he is in the wrong in some way."

How could Yu Shaotang have been in the wrong? For the life of him, Zheng Banqiao could not figure it out.

"Mister Zheng," Qiu'er suddenly asked, "Did you and lady grow up as children together?"

He couldn't tell whether or not there was something behind the question. So he replied cautiously, "We are cousins, and we lived close to each other, so we saw each other frequently from the time when we were young."

"Well ...," Qiu'er hesitated for a moment, then somewhat uneasily asked, "Since you are cousins and lived so close to each other, why didn't the two families strengthen the ties by arranging a

一句話觸及鄭板橋的痛處，强自笑道：『這都是緣分。』

『是！』秋兒似懂非懂地點着頭：『緣分！』

他想說：這一次重逢，也是緣分。然而畢竟不曾出口，因爲這一來就扯得多了；有些話，無論如何是不足爲外人道；更不足爲不解事的外人道的。

看鄭板橋神思不屬，有心事在想；秋兒很知趣地站起來，說一聲：『鄭大爺早早安置！』悄悄走了。

秋兒的話，鄭板橋不曾聽見；自然也不曾發覺她走。他確是有心事在想，想到當年的光景，信口吟成一闋《浣溪紗》：

> 硯上花枝折得香，
> 枕邊蝴蝶引來狂，
> 打人紅豆好收藏。
>
> 數鳥聲時癡卦算，
> 借書攤處暗思量，
> 隔牆聽喚小珠娘。

『雀兒算卦』說西鄰的珠娘該嫁個肖鷄的；若非一姐的打人紅豆、擲硯花枝，令人魂牽夢縈，當時娶了珠娘，倒也是一頭好姻緣。

『唉！』鄭板橋嘆口氣自語：『一誤再誤！』

marriage between you two?"

This touched a raw nerve in Zheng Banqiao. He forced a smile and said, "It was all a matter of fate."

"Yes," said Qiu'er nodding half knowingly. "It's fate."

He was on the point of saying that this reunion was also fated, but in the end he held back because one thing would only lead to another and one is liable to say too much. There were some things which were not for the ear of outsiders regardless, especially not to outsiders who lacked understanding.

Seeing that Zheng Banqiao was distracted and had something on his mind, Qiu'er discreetly stood up and said, "Rest early, Mister Zheng!" She then tiptoed out.

Zheng Banqiao didn't hear what she said, nor did he notice her departure. He really did have something on his mind, and when he thought back to the scenes of those years, a poem came without any effort to him:

> The branch of blossoms on the inkslab bowed down
>   with its fragrance;
> The butterflies attracted by the pillow dance wildly;
> And the red beans for throwing at lovers should be put away safely.
> While several birds were singing,
> Driving stalks were cast with obsession.
> At the bookstall I calculated within myself.
> And on the other side of the wall I heard someone
>   calling the name of Miss Zhu.

The "bird fortune-teller" said that Miss Zhu, his neighbour to the west, should marry a man born in the Year of the Cock. If it were not for Yijie who beat him with the red beans of love, threw away the branch of blossoms on the inkslab and bewitched him utterly, if he had married Miss Zhu, it might have turned out to be a happy marriage.

"Ah!" sighed Zheng Banqiao, muttering to himself, "I keep missing the boat!"

三天不見，彼此彷彿都有無數的話要說，礙着秋兒，只得強忍；唯有偷空多覷幾眼——彷彿覺得這三天就是三年，彼此在容顏上，必都應有甚麼改變，要把它找出來似地。

『姑太太的病，總算不要緊了。虧得你勸少棠去，老人家自己的兒子倒還不怎麼樣，就是想她那個自己餵過奶的內姪。也就為此，少棠的表兄留他住在那裏，還得兩三天，等我去接他的班。』一姐說到這裏，抬眼問道：『這兩天，秋兒照應得還好？』

『很好，很好！只是——。』鄭板橋搖搖頭，沒有說下去。

『只是少個人陪你喝酒？』

這個人是指于少棠還是指她自己？鄭板橋不明白，『一個人也好！』他言不由衷地，『靜下來可以想想往事。』

『那——，』一姐斜睇着他說，『回頭倒說給我聽聽！』

『回頭』已是二更時分，蕭蕭秋雨，宜尋好夢，鄭板橋正待解衣上床，窗紙外映出一片光暈；開門看時，是一姐持着燭台站在外面。

 Zheng Banqiao and Yijie had not seen each other for only three days, and they seemed to have so many things to say to each other. But they were inhibited by the presence of Qiu'er, and they could snatch but a few stealthy glances each in the other's direction. It seemed as though their three days of separation had been three years, and that they had to search each other's face for the changes that time had wrought.

"Aunt is much recovered now. It was fortunate that you urged Shaotang to visit her. She didn't care so much whether her own son came or not, but she missed the nephew she had nursed very much. It was because of this that Shaotang's cousin asked him to stay on for two or three days before letting me go to take over from him." At this point, Yijie rasied her eyes and asked, "Did Qiu'er take good care of you these few days?"

"Very well, very well! Only ..." Zheng Banqiao shook his head but didn't continue.

"Only there was no drinking companion?"

Did she mean Yu Shaotang or herself? Zheng Banqiao was not sure. "Well, there is something to say for being on one's own!" He did not quite mean what he said. "I had the time to reflect calmly on the past."

"Well ...," said Yijie, inclining her head to one side, "You must tell me about that presently?"

 When "presently" came around, it was already the second watch. The chilly autumn rain made it a time for sweet dreams. Zheng Banqiao was about to undress for bed when a flicker of light could be seen through the window paper. When he opened the door, it was Yijie standing outside holding a candlestick.

鄭板橋訝異多於一切，『還沒有睡？』他隨口問了一句；身子卻堵着門。

她把燭台伸了過來讓他接着；然後身子一閃，進門就說：『我不甘心！』

鄭板橋一驚：『甚麼事？』他問，『怎麼不甘心？』

『我不甘心嫁于少棠。』

這一聲在鄭板橋如當頭雷震，『怎，怎說這話？』他喘着氣說，『你們一雙兩好——。』

『你不要說昧心的話！』一姐搶白，『難道你就甘心了？』

一句話，直抉鄭板橋的心事，他像鬥敗了的公雞一般，把頭低了下去，往回退了兩步。

『在姑太太家那三天，我一夜夢見你好幾遍。我告訴我自己，我是有夫之婦，少棠待我不錯，莫做對不起他的事！』她指着熒然一燈：『燈光菩薩在這裏，我不說半句假話。我盡力忍，忍！到底忍不住；我少不得你，這是沒法的事！再在那裏住下去，要悶出一場病來。你——，』她亂眨着眼，便待流淚：『你怎麼說！』

說着，便撲了過來；鄭板橋跟扶救要傾跌的人那樣，不由自主地雙手一張；一姐便伏在他胸前，聽得見他的心跳如擂鼓。

豐腴軟滑的肉體，散射着令人無可抗拒的溫暖；不辨來自髮際還是衣襟的甜香，薰得人意亂如麻。鄭板橋竟無法駕馭自己，心裏要擺脫，手上卻把她抱得更緊了！

Zheng Banqiao's reaction was mainly one of surprise. "Still up?" his question came casually, but his body blocked the entrance through the doorway.

Holding out the candlestick, she thrust it into his hands, slipped by him into the room, and said , "It's so unfair!"

Zheng Banqiao was stunned. "What is it?" he asked. "What is so unfair?"

"It's so unfair that I should be married to Yu Shaotang."

This struck Zheng Banqiao like a bolt of thunder. "How, how can you say such a thing?" he said, panting for breath. "You two are perfectly suited."

"Don't say things you don't mean!" Yijie cut in. "Can you say that it is fair to you?"

These words gouged out the thought from Zheng Banqiao's innermost heart. He lowered his head like a cock defeated in a fight, and took a couple of steps backward.

"During the three days I stayed at aunt's, I kept dreaming of you. I reminded myself that I was a married woman and that Shaotang treated me with decency. It would be wrong of me to let him down." She pointed at the glowing lamp and said, "The Buddha of Light here will testify to the fact that I am telling the absolute truth. I tried and tried to control myself. But I just couldn't. I can't do without you. This cannot be helped. If I stayed here any longer, I'd have become ill through frustration. You ..." She blinked her eyes wildly on the verge of tears, "What do you say?"

Having said this, she threw herself into his arms. He threw out his arms involuntarily as if he were helping someone about to fall. Yijie pressed herself against his bosom, and could hear his heart beating like a drum.

Her full and plump body gave off an irresistible warmth. An agreeable fragrance, coming from the back of her hair or perhaps from her lapel, intoxicated him and left him confused in his mind. Zheng Banqiao found it beyond him to control himself. He wanted to disengage himself, but all the time he was holding her all the

『「便見也相思苦！」』一姐唸着他的詞說：『何苦「一字也何曾吐」？你害我終身！』

不講理的話，偏是教人迴腸蕩氣；而鄭板橋亦竟有自誤終身之感，不知對一姐應該是歉疚，還是怨恨。

偎依無言，各人都像摸得到對方的心；四隻腳一步一步移向床前，自然而然地倒了下去。灼熱的嘴唇密接在一起；於是鄭板橋慢慢伸手解開她的衣紐，隱然漾灩紅光，移眼看時，一根金鍊子繫着一方猩紅綢子的肚兜……。

驀地裏一聲雷震，兩人都驚得直跳起來！看到一姐的羅襦半解，鄭板橋猛然把頭扭了轉去，衝出房門，把頭從廊上伸了出去，讓湍急的簷溜，淋得一頭一臉。

身後又出現了燭光，『表哥！』一姐喘着氣斷斷續續地說：『老天有眼，不敎你我做錯事！科場裏有鬼神，做了虧心事的，再也不得中。差點誤了你的終生！我走了。』

她慢慢地走了。鄭板橋悵惘與欣慰交雜，而終於化為撐胸塞腹的無窮之恨；回到屋中，提筆寫了一首《沁園春》：

花亦無知，
月亦無聊，

tighter.

" 'When we meet, I am sick with love.' " Yijie read a line from the poem he had written, and said, "What is the point of being 'unable to come out with a single word'? You have ruined me for life!"

These are unreasonable words but they nevertheless move one to the core. Zheng Banqiao was made to feel that all his life he had been deprived. He didn't know whether he should feel apologetic or resentful towards Yijie.

Caressing each other in silence, they seemed to have got through to each other's heart. Step by step, their feet manoeuvred them to the edge of the bed, on which they collapsed with burning lips pressed fast together. Zheng Banqiao slowly reached out his hand and unbuttoned her dress. Dimly visible was a flash of red light, and when he turned his eyes on it, he saw a gold chain hanging at the waist of her scarlet brocade ...

A clap of thunder all of a sudden crashed around them. Startled, they lept to their feet. Catching sight of Yijie's half-unbuttoned silk garment, Zheng Banqiao jerked his head round. He dashed out of the room, and stretching his head beyond the hallway, he let the cascading water from the eaves wash all over his head and face.

The light of a candle emerged from behind. "Cousin," Yijie said, gasping for breath and in halting words, "Heaven's eyes were not shut. It had stopped us from doing wrong! There are gods and spirits in the examination hall, and whoever has done anything against his conscience will not succeed. I almost ruined your career. I'll go now."

Slowly, she walked away. Zheng Banqiao at first felt desolate yet relieved, but gradually these feelings gave way to an unrelenting feeling of loss that filled the pit of his stomach. He went back into the room and wrote a poem entitled "The Hush Garden Spring":

The flowers are ignorant,
The moon is idle,

酒亦無靈；

把夭桃折斷，

煞他風景；

鸚哥煮熟，

佐我杯羹。

焚硯燒香，

椎琴裂畫，

毀盡文章抹盡名，

滎陽有輓歌家世，

乞食風情。

單寒骨相難更，

笑席帽青衫太瘦生。

看蓬門秋草，

年年破巷，

疏窗細雨，

夜夜孤燈。

難道天公，

還箝恨口，

不許長吁一兩聲！

顛狂甚，

取烏絲百幅，

細寫淒清！

And the wine no longer works.
I deliberately snap the sapling peach-tree,
Just to spoil the scenery.
I cook the parrot,
To give me a cupful of broth.
I set fire to the inkslab
And burn the incense;
I smash the lute
And shred my paintings,
I destroy all my writings
And erase my literary name.
Like Zheng Yuenhe of Xing Yang —
My life is but an elegy.
Lonely, lowly, my fate is hard to change.
I laugh at myself,
An emaciated man wearing a blue gown and straw hat.
I watch the autumn grass grow behind my humble door,
Year after year, the lane becomes more run down.
A fine rain falls before the scanty window
Night after night, I sit beside the solitary lamp.
Why do the gods still stifle my plaintive words,
And prevent me from heaving a few long sighs?
Driven frantic,
I take out a hundred pieces of silk paper,
On which to write out,
All the sorrows that have befallen me.

PURPLE JADE
HAIRPIN

紫玉釵

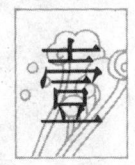『浣沙！妳聽我說，妳先坐下來息一息，我叫人拿午飯妳吃。勝業坊到西市十五里路，虧妳三天兩頭走了來，走了去；妳算是有良心的，比姓李的那個傢伙不曉得好多少倍。你們家小娘子也可憐，癡心女子負心漢——燒香拜佛、打卦問卜，統通都是白搭。落到這步田地，還不死心，也太傻了。妳該勸勸她，兩年不來，不會來了！聽說那姓李的疑心病極重、奇妒；這種人就算嫁了他，也不會有好日子過。又聽說他自吹是乾元年間宰相李揆的姪子，我倒不大相信。

我侯景先沒有開這「寄附舖」以前，在緊挨東宮的光宅坊住過，李揆的賜第就在那裏，我見過他——當朝的宰相，一點都不擺架子，而且最明白事理。可惜，好人不走運，一貶貶了出去，流落江淮十幾年不得回來。那都是因為跟元載結了怨的緣故。妳知道元載跟李揆是怎麼結的怨？』

『侯伯伯！我不知道，我也沒有心思去打聽；我不懂這些。侯伯伯，我還要趕回去，怕遲了坊門會閉。這支紫玉釵……。』

『這紫玉釵一時那裏賣得了？』

『啊呀，那怎麼辦呢？我家小娘子的病又重了，等着賣了這支釵去請醫生呢！侯伯伯，你行行好，算是幫我浣沙的忙吧。』

『鬼丫頭！我那次不幫妳的忙？我開這「寄附舖」，來來往往投宿的人，不過是些小本經紀的行賈，別的衣服首飾，脫手還容易；這支紫玉釵，妳要賣六萬錢，一時那裏去找這樣的大主顧？』

『六萬錢不貴；是我家小娘子家傳的寶物。』

"Huansha! Take my advice. But first sit down and take a rest. I'll send someone to get you lunch. It's fifteen miles from Shengye Lane to the West Market. In the last three days, it was you who kept running back and forth. You are really a very faithful girl, a lot better than that fellow Li. Your lady is so miserable. It's really a case of an infatuated girl being deserted by a heartless man. Burning incense or fortune-telling simply won't help. She's very stupid not to have given him up when she's come to such a pass. You should tell her that if he doesn't come back in two years, he'll never do so! I learned that this fellow Li is extremely suspicious and jealous. Even if she marries him, she won't enjoy a good life. I also learned that he claims to be the cousin of Li Kui, Prime Minister during the Qianyuan period. I don't quite believe him.

"Before I opened this inn, I lived in Guangzhai Lane, right next to the East Palace where Li Kui used to live. I'd seen him before —though he was Prime Minister then, he didn't put on any airs and he was most reasonable. It's an irony of fate that good people often run into bad luck. He was exiled to Jianghuai for more than ten years and never returned home, all because of his feud with Yuan Zai. Do you know how the feud started?"

"Uncle Hou, I don't know, and I am in no mood to find out. I don't understand any of this. Uncle Hou, I must hurry back or else the gate will be closed. About this purple jade hairpin ..."

"How can I sell this purple jade hairpin right now?"

"What can I do then? My lady is very sick again. We have to sell this hairpin to pay for a doctor. Uncle Hou, please try to help me."

"Silly girl! When have I ever failed to help you? All the people who stay in my inn are iternary traders with small means. It is easy for me to sell other items of clothing or ornament. But you want sixty thousand cash for this purple jade hairpin. Where can I find such a big buyer right now?"

"Sixty thousand cash isn't too much to ask. It's my lady's

『我知道不貴；我也知道它是好東西。啊，啊……有路子來了，妳看，老何！』

『老何是甚麼人？』

老何是大內的玉工；侯景先的朋友。他把他請進舖內櫃房，顧不得寒暄，也先不忙着替浣沙引見；拿她帶來的一個布包解了開來，裏面是一個六寸長、兩寸寬，蜀錦牙籤的盒子；打開盒蓋，揭起吳棉，才看到一支晶瑩溫潤的鳳頭玉釵，通體淡紫，不含雜色；雕琢之工的精細，幾乎叫人碰一碰都不敢。

『啊——！』老何倏然動容，長長地讚嘆。

『不壞吧？老何？』

『甚麼叫不壞？你簡直不識貨！』老何吵架似地對侯景先說，『我老實告訴你，我也還是第一次開眼；不過我聽我爺爺不知講過多少次了，高宗、武后年間，他在內廷當差二十年，手裏不知經過多少好玉；琢磨得最得意的，就是這支紫玉釵。』

侯景先失笑了：『你說得真玄！上次那波斯胡賣個羊脂玉玦，你說是你爸爸雕的；這會兒索性把你爺爺也搬出來了。』

『你以為我吹牛？我還你個娘家！』老何有些火了，指着紫玉釵，厲聲說道：『你曉不曉得，這是霍王家的舊物！』

僅一提『霍王』二字，侯景先立刻改變了表情；向浣沙點一點頭，說：『浣沙，見過何伯伯！』

『何伯伯！』浣沙扯一扯青布衣襟，拜了一拜。

family heirloom."

"I know it's not too much, and I also know that it's a treasure. Ah, ah ... you are in luck! It's Old He!"

"Who's Old He?"

Old He, a friend of Hou Jingxian's, was a jade carver in the palace. Hou invited him into the cashier's room without exchanging formal greeting or introducing him to Huansha. He unknotted the cloth bundle she had brought and took out a brocade ivory box six inches long and two inches wide. He lifted the lid and the silk cotton cover, revealing a crystal-clear, smooth, phoenix-headed hairpin. The body of the hairpin was a light purple. The craftsmanship was so fine that one felt a reluctance to touch it.

"Oh my ...!" Old He was astonished and gave a long sigh of admiration.

"Not bad, eh? Old He?"

"Did you say 'not bad'? You're quite an amateur!" Old He said to Hou Jingxian as if he were quarrelling. "Honestly, even to me this is a real eye-opener, though I heard about this hairpin from my granddad long ago. During the reigns of Emperor Gaozhong and Empress Wu, my grandfather, who served as a palace jade carver for twenty years, completed numerous exquisite jade pieces. Yet of all his carvings, this purple jade hairpin is the most satisfactory."

Hou Jingxian laughed. "You make it sound so intriguing. Last time that Persian guy Wu had a piece of mutton-fat jade to sell, you said it was carved by your father. This time, you're saying that it was your grandfather's masterpiece."

"You think I am bluffing? To hell with you!" Old He was getting angry. Pointing at the purple jade hairpin, he said in a loud voice, "Don't you know that this is King Huo's family treasure?"

At the mention of King Huo, Hou Jingxian's expression changed immediately. He nodded to Huansha and said, "Huansha, have you met Uncle He?"

"Uncle He." Huansha straightened the front of her blue gown

　　老何還了禮,問道:『這紫玉釵,是姑娘妳的首飾?』

　　『不是。是我家小娘子的。』浣沙遲疑了一下,又說:『我家小娘子是霍王之後。』

　　『這不就對了嗎?』老何大聲對侯景先說。

　　『你先別得意。』侯景先不慌不忙地答道,『既然你知道這支紫玉釵的來歷,而且你又走慣了大宅門的,少不得賴上了你,非給這支釵賣個好價錢不可!』

　　『這容易。祇是這位姑娘家的小娘子,到底是誰?怎麼又變賣家傳寶物?得先說給我聽聽,才好去找個好主顧。』

　　『這話也對!』侯景先想了會,對浣沙說:『我看妳今天回不去了。我叫個人到勝業坊去通知一聲;好在還有桂子在照應,妳就一天不回去也不要緊。今晚上妳跟我女兒作伴好了。』

　　『謝謝侯伯伯!』浣沙定一定神,開始講那紫玉釵的主人:『我家小娘子叫霍小玉……』

　　『小玉來也!』

　　堂東閣子有聲,屏門啓處,李益頓覺目迷五色。昨日終宵自擾,不知道鮑十一娘的話是否可信?小玉眞是那樣美得無法形容?現在,心中一塊石頭落地——但,

and greeted him with clasped hands. Old He returned the greeting and asked, "Is this purple jade hairpin yours?"

"No, it's my lady's." Huansha hesitated and continued. "My lady is one of King Huo's grand daughters."

"So I am right after all!" Old He said to Hou Jingxian in a loud voice.

"Don't be so proud of yourself yet." Hou Jingxian replied calmly. "Since you know the story behind this purple jade hairpin, and you have good connections with the rich, we have to rely on you to find someone who can offer a good price for it!"

"That's easy. But first I want to know who this girl's mistress actually is, and why she has to sell her family treasure? You must tell me the story first before I find you a good buyer."

"Of course!" Hou Jingxian thought for a while, and said to Huansha, "I think you should stay here tonight. I'll send somebody over to Shengye Lane to tell them that you won't be returning this evening. Fortunately, Guizi can take care of everything, so it really doesn't matter if you stay here one day. You can keep my daughter company tonight."

"Thank you, Uncle Hou!" Huansha composed herself, and then started to relate the story of the owner of this purple jade hairpin:

"The lady of my family is called Huo Xiaoyu ..."

"Here comes Xiaoyu!"

There was a sound at the east side of the hall and when the door was opened, Li Yi was astonished. All through the night, he had been wondering whether what Eleventh Lady Bao had said was true? Was Xiaoyu's beauty really so indescribable? Now the doubts on his mind were removed —

小玉的美還是可以形容的，李青蓮的詩：『一枝穠艷露凝香』，用來刻畫她的神韻最好。

『十郎！』長安名媒鮑十一娘，輕佻如坊里少年，她斜睨着他，伸食指向上勾一勾，示意他起身迎接。

『喔，』李益匆忙離座，迎着丁東的環珮的聲響，拜了下去，口中自介：『我，隴西李益。』

小玉避到側面回禮。等他揖罷抬身，祇見她正回眸斜睇着他，微笑低頭，然後翩然轉身，挨着她母親坐下。

那四十左右的半老佳人，有個比丘尼般的名字：淨持。她跟鮑十一娘都是薛駙馬家贖身出來的青衣侍兒——一樣知書識字、一樣嫻習禮儀、一樣大家風範，因此才能教導出一個好讀詩的女兒，『妳平常不是常在唸：「開門復動竹，疑是故人來。」』她對小玉說，『那就是這位李十郎的詩。』

『真的？』小玉的驚喜，完全呈現在那雙黑白分明，睜得極圓的大眼中，『「隴西李益」；好笑不？剛才我竟沒有想起來是甚麼人。』說完，微低着頭，以偷覷的姿態，重新打量李益；彷彿在了解了他的身份以後，他的樣子就有了改變似地。

文字見賞，而且見賞於美人，那份興奮是李益所從未經驗過的，『小娘子……。』

『叫她小玉好了。』淨持搶着說了這一句。

『喔，喔，那麼，我從命。』李益更高興了，『小玉，多謝妳。讓我敬妳一杯！』

Xiaoyu's beauty could be depicted as in a line from Li Bai's poetry — "The spring of rosy loveliness distils the dewy fragrance."

"Shilang!" Eleventh Lady Bao, a well-known match-maker in Chang'an, glanced at him like a young coquette and gestured with her index finger, inviting him to rise to meet her.

"Oh," Li Yi quickly left his seat, and with pendants jingling, he clasped his hands and introduced himself, "I am Li Yi, a native of Longxi."

Xiaoyu, half turning her face, returned the greeting. As he finished his greeting and rose, he noticed that she was also turning to steal a look at him. She smiled and lowered her head, and then spun round and sat down beside her mother.

The attractive woman in her forties had a name that sounded like a Buddhist nun's: Jingchi. She and Eleventh Lady Bao were both blue-gown maids who had bought their freedom from the Xue family, who were related to the emperor by marriage. They were both well-educated, knowledgeable in etiquette, and had the manners of ladies from respectable families, which explains how they manage to raise a daughter who was a great lover of poetry. "Don't you always recite the line: 'When the door is opened and the bamboo is rattled, I suspect an old friend of mine has come'?" Jingchi said to Xiaoyu, "This poem was written by Li Shilang."

"Really?" Xiaoyu's triumphant surprise was revealed in her big round eyes. "Isn't it funny how when he announced himself as 'Li Yi, a native of Longxi', I failed to remember him?" When she finished speaking, she lowered her head and secretly sized him up again, as if a better understanding of a person would lead to a change in his looks.

Having his poetry appreciated, especially by a beauty, brought Li Yi a thrill that he had never experienced before.

"Lady ..."

"Just call her Xiaoyu," said Jingchi, interrupting him.

"Oh, well, I will do that." Li Yi was even more pleased. "Xiaoyu, thank you. Let me drink a toast to you!"

『謝我甚麼啊？』

『多謝妳賞識我的詩。』他一飲而盡，斟上半杯酒遞給小玉。

她分兩口喝完他所敬的酒，笑道：『我也該多謝你；多謝你那些好詩，供我排遣寂寞黃昏。』說着，滿斟一杯，她自己先啜了一口，多下的遞還李益；自然，他又喝得涓滴不留。

『再喝一杯！』小玉擎着銀壺說。

『我量淺。祇是妳要我喝，我當然喝。』

『既然如此，』小玉回頭吩咐浣沙：『取那隻玉觥來！』

那隻巨觥，足容十杯；明是故意捉弄。李益真的量淺，但說出來的話不能不算；抵拚一醉，該有代價，『小玉！』他指着滿觥的酒說：『妳唱支曲，我乾了它！』

『不！』她畏縮地笑着：『我不會唱。』

『妳騙我！』李益轉臉向淨持說，『誰都不會相信她不會唱吧？』

淨持向小玉使個眼色，『妳就唱一支。』

於是，浣沙取來琵琶，交到小玉手裏，她調一調弦，向李益說道：『唱一首「北歌」。我唱你和。』

『唱甚麼？』李益問：『「紫騮馬」、「折楊柳」、還是「隴頭水」？』這些都是『北歌』中最有名的詩——李白和盧照鄰的作品。

『你聽了就知道了。』

小玉五指一揮，大小弦中灑落陣陣疾風暴雨；然後嘈嘈切切；

"Thank me for what?"

"Thank you for your appreciation of my poetry." He emptied the cup and poured half a cup of wine for Xiaoyu.

She finished this in two mouthfuls and said with a smile, "I should also thank you for all the good poems you've written which I read to dispel my loneliness at dusk." As she spoke, she filled another cup, took a sip herself and gave the rest to Li Yi. Naturally, he emptied it.

"Have another cup!" Xiaoyu said, holding the silver wine carafe.

"I can't drink too much. But if you want me to drink, I will surely comply."

"If that is so," Xiaoyu turned and instructed Huansha, "then bring me that jade carafe."

The large jade carafe could hold as much as ten cups of wine. Clearly, Xiaoyu wanted to embarrass him. Li Yi really couldn't drink very much, but neither could he eat his words. For getting drunk he had to gain something in return.

"Xiaoyu," he pointed at the pot of wine filled to the brim and said. "You sing a song, and I'll empty the pot."

"No!" She smiled, shrinking back. "I can't sing."

"You are lying!" Li Yi turned round and said to Jingchi, "Surely nobody will believe that she can't sing."

Jingchi glanced at Xiaoyu. "My dear, why don't you sing a song then?"

Huansha fetched a *pipa* and handed it to Xiaoyu. She tuned the strings and said to Li Yi, "I'll sing a 'northern song'. You sing along with me."

"What are you going to sing?" Li Yi asked, "'Purple Pony'? 'Breaking Willow Twigs'? Or 'Rivers in Longtou'? These are the most famous northern songs by Li Bai and Lu Zhaolin."

"You'll know it when you hear it."

As Xiaoyu moved her fingers across the strings, the music emerged like splatters of strong wind and torrential rain. It then

轉為怨婦私訴之聲，忽然錚錚兩響，琵琶聲寂；一縷瀏亮的清音，破空而起：

> 入夜思歸切……。

怪不得說『聽了就知道了！』唱的是李益自己的詩：『夜上受降城聞笛。』小玉的聲音太美了，他不敢相和，怕破壞了它；祇深深點頭，一半讚許，一半致謝；然後凝神靜聽着。

> ……笛聲清更哀。
> 愁人不願聽，
> 自到枕前來！

上半首唱得淒怨欲絕；下半首音節一振，變為沉鬱蒼涼：

> ……風起塞雲斷，
> 夜深關月開。
> 平明獨惆悵，
> 落盡一庭梅。

李益乾了那一巨觥酒，如牛飲般，喉間啯啯有聲。放下玉觥，祇見淚痕滿面，淨持和鮑十一娘都嚇慌了，一齊問道：『怎麼了，怎麼了？』

李益搖搖頭，他不願說他心裏的感覺，也說不明白；受降城上，

hummed like a hushed whisper, or like the quiet weeping of a deserted wife. Then, she plucked the strings twice, which was followed by complete silence. Her clear, high voice cut through the air:

The night is deep
And I am anxious to go home.

No wonder she had said "You'll know it when you hear it" — this was his own poem entitled "Hearing the Music of a Flute at a Surrendered Town in the Evening." Xiaoyu's voice was so beautiful that he didn't dare to sing along with her. He simply nodded his head vigorously to express his appreciation and gratitude. He listened in silence as she sang:

The sound of the flute is clear and sad.
I don't like to hear it
So I take a rest on my pillow.

She sang the first half of the song with deep sadness. The tone of the second half suddenly changed to gloom and loneliness:

The wind rises and the clouds at the frontier
*   scatter all over the sky.*
The night is deep and the moon over the pass
*   is clear.*
All by myself, I am sad
And covering the courtyard is a carpet
*   of plum blossoms.*

Li Yi emptied the large carafe of wine like a bull drinking water, making a gurgling sound in his throat. When he put down the jade carafe, his cheeks were covered with tears. Jingchi and Eleventh Lady Bao were shaken and asked him at the same time, "What's the matter with you?"

Li Yi shook his head. He didn't want to speak about his feelings, and he couldn't put them into words either. Over the sur-

霜月雙清，那一縷嗚嗚咽咽的笛音，勾魂懾魄，喚起無限鄉思——淡忘的記憶，此一刻在小玉的歌聲中重現。於是，情感一向脆弱的李益忍受不住了。

『都是我不好。』明白他的心境的，祇有小玉，『我不該唱十郎這首傷心的詩。』

這一說，淨持和鮑十一娘才能約略意會，『來，來！』鮑十一娘眉花眼笑地，『我也來獻獻醜。』

既老且醜的鮑十一娘也要一逞歌喉，那會唱成甚麼樣子？因此，連侍兒們都拍手嘻笑，準備看她真的『獻醜』！

『十一姨！』小玉重又扶起琵琶，撥着弦問道：『妳唱甚麼？』

『不用，不用。』鮑十一娘搖手答說：『不用妳瞎起勁，我唱「迴波樂」。』

『喲，那得要且唱且舞。快拿紅氍毹來！』

『沒有那些講究。』鮑十一娘一面說，一面手舞足蹈，擠眉弄眼地唱了起來。

迴波詞照例六言四句，中宗朝盛行於宮廷中；常由被召宴的羣臣，臨時撰詞獻舞。因此，如有諫請諷喻，不便明言，便借迴波詞寄意。最有名的一個故事是，沈佺期得罪流放嶺南，以後蒙恩召還；但一切榮典並未恢復。有一次他在中宗的筵前，獻唱迴波詞：

rendered town, both the frost and the moon were clear, and the weeping tune from the flute was so touching, arousing homesickness — all these remote memories were brought to life by Xiaoyu's singing. Li Yi, who was by nature a tender-hearted person, could not help weeping.

"It's all my fault." Xiaoyu was the only one who understood how he felt. "I shouldn't have sung Shilang's heart-breaking song."

Now it dawned on Jingchi and Eleventh Lady Bao what had happened. "Now, now!" Eleventh Lady Bao smiled, "Let me show off my skills too."

Now old and ugly Eleventh Lady Bao wanted to sing a song. How would she do? Even the maids clapped their hands and laughed, all set to watch her "show off".

"Eleventh auntie!" Xiaoyu took up her *pipa* again, plucked the strings and said, "What would you like to sing?"

"Don't ask." Eleventh Lady Bao answered, waving her hand. "Don't get so excited. I'll sing 'The Joy of Rippling Waves'."

"Oh, that song should be accompanied by dancing. Quick, go and get the red carpet!"

"I don't need that." As she spoke she began her dance, making eyes as she sang.

"The Joy of Rippling Waves" was a song set to music, which usually had four lines of six words each. It was very popular in the court during the reign of Emperor Zhongzong. Officials invited to imperial banquets would write the lyrics impromptu and present them with dance accompaniment. Officials who wanted to admonish the emperor or ridicule his administration, but were reluctant to do so publicly, could deliver their message through the song. In a classic story, Shen Quanqi was found guilty and exiled to Lingnan. He was later reinstated through imperial favour, but none of his former privileges had been restored to him. So at a banquet hosted by Emperor Zhongzong, he wrote the following song:

> 迴波爾時佺期，
> 流向嶺外生歸；
> 身名已蒙齒錄，
> 袍笏未賜牙緋。

於是，中宗復賜以緋魚袋——五品以上官員出入宮禁所用的憑證。

鮑十一娘難道也有自撰歌辭的才情？李益十分疑惑，因此格外加了幾分注意；聽她唱的是：

> 迴波爾時栲栳，
> 怕婆卻也大好；
> 『從前』且有裴談，
> 『眼下』無過李老。

唱到最後兩字，拿手直指着李益，一時滿堂大笑——那也是個有名的故事，中宗朝，以滑稽爲帝后所喜的優人臧奉，獻唱此詞取媚於韋后；當時有兩個怕老婆出了名的人，一個是御史大夫裴談，一個就是中宗。原詞是：『外頭且有裴談，內面莫如李老』，李老即指皇帝；而現在鮑十一娘卻是故意改動幾個字，跟李益開了個玩笑。

『插科打諢，祇是要博十郎一笑。』鮑十一娘替李益又斟了酒，『十郎，寬飲一杯！』

這一杯下去，李益的酒量到了極限；祇覺人影晃動，胸中翻翻滾滾地想嘔，趕緊閉上了眼，儘力按捺着。

『啊呀，眞醉了！』他聽見淨持在埋怨小玉：『十郎酒量不好，

Once Quanqi was exiled to Lingnan
And was later allowed to return by Your Highness.
My position was reinstated and my reputation cleared,
But I have not gotten back my ivory audience-tablet
   and red robes.

Emperor Zhongzong immediately presented him with a red fishpouch, a pass used by officials above the fifth rank for entering the forbidden palaces.

Did Eleventh Lady Bao have the talent to improvise such lines herself? Li Yi doubted this, so he paid close attention to her singing:

An osier bucket
How good it is to be henpecked.
In the past, it was Pei Tan.
Now it's Old Li.

As she sang the last two words, she pointed at Li Yi, and the entire audience roared with laughter. Her lyrics referred to a famous story. During the period of Emperor Zhongzong, the Empress Wei's favourite court jester wrote the above lyrics to please her. At that time, there were two well-known henpecked persons: Imperial Censor Pei Tan, and Emperor Zhongzong himself. The original version went: "Outside the court, it is Pei Tan; inside, it's none other than Old Li." Old Li, of course, referred to the emperor. Eleventh Lady Bao had deliberately changed a few words to poke fun at Li Yi.

"I changed a few words just to give you a good laugh." Eleventh Lady Bao poured wine for Li Yi. "Shilang, have another cup!"

When he finished drinking, he realized that it was more than he could handle. He saw human shadows moving around before him, while his stomach felt so disturbed that he wanted to vomit. He quickly shut his eyes and tried to control himself.

"Aiya, he's really drunk!" he heard Jingchi blaming Xiaoyu.

妳不該灌他那一觥。』

『醉了怕甚麼?』是鮑十一娘在替她辯護,『來!浣沙,桂子,把十郎扶進去睡!』

胸中作嘔,心裏卻清楚,李益一半無法睜開眼來,一半卻是故意裝糊塗,看她們把他扶到那裏去?

扶到一個香味馥郁,衾枕軟滑的地方;不用說,那是小玉的臥房;但又怕不是。想睜開眼來看一看,不知怎麼又不敢,仍舊閉着眼,聽任那些柔滑的手,替他脫靴卸袍,安置在床上。

心中疑疑惑惑一直在想自己身在何處?但到底不勝酒力,漸漸地甚麼都不知道了。

一覺醒來,銀釭微明,照見紅羅帳中、鴛鴦枕上一彎黑髮;隨即又聞到甜甜的肉香。手一動,驚醒了小玉。

『睡得好沉!』她說,『酒該醒了吧?』

『嗯,嗯。』李益歉意地笑道:『荒唐失禮之至!』

『渴不渴?我倒茶你喝?』

『謝謝。給我涼涼的,來一大杯。』

小玉掀開帳子下床,剔亮了燈替他倒茶。她穿一條綠綾的短襖,窄細腰肢,卻有個豐滿的胸脯。頰上枕痕猶在;長睫毛掩蓋着惺忪的眼,那嬌慵的韻緻,使他更覺得渴了!

『當心,別潑出來!』她小心翼翼把一滿鍾茶湯捧到李益面前。

他不忙着喝茶,先伸手握住了她;彷彿怕她逃跑似地。然後就

"Shilang can't drink too much. You shouldn't have made him drink the entire carafe."

"Why worry about him getting drunk?" Eleventh Lady Bao defended her. "Come, Huansha and Guizi, help him to bed."

Though he felt like vomiting, he was still somewhat sober. Partly because he couldn't open his eyes, and partly because he wanted to appear muddled and know where they were taking him.

They escorted him to a place where the fragrance was strong and the quilt and pillow were soft and silky. This, needless to say, was most likely Xiaoyu's bedroom. But he couldn't be sure. He wanted to open his eyes and look around, but somehow he dared not to. So he kept his eyes shut and let them take off his shoes and clothes with their tender hands. He was then helped onto a bed.

He kept wondering where he actually was, however, and overcome with drunkenness he gradually lost consciousness.

When he woke up, he noticed the dim light from silver candlesticks shining on some black tresses spread over the mandarin duck pillows inside the red brocade bed curtains and he smelt a fragrance coming from her body. He moved, and Xiaoyu was waken.

"You had a sound sleep!" she said. "You must be sober now."

"Yes, I am." Li Yi smiled apologetically. "It was really most impolite of me!"

"Are you thirsty? Do you want me to get you some tea?"

"Thank you. Please give me a large cup of cold tea."

Xiaoyu raised the bed curtain and got out of bed, turned up the light, and got him some tea. She wore a short green brocade jacket. Her waist was slim but her breast were full. There were pillow marks on her cheeks, and her long eyelashes shaded her sleepy eyes. Her languorous charm made him even more thirsty.

"Be careful, don't spill the tea!" she said as she handed the cup to Li Yi.

He didn't drink it immediately, but stretched out his hands

她手中把一鍾茶喝光，喘口氣舒暢地笑道：『小玉，多謝妳的甘露。』

『「渴者易爲飲」。祇怕──。』她突然頓住，回身把茶鍾放在桌上。

『祇怕甚麼？』他拉緊了她的手追問。

『祇怕你對我──。』她正一正臉色，輕輕地說：『你心裏該明白。不要明知故問。』

『小玉，我明白妳的意思。』李益斬釘截鐵地說：『我不是那種人。』

『那麼，你是那一種人呢？』

『妳上床來！春寒料峭，別凍着了！咱們倆好好談一談。』

於是小玉仍舊上了床，兩人各擁一衾，披衣並坐，側面相對。

『從何談起呢？』他躊躇地說。

『先從你自己開始。』

『我，李益，字君虞，隴西姑臧人。叔父單名一個揆字，乾元年間的宰相。我是去年中的進士。』他停了一下，似乎很不願意地說：『但慚愧得很；吏部「釋褐」試，還未能入選……。』

『功名有遲早。』小玉安慰他說，『你今年才二十出頭，俗語說：「三十老明經，五十少進士」，你已進士及第，而且有那樣的聲名，怕不是一片錦繡前程在等着你？』

『妳說得我那樣好，』李益興奮地說，『其實，我此刻對吏部一試，能不能入選；倒不怎麼在乎了。』

『爲甚麼？』

『有了妳，富貴在我像浮雲一樣。』他有些言不由衷了。

and held hers as if she might run away if he didn't do so. He drank up the cup of tea she was holding and said with a smile of relief, "Xiaoyu, thank you for the sweet dewdrops."

"'Those who are thirsty are easily satisfied.' Only I am afraid ..."

"What are you afraid of?" He held her hands tighter.

"I am afraid that you might not ..." she suddenly became serious and said softly, "You know perfectly well. You don't have to ask me."

"Xiaoyu, I know what you mean." Li Yi said decisively. "I'm not that kind of person."

"Well, what kind of person are you then?"

"Get into bed. It is chilly in spring, don't catch a cold! Let's have a chat."

Xiaoyu got into the bed. Each holding a quilt, they sat side by side with their clothing on.

"Where do we begin?" he said hesitantly.

"Begin with yourself."

"I'm Li Yi, styled Junyu, a native of Guzang in Longxi. My uncle, whose name is Kui, was the Prime Minister during the Qianyuan period. I received the degree of *jinshi* last year ..." He paused, then continued reluctantly, "Much to my disappointment, I failed the 'Civil Office Test' and was not selected ..."

"The recognition you deserve will come sooner or later." Xiaoyu comforted him. "You're just over twenty. As the saying goes, 'To be a *mingjing* at thirty is old; but to get the degree of *jinshi* at fifty is young.' Now you're a *jinshi* with a considerable reputation, isn't there a bright future in store for you?"

"You paint me with such bright colours," Li Yi said in excitement. "In fact, I am now hardly concerned about my failure at the examination for the Board of Civil Office."

"Why?"

"Now that I have you, fame and fortune are like floating clouds to me, " he said half-heartedly.

小玉不答。她心裏矛盾得很，李益一直是她所仰慕的；又如此年輕多才，能託終身，自然心滿意足。可是，又怕他功成名就，匹配高門，自己的姻緣落空。

『小玉！』他緊握着她的手，挨近了些，『我要重重酬謝鮑十一娘——替我做這麼好一個媒。』

『哼！』小玉故意冷笑道：『像你這樣門第清華，誰配得上你！』說着掙脫了他的手。

『妳怎麼說這話？』李益重又捉住她的手，發急似地說：『本朝婚娶，好講門第，我最不以爲然了。再說，妳不也是霍王之後麼？』

『可是我不姓李。姓鄭，姓霍。』

『怎麼弄出兩個姓來了？』

『你想知道？』

『自然。』李益說，『關於妳的每一件事，我都想知道。』

於是，小玉講她的身世——。

高祖李淵第十四子元軌，封霍王，才德最美，是太宗最鍾愛的一個弟弟，特爲他聘魏徵的女兒作妃子。垂拱四年，越王起兵討武后，據說霍王同謀。越王兵敗，位列司空的霍王流放黔州；檻車到了陳倉地方，上了年紀的霍王，在那裏得病而死。

霍王生前的寵婢，這時有孕在身；霍王的六個兒子，都不願意要這個尚未出生的小弟弟或者小妹妹。於是那寵婢帶着一大筆錢，和霍王的骨血，悄然離去。不久，生下一個兒子；又不久，嫁了個

Xiaoyu didn't say anything. She was confused. She adored Li
Yi. To be married to such a young and talented man should be a
source of great satisfaction to her. But she was also afraid that once
he became powerful and famous, she wouldn't be able to match
him and their marriage would come to nought.

"Xiaoyu!" He moved closer to her, holding her hands tight, "I
have to thank Eleventh Lady Bao for being our match-maker."

"Humph!" Xiaoyu said dryly, "What family can match such a
prominent family as yours?" She freed her hands from his grip as
she spoke.

"How can you say such a thing?" Li Yi grabbed her hands
again and said, "Nowadays, it is common practice to match people
of equal family standing. But I am against it. Isn't it true that
you're King Huo's grand-daughter?"

"But my family name is not Li. It's Zheng and Huo."

"How come you've two family names?"

"Do you want to know?"

"Yes," Li Yi said. "I want to know everything about you."

So Xiaoyu started to tell him the story of her life:

Xiaoyu's ancestor, Yuan Gui, the fourteenth son of Li Yuan, the
founder of the Tang Dynasty, Emperor Gaozu, was crowned King
of Huo. Emperor Taizong loved his talented and virtuous brother
so much that he selected Wei Zheng's daughter to be King Huo's
consort. After four years of peaceful rule, King Yue revolted
against Empress Wu, and King Huo was accused of being involved in the conspiracy. When the revolt failed, King Huo, who
was then Minister of Public Works, was exiled to Qianzhou. When
the prisoner's cart reached Chencang, the aged King Huo died of
illness.

King Huo's favourite concubine was already pregnant before
he died. His six sons, however, did not want this new addition to
the family, be it a boy or a girl. The concubine, therefore, had to
flee quietly with a large sum of money with King Huo's unborn
child. Eventually, she gave birth to a son, and not long after that

姓鄭的商人；霍王的小兒子便也改姓了鄭——他，就是小玉的祖父。

　　小玉的母親淨持，不是她父親明媒正娶的嫡室：那種曖昧的關係，隨着她父親的暴卒而消逝。因此，淨持不願再讓小玉姓鄭，但也不敢說是王室庶支，復姓爲李；這樣，姓霍便最恰當了。

　　『照此說來，妳眞是霍王的曾孫女；』李益感嘆地說，『高祖皇帝的玄孫，地地道道的金枝玉葉。倒是我高攀了！』

　　『你壞！』小玉嗔責地，『我原不肯告訴你的。告訴了你，你又挖苦我。』

　　『我怎麼敢，眞的，妳自己去算算輩份，不是金枝玉葉是甚麼？照規矩，該封妳個「縣主」！』說着，他自然而然地一把拖住了她。

　　『還要笑我！還要笑我！』小玉扭着身子，要伸出手去打他。

　　兩人就此糾纏着笑作一團；錦衾凌亂——結果，兩條衾併作一條衾；然後聲音低了下來，低低地笑和低低的喘息。

歡娛的高潮，在李益是很快地消失了；但對小玉來說，卻是餘波蕩漾，化作漣漪，一圈一圈地在心湖中推展、擴大，久久不能平息。

she married a merchant named Zheng. King Huo's son therefore had to change his family name to Zheng — this was Xiaoyu's grandfather.

Xiaoyu's mother Jingchi was not her father's legal wife; her marriage had not been properly arranged by a go-between. That relationship came to an end with the sudden death of her husband. Jingchi would no longer let Xiaoyu bear the family name Zheng, nor would she dare to use the family name Li, for that would suggest a direct lineage with the royal family. The most proper choice, therefore, was to use the family name Huo.

"In that case, you're King Huo's great-grand daughter," Li Yi said with a sigh. "A great-great grandchild of Emperor Gaozu is truly of royal lineage. It is I who don't match you!"

"Don't be so naughty!" Xiaoyu said, somewhat displeased. "In fact, I didn't want to tell you any of this. Now that I've told you, you make fun of me."

"How dare I! Really, aren't you an imperial grandchild? According to ancient practice, you should bear the title *xianzhu*." As he spoke, he put his arms around her.

"You're still making fun of me! You're still making fun of me!" Xiaoyu, twisting about, wanted to hit him.

Thus entangled, the two of them laughed as they embraced each other. The brocade quilts were knotted together, and in the end, the two quilts became as one. Then, their voices became lower and lower, and all that could be heard was their soft giggling and panting.

 For Li Yi, the climax of ecstasy soon vanished. To Xiaoyu, however, the ecstasy lingered on and on until it became circle upon circle of ripples which kept expanding outward in her mind.

昏昏的燈燄，沉沉的長夜；如果不能尋得好夢，便會尋得煩惱。
第一惱人的是，與她在同一個枕上的人的勻稱的鼻息；在她的經驗
中，幾乎每一個男人都是一樣的，可以一下子由熱變冷，由眉花眼笑
變得毫無表情，由說不盡的甜言蜜語變得隻字不出。然後，眼一閉，
翻個身，管自己睡得像死豬一樣，彷彿根本不知道還有一個人在他
身旁似地。

那常使她生出反感，覺得那是男人自私無情的表現。但這份反
感每每也是極短暫的；不像此一刻，一直盤踞在心中。

她知道，那是因為她對他跟對別的男人不一樣的緣故。『李益』
這兩個字，鏤刻在她心頭已久，每當細讀傳鈔的他的詩篇；或者凝
神靜聽教坊樂工，勾欄嬌娃奏唱他的新作時，腦中總會浮起一個瀟
灑風流的少年男子的形像，而視之為她唯一的情郎。

她相信他一定會到長安來的。天下的才人，一生至少要來長安
一次，而且也一定是在二十歲至三十歲的年輕時候——他們來角逐
那一名四海艷羨的進士。她更相信，祇要他到了長安，一定有相遇
的機會，他不會隱在終南山的古寺中去讀書用功；走馬章臺，遍閱
長安名花，他該知道小玉的不凡，登門探訪。就算他不來，以他那
樣的聲名，在長安的人海中也是隱藏不住的，當然有辦法可以把他
找了來。

見面以後又如何呢？她也常常這樣自問着。祇為了一次相思債
嗎？不是的！她沒有忘掉她自己是霍王之後，從小，她母親就這樣

If dim lights and long nights don't inspire sweet dreams, they inspire troubles. The most troublesome thing was the even breathing of the man who slept next to her. In her experience, almost every man was the same: they went from warm to cool in a second, from all smiles to a straight face, and from endless outpourings of sweet words to speechlessness. Then they closed their eyes, and fell into a sleep so deep that they seemed unaware they were not alone.

This behaviour often aroused her aversion, for it appeared to her as a manifestation of masculine selfishness and heartlessness. Usually, her aversion was just momentary. But now, it remained stuck in her mind.

This, she knew, was because she treated him differently from other men. The name Li Yi had been deeply engraved in her mind for a long time. Whenever she read his poems, or when she listened attentively to street musicians and courtesans playing his songs, the image of a handsome and smart youth always appeared in her mind's eye, and she looked upon him as her one and only lover.

She believed that he would come to Chang'an. Talented men from all over the empire would come to Chang'an at least once in their lifetime, usually between the age of twenty and thirty, to seek the much-coveted *jinshi* degree. She also believed that when Li Yi came to Chang'an, she would have a chance to meet him, since she thought he would not shut himself up and study at an old temple on Zhongnan Mountain. When he visited the pleasure houses of Chang'an, he would come to realize how exceptional Xiaoyu was, and would surely pay her a visit. Even if he didn't come, there would certainly be a way for her to discover the whereabouts of such a famous person.

"What would happen after the meeting then?" she always asked herself. Was it for the sake of meeting her dream lover? Certainly not. She never forgot that she was a granddaughter of King Huo. Ever since childhood, her mother Jingchi kept remind-

一遍又一遍地告訴她——淨持，似乎特別看重這一點。小玉知道她母親的力爭上游的志氣；可是生活逼人，終於淪落爲娼家，這是她們母女心頭最大的隱痛。

然而，那也不能說是一無是處。兩年來，一曲紅綃，纏頭無數，聚積了千把貫的家財，可算小康。霍王之後的身份，加上可供半世溫飽的衣食之資，能夠平衡她的勾欄出身的缺點了！

於是，她也有了力爭上游的志氣，要脫出娼家女子不能成爲讀書人的嫡室的傳統，跟李益做白首偕老的花燭夫妻。不如此，她寧願把他當做夢裏情郎，悵惘終生。

自從有了這樣的決定，她就知道見了面該如何自處了。她要端莊穩重，像個名門淑女；讓李益祇記得她是霍王之後，忘卻她現在的營生。然後，儘力幫助他讀書成名——她已打聽出來，李益是式微的世家子弟，境況清苦；她要待之以情而持之以禮，使他在感激愛慕之中，有着一份不敢褻瀆的尊敬，才像個敵體的嫡室的樣子。

這些深思熟慮得妥妥貼貼的念頭，果然一步一步實現了：李益到了長安，通過鮑十一娘的靈活的手腕，做成了媒。但剛是相見的第一面，她就把那些想得極透澈的做法，忘記得乾乾淨淨！

現在她明白了，不該唱他的詩，不該灌他的酒，不該讓他進入自己的臥房；更不該說那些自卑自賤的話，尤其不該……

ing her of her imperial pedigree. Naturally, Xiaoyu was familiar with her mother's aspirations to rise high. But life was harsh. Xiaoyu had fallen into prostitution and this was a hidden sorrow shared by both mother and daughter.

Nevertheless, prostitution wasn't entirely unrewarding. In the last two years, Xiaoyu had accumulated a fortune of about one thousand taels of gold, which could provide her with a comfortable life. Her status as King Huo's granddaughter and her fortune, sufficient to support her for the rest of her life, balanced out all the shortcomings of being a courtesan.

So she also had aspirations to rise high, and wanted to break the tradition that a courtesan could not become the legal wife of a man of letters. She wanted to be legally married to Li Yi and enjoy marital bliss to the end of their days. If she failed to achieve this, she would rather have him as a lover in her dreams and remain single for the rest of her life.

Having made up her mind, she knew how to deal with Li Yi when she met him. She would behave like a lady from an aristocratic family so as to remind him that she was a grandchild of King Huo and make him forget her present occupation. Then she would try to help him achieve fame through scholarship. She already knew that Li Yi was the son of a noble but poor family, and was now leading a miserable life. She would give him love and treat him with propriety so that he would, out of gratitude and adoration, show her his respect. In this way, she could appear like a wife of equal status for him.

All of her well-thought-out plans were realized one by one. When Li Yi arrived in Chang'an, through clever manoeuvering on the part of Eleventh Lady Bao, they finally met each other. But at their first meeting, Xiaoyu completely forgot what she had set out to do.

Now she realized that she shouldn't have sung his songs, plied him with wine, allowed him into her bedroom, and most importantly, said so many self-derogatory things to him. And what's

　　她，她發現她對待李益的，跟對待任何一個生張熟魏的狎客的，並沒有絲毫的不同。而他，他的反應，也像任何一個生張熟魏的狎客在高潮消失以後所表現的，完全一樣。在他心目中，她至多不過是一個名妓而已。

　　『該死！我做了些甚麼混帳的事！』椎心般痛悔着的小玉，一伏身埋頭在錦衾之中；錦衾爲淚水濕了一大片。

　　嚶嚶的啜泣，吵醒了李益。『怎麼啦？小玉？』他驚疑地問。

　　不問還好，一問更使她感到有口難言之苦，哭得更兇了！

　　李益的疑懼更甚，『小玉！』他使勁地搖着她的肩說：『妳快告訴我，究竟是甚麼事傷心？』

　　『我悔，我做錯了！』她哽咽着說。

　　『做錯了？做錯了甚麼？』

　　『我不要說！』她哭着喊道：『你一定在心裏看不起我！』

　　李益有些明白了，大概是她自己觸起身世之痛。他默然無以爲答，因爲他實在還沒有想到過這一點。

　　而在表面上，他似乎默認了她的話，因此，她再度泣不可仰。

　　夜靜更深，羅帳中的哭聲，傳到外面，將會引起他人極深的訝異。李益急於想收拾這個尷尬的局面，便一把把她攬倒在懷中，用一塊錦帕替她拭着眼淚，同時溫柔地喊道：『小玉，小玉！』

　　這對小玉發生了撫慰鎮靜的作用，她慢慢地住了哭聲。

more, she shouldn't have ...

She realized that she had treated Li Yi the same as all the other pleasure-seekers. And, worse still, his reactions were the same as the other pleasure-seekers once the climax was over. To him, she was nothing more than a notable courtesan.

"Damn it! What the hell have I done?" Sorrow stricken, Xiaoyu buried her head in the brocade quilt which was soaked with her tears.

Her sobbing awoke Li Yi.

"What's the matter, Xiaoyu?" he asked in astonishment.

It would have been better for him not to have asked. For upon hearing his words, she felt so bitter about the many things she couldn't express that she cried even harder.

Li Yi became even more perplexed. "Xiaoyu," he shook her shoulders vigorously and said, "Tell me what is it that makes you so unhappy?"

"I hate myself for all the wrong things I've done!" she said in tears.

"For all the wrong things? What wrong things have you done?"

"I don't want to talk about it!" she said, crying. "You must have the greatest contempt for me!"

It began to dawn on Li Yi that Xiaoyu was upset about her origins. He remained silent and didn't answer her, simply because he hadn't thought about the matter himself.

Since it appeared that he had actually agreed with her, she cried even harder.

Crying from the confines of a brocade bed curtain transmitted to the outside in the depths of the night could easily arouse people's curiosity. Li Yi was eager to resolve this embarrassing situation, so he embraced her, wiped her tears with a brocade handkerchief, and said to her softly, "Xiaoyu, Xiaoyu!"

The way he spoke her name soothed her, and she soon stopped crying.

『到底爲了甚麼？哭得這樣叫人心痛！妳倒是說給我聽聽！』

『你知道的，』小玉容顏慘淡地答說，『我不過是個娼家女子，配不上你。眼前相好，不過是你拿我當個玩物；一旦人老珠黃不值錢，就像秋天的團扇一樣，你再也想不起它了！』

原來如此！李益懷疑她是故意做作的一條苦肉計。但當初託鮑十一娘做媒時，人家已說得清清楚楚，雖是霍王之後，卻不幸淪入娼家，祇是色藝雙全，並且手頭頗有積蓄，如果看中了，卻要明媒正娶。而自己已是滿口答應了的；此時如果沒有確切的表示，明顯著有負心之意，那麼，一切的一切，就都算終結了！

『不行！』他立刻在心中警告自己。儻來艷福，予而不取；而且，吏部一試，也還沒有把握，『長安居，大不易。』有這樣一個不愁衣食的溫柔鄉可住而不住，天下那裏找這樣優的人去？

於是，他鄭重肅穆地說：『小玉，我現在就改了對妳的稱呼：夫人！』

『夫人?』小玉失驚地叫了一聲，含着淚珠的雙眼，映着殘燄，閃閃生光，疑多於驚，驚多於喜，她終究還不能相信。

『夫人！』李益又說：『從安史大亂以後，婚姻門第之說，已不大講究了。我李益，更不是那種陳腐頑固的人，平生自誓，不娶則已，要娶，一定得是個絕色的美人。承妳不棄，平生大願，算是圓圓滿滿地達到了，妳怎麼反而疑心我的誠意呢？我有個朋友叫孟郊，他新近做了一首詩，題目叫做「結愛」，我唸開頭跟結尾的四句

"What's the matter? You're crying so hard it hurts me! Why don't you tell me about it?"

"You know already." Xiaoyu said dispirited. "I am a mere courtesan and can never match you. We're happy now because you treat me like a plaything. But once I'm old and ugly and worthless, I'll be like a fan in autumn — you'll soon forget me!"

So this was the reason. Li Yi suspected that she might be playing a trick just to impress him. But when he had spoken to Eleventh Lady Bao about acting as go-tween, she had made it clear to him that Xiaoyu was a granddaughter of King Huo who had fallen into prostitution. She was beautiful and talented, and had saved up some money. If she was the right person for him, he had to marry her with a go-between and a proper marriage ceremony, all of which he had promised Bao to do. If he made no indication now, he would be eating his words, and everything would come to an end.

"No!" he warned himself. Why refuse to follow good fortune when it befell him? What's more, he was far from confident that he would pass the examination at the Board of Civil Office. As the saying goes, "Life in Chang'an is difficult." Only a fool would move away from this love nest free from worldly care.

Having made up his mind, he said solemnly to Xiaoyu: "Xiaoyu, I'll change the way I address you and call you 'wife' now."

"Wife?" Xiaoyu cried out in surprise. Her eyes, filled with tears, glistened in the dim light. Both suspicious and surprised, she couldn't believe her ears.

"Wife!" Li Yi continued. "Since the An Lushan Rebellion, few people would still talk of matching social status in marriage. I am not a bigot myself. I swear that if I ever marry, I must have a beautiful lady for my wife. Thanks to your kindness, I have achieved my goal. How can you still doubt my sincerity? I have a friend called Meng Jiao who has written a poem entitled 'Hearts Linked Together'. Let me read you the first and the last two lines:

給妳聽：「心心復心心，結愛務在深，坐結行亦結，結盡百歲月。」
這四句詩，就是爲妳我而詠的。』

『「心心復心心，結愛務在深。」』小玉悄悄地唸着，嘴角綻開
了甜笑，但眼中還有些微的懷疑。

『如果妳再不信，我寫一篇誓約給妳。』

『眞的？』

『這是何等大事？豈敢戲言！』

於是，小玉盡歛笑容，低眉捧心，以極莊重的聲音說道：『十
郎！不是我不相信你，祇是我把我的終身看得極重，如果你眞的無
絲毫嫌棄我的心，你就隨便寫幾個字給我，叫我放心，我會終生感
激你。若是你覺得有些勉強，那就不必多此一擧了！』

『妳這叫甚麼話！』

『那麼，你是願意寫了？』

『是的。』

『寫了的話，可不能沒有一個字做不到？』

看她這樣子釘住了問，李益倒有些疑疑惑惑，怕有甚麼別的用
意在內。但事已如此，不容猶豫，他咬一咬牙，答道：『絕對做到！』

小玉點點頭，下了床喚起侍兒，開了箱子取出一幅烏絲欄的素
縑，長可三尺，色澤微黃，那是地地道道的霍王家的舊物。

鋪好素縑，浣沙在傍磨墨。這時，李益也已披衣下床，他怕是

Your heart and my heart,
Our hearts are closely linked.
Sitting or walking,
Our hearts are closely linked;
Linked together
For as long as a hundred years.

These lines were written for us."

" 'Your heart and my heart/Our hearts are closely linked,' "
Xiaoyu intoned these two lines quietly. A trace of a smile appeared
at the corner of her mouth, but there was still some doubt in her
eyes.

"If you still don't trust me, I'll give you my oath on paper."

"Really?"

"This is a serious matter, how could I be playing games?"

Xiaoyu's smile disappeared, and lowering her eyebrows, she
said solemnly, "Shilang, it isn't that I don't trust you, just that I
take marriage very seriously. If you really have no intention of
deserting me, you might as well write down a few words, just to
put my mind at rest. For this, I would be most grateful. If you are
reluctant to do this, then don't bother."

"How can you say such a thing?"

"Well, that means you are willing to do it!"

"Of course I am."

"If you put it down in black and white, you must keep your
word."

Seeing how she was trying to pin him down, Li Yi suspected
that she might have some ulterior motive. But he had reached the
stage where he could no longer back out. So he gritted his teeth
and said, "I will keep my word for sure."

Xiaoyu nodded, rose and sent for her maids. From a wooden
box she took out a piece of white silk some three feet long, a
genuine heirloom from the family of King Huo.

The silk was spread out on the table, and Huansha stood
beside it grinding ink. By that time, Li Yi had gotten dressed and

小玉已對他發生懷疑，心裏警惕，得要寫得特別堅定誠懇，才能袪除她的疑慮。

『行了！』他試一試墨色說。

浣沙住了手，剔一剔銀釭中的燈芯；『卜』地一聲，燈花爆了！

『「燈花爆而百事喜」，夫人，好吉兆！』李益又說：『《西京雜記》中說：「火華則拜之。」火華就是燈花。妳我一起來拜！』

小玉欣然樂從，兩人並肩立在燈前，雙雙下拜，默默禱祝，小玉祝告神靈庇佑，夫婿永不變心；李益卻祝的是早日發財——《西京雜記》中說：『燈火華得錢財。』這個徵兆，他自己心裏明白，祇不便說給小玉聽。

拜罷起來，李益拈筆在手，寫下永不變心的誓約——如果變心，『神人共棄，爲厲鬼擊腦而死！』

『夫人，妳好好收起來！』李益捲起素縑，雙手捧給小玉，『等妳我晚年，拿出來給兒孫看，給他們做個堅貞的榜樣，也算是人間的佳話。』

『十郎！』小玉噙着眼淚答道：『你這樣待我，我眞不知道怎麼樣才能報答你！』

她所報答李益的是，豐衣美食，柔情嬌笑。兩年之中，李益像做了皇帝一樣；但也像做了乞兒，自卑感越來越重，他一直在懷疑，所有相識的人——甚至包括小玉在內，都看不起他；把他看成個沒用的人；把他看成娼家豢養的『廟客』……

out of bed. Fearing that Xiaoyu might already be doubting his sincerity, Li Yi reminded himself that he should write something forceful and sincere to drive away her suspicion.

"It's all right now," he said as he tested the ink.

Huansha stopped grinding and trimmed the wick in the silver lampstand. With a "pop", the snuff sputtered.

"'When the snuff sputters, everything goes fine.' My dear, it's a good omen!" Li Yi continued, "In *Miscellaneous Notes on the Western Capital*, it is written that: 'Kneel down and pray to the gods when the fire sputters.' The fire here means the snuff. Come, let's kneel down and pray to the gods together!"

Xiaoyu followed willingly. Shoulder to shoulder, they stood before the lamp, kneeled down together and prayed to the gods in silence. Xiaoyu prayed for the eternal loyalty of her husband, while Li Yi prayed for the quick acquisition of wealth. In *Miscellaneous Notes on the Western Capital*, it is also written that "When the snuff sputters, it means you will get rich." He knew what the sputtering meant, but he didn't want to tell Xiaoyu.

When they rose, Li Yi wrote an oath to pledge his eternal loyalty to Xiaoyu. Were he to be disloyal, he would be "deserted by gods and men, and die willingly by being struck on the head by fierce ghosts."

"My dear, keep this in a safe place!" Li Yi rolled up the silk cloth and presented to Xiaoyu with two hands. "When you and I grow old, we'll take it out and show it to our grandchildren, as an example of fidelity. This fine story will be on everybody's lips."

"Shilang!" Xiaoyu answered in tears, "I really don't know how to repay your kindness!"

Xiaoyu repaid Li Yi with fine clothes, good food, tenderness and happiness. For two years, Li Yi lived like a king, though at the same time he felt he was living like a beggar. His inferiority feelings intensified with the passage of time. All along, he suspected that everyone he knew — including Xiaoyu — looked down on him, and regarded him a useless person, a parasite kept

因此，他急於想通過吏部的釋褐試，一官榮身，洗刷寄人籬下
的恥辱。

第一年釋褐試未能中式，轉眼第二年的試期又到了。

釋褐試每年自十一月初一開始。官額有限，而每年
各科取中的貢士，以及軍功、徵辟、奏薦、或者恩賜出
身，具有出仕資格的人卻是越積越多；仕途壅塞，平均
八九個人爭一個官位，以致於每年吏部釋褐試，有五六千人參加，
分批考試，要到第二年三月底才能完事。

考試分筆試和面試兩部份，每一部份又各分兩個項目。筆試的
項目，第一是『書』，取其楷法遒美；第二是『判』，取其文理優
長。面試的項目，第一是『身』，取其體貌豐偉；第二是『言』，
取其言詞辨正。

筆試的日期在年底，到了那一天，李益一大早就已出門，小玉

by a courtesan.

Li Yi was eager to pass the examination for the Board of Civil Office. Once he had an official position, it would wipe away the shame of living under someone else's roof.

4   Li Yi didn't pass the placement examination on the first year, and in no time, the examination for the second year rolled around.

The examination began on the first day of the eleventh month. Due to the limited number of posts, the number of people qualified for posting grew in number. These included *gongshi*, or "entered scholars" from various areas and those who qualified through military achievement, recommendation, or imperial favour. As so many people competed for so few posts, on the average only one out of eight or nine candidates would finally obtain a post. That is why every year some five or six thousand candidates sat for the placement examination. They had to take the examination in groups, with the entire exercise lasting until the end of the third month of the following year.

The examination was divided into two parts: a written examination and an interview, each of which consisted of two sessions. The first session of the written examination tested the candidate's calligraphy to determine whether he could write a good hand. The second tested knack in making judgments, or the ability to reach legal decisions without error. The first session of the interview tested the candidate's appearance to determine whether his looks were sufficiently imposing for him to rule over the populace. The second tested language, or talent for eloquence.

The written examination took place towards the end of the year. On that day, Li Yi set out early. Xiaoyu saw him off at the

送到路口，殷殷叮囑早回，他敷衍了兩句，揮一揮手，匆匆趕到吏部。四試俱畢，卻不知道結果如何？得失縈懷，心情如待決之囚，這個年過得可真不舒服！

過了元宵，可發榜的日子到了！

一棒鑼響，坊里間掀起一片雜沓的人聲，倒像誰家失了火似地。細聽卻又不像，失火告警是亂鑼。而這是有節奏的——鏜、鏜、鏜地越來越響，及門而止。

『十郎、十郎！』桂子一路喊着奔了進來，一見李益又喘又笑地說：『報喜的來了！』

李益心頭陡覺一陣陣發緊，恨不得一把摟住桂子，狠狠吻她一吻，才能發洩心中那股搔不着、摸不到的歡喜勁兒。

『快嘛！十郎，報喜的人等着見你呢！』

就這時，一家上下幾乎都集中在他面前了；亂哄哄一片嘻笑聲中，簇擁着他來到堂前。

堂前院中，擠滿了左鄰右舍看熱鬧的；階上廊下，一名青衣中年漢子，一腿屈膝，半跪着高擎一張朱箋，望見李益，便即朗聲背唸箋上所寫的字：『捷報貴府郎君吏部銓選書判高中第七名——。』

應筆試的總有六千人，大約錄取十分之一，也有五六百人；第七名的名次確是很高的了。一時喜出望外，竟忘了說話。

junction of the road, and urged him to return early. He muttered a few words, waved goodbye, and swiftly made his way to the Board of Civil Office. After completing all four sessions of the examination, he still had to wait for the results. Obsessed with the outcome of the examination, he felt like a prisoner about to be executed, and spent the New Year Festival in great misery.

After the Lantern Festival, it was time to announce the list of successful candidates.

With the clang of a gong, a bustling of voices rose up in the streets, as if a house was on fire. On second hearing, it seemed to be something different, for the fire alarm signal was a much irregular clanging. This time, the sound was rhythmic — clang, clang, clang. It got louder and louder until it reached as far as Xiaoyu's house.

"Shilang, Shilang!" Guizi rushed shouting. When she met Li Yi, she said, smiling and panting at the same time. "The good-news messenger has come!"

Li Yi immediately felt a throb in the heart. If he could, he would have hugged Guizi and given her a big kiss to vent his happiness, the happiness he wanted so much which still remained out of his grasp.

"Come on, Shilang! The messenger is waiting to see you!"

At that moment, the whole family gathered round him: in the midst of all this happiness, he was ushered to the main hall.

The courtyard of the hall was crowded with neighbours who came to watch the celebration. On the staircase under the roofed corridor was a middle-aged man dressed in blue. Half kneeling, he held up a piece of vermilion paper when he saw Li Yi, and read its contents: "This is to report that the master of this house has been ranked seventh by the examiners of the Board of Civil Office ..."

There were altogether about six thousand candidates taking the written examination. Around ten per cent of them could pass the examination, or a total of five or six hundred candidates. The seventh place was very high indeed. Li Yi was so happy that he

『放賞。』淨持輕聲提醒他說。

『喔!』他大聲吩咐:『放賞!賞兩貫!』

於是,打發了報喜的人,款待賀喜的人;從厨房到廳堂,洋溢着歡暢的笑聲,直到起更時分,才靜了下來。

而小玉的臥室中還高燒着紅燭,燭光下,小玉笑盈盈地下拜:『恭喜十郎!』

『同喜、同喜!』李益雙手攙扶着她說,『多虧夫人的內助,該我向妳拜謝。』說着,放開了手,眞的要向小玉下拜。

『使不得!』小玉趕緊閃身躲避,『你別折殺了我。』

『其實稱賀也還早。』李益矜持地笑着,『「身」、「言」兩字如何?還不知道。』

『你過慮了!憑你的儀表、口才,那有不中選留用之理?』

小玉的話不錯,吏部面試銓察一關,輕易通過。出仕已成定局,祇不知放一個甚麼官兒?這,李益關心,小玉更關心。

『若是外官,可怎麼辦?』小玉憂心忡忡地問;她,未聞驪歌,已預支了別怨離愁。

『「注唱」時我會要求內用。我的名次高,該有權選擇。』

小玉不明白甚麼叫『注唱』?但『名次高,該有權選擇』的話

was speechless.

"Give him a tip," Jingchi reminded him softly.

"Oh, yes!" he instructed loudly, "Give him a tip! Give this man two strings of copper coins."

The messenger left and those who had come to congratulate him were entertained sumptuously. Everywhere from the kitchen to the main hall, joyful laughter filled the air until late in the evening.

In Xiaoyu's bedroom, a pair of red candles was lit. In the candlelight, Xiaoyu kneeled and said with a smile, "My congratulations to you, Shilang!"

"Let's share the joy! Let's share the joy!" Li Yi helped her up with both hands as he said, "My wife, this is all due to your assistance, so I should kneel to you to express *my* gratitude." As he spoke, he freed his hands and started to kneel down.

"No, you can't do that!" Xiaoyu chided him, "You overwhelm me with more than I deserve!"

"In fact, it's actually too early to congratulate me," Li Yi said reservedly with a smile. "I still don't know how I'll fare in the physique and language tests in the interview."

"You worry too much. With your fine appearance and eloquence, there is no reason why you shouldn't be chosen and posted!"

Xiaoyu was right. Li Yi easily passed the interview at the Board of Civil Office. His posting was not a problem, only he didn't know what post he would be assigned to. Li Yi was very concerned, but Xiaoyu was even more worried.

"If you're assigned outside the capital, what can I do?" Xiaoyu said anxiously. She sensed the sorrow of parting even before the farewell song was actually sung.

"When they do the 'placement registration and calling of names', I'll request a post in the capital. Since I'm high on the list, I should have the right to make a choice."

Xiaoyu didn't understand what "placement registration and

是聽懂了的。於是愁懷一放，欣欣然指望着李益成一名京官，留在長安，永相廝守。

然而，李益卻說的是假話——真話，祇在『注擬』以前向吏部郎中去說。

『請問，志願如何？想外放，還是內用？』

『想到外面去歷鍊歷鍊。』李益回答。

『地方呢？』

『江南。』他久已嚮往江南的繁華；而且叔父李揆也在江南，所以作此要求。

『想到江南去的人真多！』吏部郎中搖搖頭，『且「注」下再說。』

事情未可樂觀，不覺憂形於色。小玉卻以爲內用的要求被駁；默默在心中另作盤算了。

三天以後，可見分曉。到那一天，李益一大早趕到吏部，舉目望去，徘徊在音聲樹下的人，一個個無不像他一樣，患得患失的表情，都擺在臉上。

『隴西李益——。』

唱名唱到了，他趕緊擠上前去，側耳靜聽。

『隴西李益，年二十三歲，大歷四年進士。外放嶺南道、崖州、珠崖郡、文昌縣主簿。』

一聽放了這樣一個官職，李益頓覺心灰意冷。文昌在百粵極南，炎方瘴癘之地，決計不去！

calling of names" meant, but she knew that by being "high on the list, he should have the right to make a choice." So she felt relieved and happily waited for the day when Li Yi could be a metropolitan official and remain in Chang'an to enjoy a happy marriage.

In fact, what Li Yi said was *not* true — he would only tell the truth to the Minister of Civil Office at the placement registration.

"Please give me your choice. Do you wish to be a provincial official or a metropolitan one?"

"I would like to leave the capital and experience life," answered Li Yi.

"Where would you like to go?"

"To Jiangnan." He had been looking forward to seeing prosperous Jiangnan; Li Kui, his uncle, was also there.

"So many candidates want to go to Jiangnan!" The Minister said, shaking his head. "I'll note it down first and see what can be done about it."

As his request might not be met, he couldn't help feeling worried. Xiaoyu, however, thought that his request for a metropolitan assignment had been turned down, so she secretly made her own plans.

The examination results were to be announced in three days. On the day of the announcement, Li Yi went to the Board of Civil Office early in the morning. When he looked around, he saw that like himself, everyone was pacing back and forth under the tree with expressions of concern on their faces.

"Li Yi of Longxi ..."

His name was called. He forced his way to the front and listened attentively.

"Li Yi of Longxi, aged twenty-three, holder of the degree of *jinshi* from the fourth year of Dali, is now assigned to Lingnan, Yazhou, Zhuyaqun, and Wenchangxian as Registrar."

Upon hearing this, Li Yi was very disappointed. Wenchang was located at the southern tip of Guangdong, a place with a hot climate and many epidemic diseases, somewhere he definitely

不去是允許的。依例得上書申訴，改注改唱；再不滿意，還可以申訴一次，共是『三注三唱』。如果依舊不符所願，那麼當年『冬集』，重新再參加銓選，亦爲法所不禁。

於是，他以『親老家貧』的理由，請求改調。吏部重新調整，改授河南鄭縣主簿。他的母親住在洛陽，離鄭縣不遠；這一來，再無理由要求到江南了。

李益得意的開始，恰是小玉噩運的臨頭。就在他得官的第三天，淨持遽得暴疾，來不及延醫便已一瞑不視。

小玉哭得死去活來，李益也大爲喪氣。名份未定，他不便出面主持喪事，請了鮑十一娘來經紀一切：他——新任的鄭縣主簿，天天在外面赴餞別的宴會，從曲江醉到平康，常時就宿在三曲，幾乎都想不起小玉了。

而小玉雖遭大故，也還是把一顆心都放在他身上，置行裝、辦

would not go to.

Refusing to accept an assignment was permitted. According to the regulations, one had to submit a request to alter the placement registration and the calling of names. If the second assignment was unsatisfactory, one could submit another request. The maximum was three placement registrations and three name-callings. If the assignment still failed to meet one's expectations, one could sit for the "winter examination" and take the placement examination again.

Citing the pretext of looking after his aged mother and supporting his poor family, Li Yi asked to be reassigned. After consultation by the Board of Civil Office, he was given the post of Registrar of Zhengxian in Henan. Since his mother lived in Luoyang, which was not too far from Zhengxian, he had no other reason to be assigned to Jiangnan.

 Just as Li Yi was beginning to enjoy his stroke of luck, Xiaoyu had her darkest spell. Three days right after his assignment, Jingchi suddenly fell ill, and passed away before a physician could be fetched.

Xiaoyu cried her heart out and Li Yi was also very depressed. As they had not yet legally married, it was not proper for him to take charge of the funeral, so the task fell on Eleventh Lady Bao. Li Yi, the newly appointed Registrar of Zhengxian, could thereorfe attend farewell parties day after day. He ate and drank his way from Qujiang to Pingkang. Normally, he stayed at Sanqu, and nearly forgot Xiaoyu entirely.

Although Jingchi's death had been a great loss for Xiaoyu, still she took care of everything. She helped Li Yi to pack his luggage, hired the cart and horses, and personally saw to it that everything

車馬，一一親自檢點。向晚燈下，在她母親靈前哭奠完了，就坐在素幃之下，一個人千迴百折地想心事。

『小玉！』終於鮑十一娘看不過去了，問她：『十郎可有句話？』

『甚麼話？』她語聲緩緩地明知故問。

『當初我做的媒，答應了的明媒正娶。以前，祇說尚未出仕，等做了官風風光光娶妳——如今，做了官怎不提這話？妳母親可是撒手丟下妳了；別讓那活着的也丟下了妳！』

一番話勾起小玉的死別生離之痛，嗚嗚咽咽地，越哭越覺得委屈。

『怎麼？』鮑十一娘看出情形不妙，『十郎說了甚麼？』

『他沒有說，一句話也沒有說！』小玉忍淚吞聲相答。

『他不說，妳該問他！我是見證。』

『我——，』小玉再一次號啕大哭，『我好悔！』

『悔？』鮑十一娘倒詫異了，『莫非後悔不該託我替妳做這個媒？』

『不是！』小玉抬起婆娑的淚眼，『我祇悔不該拖延着；現在，現在身份更差得遠了！』

鮑十一娘默然。

『小娘子！』浣沙在傍邊說了話，『妳該聽十一娘的勸，有話該跟十郎早說——今晚就說。』

這晚上李益回來得早，也少醉意，恰是說正經話的好時候。小玉哭去了心中的塊壘，下了遲疑已久的決心，而說話的態度也是平靜的，照舊舖床、照舊疊被，照舊晚妝——祇是更着意修飾，一身

was in order. In the evenings, when she finished praying to her mother, she would sit under the white hangings and think of the many complex things that had happened around her.

"Xiaoyu!" Eleventh Lady Bao could remain silent no longer. "Has Shilang said anything to you?"

"To … me?" She deliberately drawled out her reply.

"When I made this match, Li Yi promised to marry you with the proper ceremonies. In the past, his excuse was that he didn't have a post and promised to hold a grand marriage banquet when he got one. Now, he has what he wants, so why hasn't he mentioned marriage? Your mother has already left you, don't let him do the same thing to you!"

These words intensified Xiaoyu's sorrow about death and parting. She started to cry.

"Well?" Eleventh Lady Bao felt that something had gone wrong. "What did Shilang say?"

"He didn't say anything. Not a word!" Xiaoyu answered, holding back her tears.

"Even if he didn't say anything, you should have asked him! I am the witness."

"I … ," Xiaoyu howled, "I have so many regrets."

"Regrets?" Eleventh Lady Bao was surprised.

"Regrets that you asked me to be go-between?"

"No." Xiaoyu raised her tearful eyes. "I only regret that I delayed the marriage. Now, his social position and mine are worlds apart!"

Eleventh Lady Bao remained silent.

"My lady!" Huansha, who was standing aside, cut in, "You should follow Eleventh Lady's advice and talk to him about the marriage as soon as possible. Why don't you ask him tonight?"

That evening, Li Yi returned early, but was only a bit tipsy. It was an appropriate time to discuss serious matters with him. Xiaoyu, having washed away her depression in tears and made up her mind, spoke calmly. As usual, she made the bed, folded the

縞素、窄瘦腰肢；臉上敷粉而不施朱，在窗前迎着初夏的薰風，彷彿洛水之濱的凌波仙子。

這把李益看傻了！算來平康佳麗，都不及小玉。他在心裏說。

『十郎！』小玉回頭凝視着他：『我有話說。』

『是，是！夫人。』

『從今後再休提「夫人」兩字。……』

『何來此言？』李益打斷她的話問。

『十郎，你得平心靜氣聽我說，否則，你我明天再談。』

『喔！』李益定一定神答道：『妳說，我不打岔。』

『我澈頭澈尾想透了！』小玉倚着窗戶，徐徐說道：『以你的門弟、才華、聲名，定有高門大族，願結婚姻。而況你此一去，上有白髮太夫人，內無主持中饋的家婦，自然得要辦了這件大事。』她停了一下，微露苦笑：『所謂「誓約」，祇是空話。但是我另外有個小小要求，不知道你肯不肯聽？』

『妳儘管說。』李益不知是驚是喜，聲音中略帶迷惘，『妳先說了再談。』

『我在想，我今年十九，你今年二十三；男子「三十而娶」不算晚，有七年的時間可以給我。』小玉慢慢激動了，『我拿一生來換你的七年。到你三十歲，儘管另選高門名媛；我，』她握着長長的髮絲又說：『那時我剪了這把頭髮，給你留個紀念；從此黃卷青燈，了我殘生，也沒有甚麼遺憾了！』

quilt, and did her evening make-up — only she put on more make-up than usual and wore white. She applied powder to her face but put on no rouge. When she stood in front of the window with the early summer breeze caressing her, she was as charming as the Goddess of River Luo.

Li Yi was dazzled by her beauty. He thought to himself: in all fairness, none of the courtesans in Chang'an could match her beauty.

"Shilang!" Xiaoyu turned round and gazed at him, "I would like to have a word with you."

"Yes, my wife."

"From now on, never say 'my wife' ..."

"Why is that?" Li Yi interrupted her.

"Shilang, you have to listen to me calmly. Otherwise, we can simply discuss the matter tomorrow."

Li Yi composed himself and said, "Go on, then. I won't interrupt."

"I've thought the matter over." Leaning against the window frame, Xiaoyu said slowly, "With your social status, talent and reputation, some prominent family will certainly be willing to take you as son-in-law. What's more, once you assume your post, you will have to marry since you have an old mother to look after and need a woman to take care of the household chores." She paused for a while and continued with a bitter smile, "Your so-called 'oath' is nothing but empty words. I have a little request which I don't know if you will accept?"

"Just say it." Li Yi was rather confused now. "You tell me first and we'll discuss it then."

"It occurs to me that I am now nineteen and you're twenty-three. It isn't too late for a man 'to marry at thirty', so I can wait for seven years." Gradually, Xiaoyu became more emotional. "I'll give my entire life in exchange for seven years of your life. When you're thirty, you can marry a girl from a prominent family, and I ..." She held her long hair and continued, "I'll cut off my hair and give it to

看她說得那樣決絕，卻又那樣委婉；那盈盈欲涕，萬千幽怨，齊聚眉端的淒楚神情，叫李益想起了如果變心，『神人共棄，爲属鬼擊腦而死』的誓約，也想起了她兩年來所給他無數的柔情蜜意。他不能不感動，不慚愧！

『小玉！』他流着眼淚叫道，『我跟妳的誓約，生死以之，永不可改。我不會三心兩意的；至遲到桂子香時，我一定來接妳——中秋，天上人間一齊團圓。』

『你？』小玉困惑地，『你叫我怎麼說呢？』

『妳不必說甚麼？妳祇把我的話擺在心裏，相信我，相信我……。』

他奔過去緊抱住她，雨點般吻着她的髮和後頸。她畏縮地仰起了臉，在月光的映照下，彷彿看得見她自己睫毛上所沾染的淚水，像草間晞露似地在朝陽影裏閃耀着。

『那麼，八月裏來了沒有呢？』老何問浣沙。

『鬼影子都不見！這個死沒良心的東西，比畜類都不如！』浣沙破口大罵，『最喪良心的是，我家小娘子明明已經看穿了，他還要騙她一騙。何伯伯，你想，小

you as a souvenir and go live in a nunnery for the rest of my life. Only in that way will I have no regrets!"

Li Yi was impressed by her determination and consideration. The tearful and sorrowful expression visible at the tips of her eyebrows reminded him of the oath in which he swore to be "deserted by the gods and men, and die willingly by being struck on the head by fierce ghosts" if he failed to be faithful to her, and he also thought about all the tenderness and care that she had showered on him over the last two years. He couldn't remain unmoved and felt sorry.

"Xiaoyu," he cried, "I will honour my oath for the rest of my life. I love you with total devotion. At the latest, I will marry you when the osmanthus turns fragrant; that is, at the Mid-Autumn Festival, when heaven and earth rejoice in their union."

"You …" bemused, Xiaoyu asked, "you tell me what I should say?"

"You don't have to say anything. Just remember what I said and trust me …"

He rushed over and embraced her tightly, showering her hair and the back of her neck with kisses like pouring rain. She drew back and raised her head. Under the moonlight, the tears on her eyelashes glistened like dewdrops on the blades of grass in the morning sunlight.

 "Well, did he come back in the eighth month or not?" Old He asked Huansha.

"Not a trace of him! That damn heartless fellow is even worse than a beast!" Huansha rapped out. "What's worse is the way my lady has already seen through him, yet he still went ahead and deceived her. Uncle He, just think, my lady has

娘子已經說了，那誓約不過是空話，他偏還要那樣拿死來賭咒；若不是眞心，何用如此？因此，小娘子那顆死而又活的心，自然又讓他騙得死心塌地了！』

『那麼，沒有去打聽一下？』

『怎麼沒有打聽？』侯景先接口說，『姓李的那傢伙，先說回洛陽省親；到了九月裏託人去打聽，說到江南去了，不知道甚麼時候回來。年底到鄭縣去打聽，那傢伙避而不見；以後，小玉又託人帶信給他，連個回信都沒有。』

『旣然如此，小玉該死了這條心了吧？』

『那裏死得了?』侯景先把顆白髮皤然的頭，搖得博浪鼓似地，『求神問卦，燒香拜佛，搞得失神落魄，弄出一場大病，到現在沒有好。生了病，還在東託人，西送禮，想拜託那傢伙的親戚朋友，通個消息；可是誰理她？祇有個姓崔的──李益的表兄，還好；有時候有姓李的信息。不過，也是畫餅充饑，當不了事。』

『唉！』老何長嘆一聲，站起身來說：『浣沙，我帶妳去個地方。到了那裏，妳實話實說好了。』

於是老何把她帶到延先公主的第宅，那一枝紫玉釵加上那段悽楚的故事，賣得了很好的價錢──一百二十貫，合十二萬錢。

半年來，小玉是第一次如此富裕。剛吃了藥，精神稍爲好些，便即想到崔允明──一位『明經』，就是李益的表兄，在長安候選了三年，還沒有選上一個官兒，境況十分清苦。

said that his oath is no more than a bunch of empty words, yet he still made the curse to deceive her. If he wasn't sincere, what was the point of going so far? So my lady's heart went from cold to hot again, and she was cheated by him once again!"

"Well, why don't you ask around for his whereabouts?"

"You think we haven't done that?" Hou Jingxian cut in. "That fellow Li first said he was going to Luoyang to see his mother. In the ninth month, we asked someone to locate him and were told that he had gone to Jiangnan, and no one knew when he was going to return. Towards the end of the year, we went to Zhengxian to look for him, but he evaded us. From then on, Xiaoyu sent him letters through friends but there's been no reply."

"If that's so, Xiaoyu should just give up."

"How could she give up?" Hou Jingxian shook his grey-haired head vigorously. "She sought help from the gods, consulted fortune-tellers, burned incense, and prayed to Buddha. She acted foolishly and got very ill, and she hasn't recovered. During her illness, she still tried to get information about him through his relatives and friends by entreating them or giving them gifts. But who would pay any attention to her? Only a Mr Cui, a cousin of Li Yi, offered to help, and gave her some news about him from time to time. But that was like drawing a cake on paper to allay hunger."

Old He heaved a long sign and stood up, "Huansha, I'll take you to a place where you can simply tell them the whole truth."

So Old He took her to the residence of Princess Yanxian. The purple jade hairpin, plus the sad story, earned her a good price —one hundred and twenty strings of copper coins, the equivalent of one hundred and twenty thousand cash.

This was the first time in six months that Xiaoyu had so much money in her hands. After she had taken the medicine and began to feel better, she immediately thought of Cui Yunming. Cui, Li Yi's cousin, was a Graduate in Classics, who had been waiting for a posting in Chang'an for three years without success, and had

『浣沙！』小玉微微喘息着說：『秋深了，崔郎的寒衣，怕還在西市的質肆裏；妳，妳送一萬錢去給他。』

自顧不暇，還拿艱難得來的錢，大把送人；浣沙心裏有氣，便故意不理她。

『浣沙，浣沙……。』

『知道了！』浣沙不耐煩地答了這一句。

『那麼，妳去嘛！』小玉伏在被上喘了半天，斷斷續續地說：『崔郎是好人。我，我還指望着他爲我幫忙。好妹妹，妳算是體恤我──去一趟，說那天空了，來看看我，我有話說。』

看着她那隱在舊羅被下面，瘦得幾乎顯不出來的身子，和那蒼白的臉色以及失去了光澤的頭髮，還有那充滿了無限辛酸的眼，浣沙心如刀割，再也不忍拂她的意了。

　『浣沙！』崔允明托着一個開元錢在手裏，容顏慘淡地說，『這一文錢，就像一斤金子那麼重！我眞不願意用妳家小娘子的錢，可又沒有辦法不用。我常常有個癡想，但願我死了，回到我的前生──生在開元年間。』

『祇有巴望來生的，那有想回到前生的。』浣沙斂一斂笑容，又說：『開元年間的日子好過？』

『當然好過，太好過了。像我這樣一名「明經」，何愁沒有官做？至於如李──。』

been leading a miserable life.

"Huansha," Xiaoyu, somewhat out of breath, said, "it's late autumn now. Mr Cui's winter clothes might still be in the pawnshop at the West Market. You ... you go and give him ten thousand cash."

While in straitened circumstances, Xiaoyu still gave away her hard-earned money. Huansha was displeased and didn't bother to answer.

"Huansha, Huansha ..."

"All right!" Huansha answered impatiently.

"Go then!" Xiaoyu rested on the quilt, still wheezing, then continued in stops and starts. "Mr Cui is a nice person. I ... I can still count on him to help me. Good sister, just do it for my own sake. Go and tell him to come and see me when he is free. I want to speak to him."

Huansha looked at her, pathetically emaciated and hiding under an old quilt, with her pale face, lacklustre hair and sad eyes, and felt as if a knife were cutting through her heart. She couldn't bear to go against her wishes.

 "Huansha!" with a coin from the Kaiyuan reign in his palm, Cui Yunming explained grimly, "this one-cent coin is as heavy as a catty of gold in my hand! I really don't want to spend your lady's money, but I have no choice. I always get this silly idea in my head: I wish I were dead and could return to a previous life in the Kaiyuan years."

"We can only hope for future reincarnations, never previous ones." Huansha stopped smiling and said, "Were the Kaiyuan years better?"

"Of course, a lot better. A Classics Graduate like myself

他突然頓住了。她明白，是不願提到李益——然而，別人都厭棄那負心漢，小玉卻還念茲在茲，這片癡情，簡直癡得可怕！

浣沙最明白小玉是怎麼回事？她是用李益遺留給她的那把感情的刀，一寸一寸在切割自己的生命。到現在已所剩無幾了！但那怕知道她明天就要死，今天也不能不盡全力去救她。

怎麼救呢？延醫服藥，禱告神靈，求巫作法，統通無用——祇有一味起死回生的藥：一個情多意重、溫柔體貼的李十郎，擺在她面前。

而這味藥是比甚麼成形的何首烏，或者千年的肉芝都難尋覓的。誰也沒有見過樣子像人的何首烏，更沒有見過如白胖娃娃、會跑會跳的肉芝。世上根本沒有這兩樣東西；世上——。

世上也根本沒有個情多意重、溫柔體貼的李十郎！浣沙一下子想通了：『讓她死了這條心吧！』

『妳是說妳家小娘子？』

浣沙點一點頭，凝神靜慮抓住她那個突如其來的意念，反翻推敲，越想越有道理，『崔郎，以前錯了！』浣沙的聲音像個經歷過滄桑的中年人，『大家都怕小娘子經不起刺激，所以明知道李十郎不會再來了，永遠不理她了，卻還是編出許多說詞來騙她，懸着那游絲一線似地的希望，吊着她的脖子看她死。這，這連崔郎你也有錯處！』

wouldn't have to worry about placement. As for Li ..."

He suddenly paused. She knew that he wouldn't mention the name Li Yi. While others despised that heartless fellow, Xiaoyu still loved him deeply. Her infatuation was truly beyond belief.

Huansha knew perfectly well why Xiaoyu was behaving like this. Inch by inch, she was using the emotional knife that Li Yi had left her to slice herself up until very little of her remained. But even if she knew that Xiaoyu was going to die tomorrow, Huansha would still try her best to save her today.

But how to save her? Getting a doctor, taking medicine, praying to the gods, asking a witch to do magic were all totally useless — there was only one medicine that would bring the dying back to life: a loving , tender Li Shilang standing before her.

But this medicine was even harder to find than a human-shaped tuber of multiflower knot-weed, or a fleshy glossy ganoderma, which took a thousand years to mature. Nobody had ever seen a human-figured knot-weed, or a white child-like glossy ganoderma which could jump and run. In fact, these two things did not exist in this world; and in this world ...

In this world, a loving, tender Li Shilang was also nonexistent. Something suddenly dawned on Huansha, and she said, "Let her have no more illusions."

"Are you referring to your lady?"

Huansha nodded and started pondering the idea that had just cropped up in her head. As she thought it over, the idea became more and more convincing.

"Mr Cui, we were wrong in the past."

She sounded like a middle-aged woman who had experienced all the vicissitudes of life. "We are all too concerned about my lady getting upset. Though we know Li Shilang will never come back, never love her again, we still make up a lot of excuses to deceive her, and give her threads of false hope with which she'll eventually hang herself. This, I must say, also has got something to do with you!"

　　崔允明不防浣沙能說出這麼一番鞭辟入裏的話來，紅了臉，囁嚅着承認：『妳，妳說得不錯。』

　　『那麼，我有個主意，說出來請崔郎斟酌；要有那麼一封信，能讓小娘子死了那條心！』

　　『嗯，嗯！』崔允明點頭說道：『這不失為破釜沉舟之計。妳再說，要有怎樣一封信，才能讓她死心？』

　　『要有李十郎一封信，說得決絕些。』

　　『怕我那表弟，已有負心之實，卻不願擔負心之名，不肯寫這封信的。』

　　『這就看崔郎你了。假造啊！假造李十郎的筆跡。』

　　『這倒使得。』崔允明答道，『信中寫些甚麼？』

　　『就說，已另選高門，成親在即；叫我家小娘子，不必癡心妄想了！』

　　『「另選高門，成親在即。」』崔允明茫然唸着這兩句話，往來踱躞——這讓浣沙疑惑了，剛想動問，他停住了腳，說：『「另選高門，成親在即。」妳說得一點不錯，是事實，千真萬確的事實！』

　　『甚麼？』浣沙睜大了眼問：『崔郎，你這話從何而來？新得的消息，還是早就知道了的？』

　　『早就知道了。』

　　『既然如此，何不早說？』浣沙厲聲詰責：『難道你也像令表弟一樣，從不知良心二字怎麼寫？』

　　『浣沙，妳責備得對。不過，我也有我的想法，我總希望我那

Cui Yunming was totally unprepared for this inciteful remark, and with a reddened face, he admitted: "Indeed, you're right."

"Well, I've an idea about which I want to have your views. We've got to get a letter that will make her give up hope once and for all!"

"Yes, yes," Cui Yunming answered, nodding. "This is a once-and-forever solution. Go on, tell me, what kind of letter will make her give up hope?"

"A decisively heartless letter from Li Shilang."

"My only worry is that although my cousin is heartless in deed, he would never want to be heartless in name, so he'll never agree to write such a letter."

"That depends on you, Mr Cui. Forge it. Forge Li Shilang's handwriting."

"That can be done," Cui Yunming answered. "What should I write in the letter?"

"Just say that he has just chosen a girl from a prominent family and is going to marry her. And tell my lady to have no more illusions about their marriage!"

"Chosen a girl from a prominent family and is going to marry her." Cui Yunming repeated these words absent-mindedly as he paced back and forth. This baffled Huansha. Just as she was about to ask him something, he paused and said once again, "'Chosen a girl from a prominent family and is going to marry her.' What you've said is exactly the case. A fact. A true fact!"

"What?" Huansha asked with her eyes wide-open, "Mr Cui, why did you say that? Did you just hear it or is this something you've known for a long time?"

"I've known it for a long time."

"If so, why didn't you tell us then?" Huansha scolded him.

"Seems you're just like your cousin, you don't know what the word 'conscience' means."

"Huansha, you're right to scold me. But I have my own way of thinking. I had always hoped that my cousin would change his

表弟，還能回心轉意——至少，也有個比較妥善的安排，所以不肯
透露實情，怕演成決裂得無可轉圜的僵局。』

　　聽他這樣解釋，浣沙的氣平了些，冷笑一聲道：『且看看那家
有福氣的名媛，嫁得這麼位多情多義的才貌仙郎？』

　　『是他的表妹，姓盧——。』

到任的第二天，李益便上書乞假半年省親。進士出身，
自然蒙長官另眼看待；而且在京師候選，年復一年，稽
延日久，人子承歡膝下的孝道久曠，所以省親的假期雖
長了些，還是被准許了。

　　李益的老家在隴西，他的母親卻久住洛陽；式微的世家，唯恐
為人看不起，非萬不得已，不肯回鄉。然而在繁華的東都，亦像『長
安居』一樣，大不容易，因此，李太夫人五十剛過，即已滿頭白髮。

　　李益懍然心驚！意會到那滿頭白髮中所蘊藏的辛酸，哽咽着叫
了一聲：『娘！』便甚麼話都說不下去了。

　　嚴峻剛毅的李太夫人，很少把感情擺在臉上，祇說：『你可回
來了！總算還想到了家，想到了老娘。』

　　『娘！』李益激動地說，『我接妳老人家到任上去住，也讓妳
過幾天舒服日子。』

mind — or, at least, make a better arrangement for himself than this one. That's why I didn't want to disclose the facts for fear that the situation with Xiaoyu would be totally irreparable."

Upon hearing his explanation, Huansha calmed down a little bit and said sarcastically, "I'll see who the lucky lady is he going to marry, such a loving, talented, good-looking gentleman."

"It's his cousin, whose family name is Lu ..."

 The day after he had reported for duty, Li Yi applied for a leave of six months to look after his mother. As a graduate of the palace examination, he was naturally treated as a special case by his superior. Moreover, as he had waited for posting in the capital for many years, his display of filial piety to his mother was long overdue. So even though his leave was longer than usual, it was still granted.

Li Yi's native place was Longxi, but his mother had been living in Luoyang for a long time. As his family was already on the decline, he had a fear of being looked down upon. So unless it was absolutely necessary, he preferred not to return to his native place. But, as it says in the poem "Living in Chang'an", living in the prosperous Eastern Capital was by no means easy. That was why Mrs Li, who was just over fifty, was already grey-haired.

Li Yi was shaken. He could imagine all the bitterness that hid behind her hoary looks. So by the time he called to her, he was so choked that he couldn't speak.

The stern and strong-willed Mrs Li seldom showed her feelings. All she said was, "So you're back, at last. In the end, you haven't forgotten your family and your old mother."

"Mum," Li Yi said emotionally, "I'll take you to my official residence and let you live out your days in comfort."

李太夫人立刻放下臉來斥責：『你是多大的官兒？說話不知輕重？憑你，一個主簿，就敢說讓我過幾天舒服日子？不怕人笑掉了大牙？』

這話說得李益刺心！連自己的母親都看不起兒子；權勢眞是可怕——然而，也是可愛的，權勢就是一切！他第一次確實地掌握住了這一個了解。

『去吧！』李太夫人吩咐：『去拜了祖先，該到親戚家去走一走。叫李林陪你去，該到那一家，他都知道。』

李林是他家的老僕，陪着他去拜了兩天客。親戚們看他衣冠華麗，意態軒昂，都出以熱誠的接待；跟他兩年前進京辭行時所受的冷落，大不相同。

李益還是李益，祇不過新選了官，而且外表也還不寒酸而已。他在心裏冷笑，卻更熱中於權勢了。

到了晚上，關在他舊時的書齋中，在燈下重溫夜讀的趣味；宵深人倦，剛想上床，門上剝啄兩下，他問道：『誰？』

『我。』

『啊！』他趕緊去開了門：『娘沒有睡？』

『唉，我那裏睡得着？』李太夫人顫巍巍地跨進門檻。

李益的心一沉，不敢多說，祇把她扶着坐下。

在這沒有第三者在旁邊時，做母親的才不太掩飾她的感情：『這兩年你在外面，那曉得做娘的苦楚……。』

Mrs Li pulled a long face and said, "How high is your post? Mind your words! How dare you, a mere Registrar, say that you will let me live out my days in comfort? Aren't you afraid of people laughing off their teeth when they hear that?"

These words hurt Li Yi deep and hard: even his mother didn't think very much of him. Power was terrifying — but also admirable. Power was everything. This was the first time that he truly understood this.

"Go!" Mrs Li instructed. "Go and pay homage to ancestors, and you also ought to go to see your relatives. Ask Li Lin to keep you company, he knows which relatives you should see."

Li Lin, an old family servant, accompanied Li Yi as he visited his relatives for two days. When they saw his fine clothing and smart appearance, all his relatives greeted him with great enthusiasm. This was in stark contrast to the cold send-off he had gotten when he bid them farewell before his departure for the capital.

Li Yi was still his same old self: the only difference was that he had just been granted an official post, and didn't look as poor and mean as before. He laughed to himself, truly enjoying his new-found power.

In the evening, he shut himself up in his study, enjoying once again the pleasure of reading by candlelight. He got tired as the night grew deeper. Just as he was going to bed, there were two taps on the door. "Who is it?" he asked.

"It's me."

"Oh!" He hurried to open the door. "Mum, you're still up?"

"Ai, how can I sleep?" Mrs Li, somewhat unsteady on her feet, entered the room.

Li Yi's heart sank. He didn't dare say anything, but simply helped her to her seat.

Alone with her son in the room, Li Yi's mother felt free to express her inner feelings, "How can you know the suffering I've experienced during the last two years when you were away?"

『我知道的。』李益搶着說。

『你知道甚麼？你怕連我爲甚麼要費盡心血，維持這個排場，都不知道。』

這有甚麼不知道的？無非因爲『隴西李家』的名望，不得不然。

『我是爲你！』李太夫人說：『我有一個兒子，不是沒出息的，我要替「他」做面子；將來得意了，儘量舖排，才不顯痕跡。要不然，成了暴發戶的樣子，叫人看不起！』

李益這才眞正明白母親的操持的苦心；而這番苦心，現在是該輪到他報答的時候了。一想到此，頓覺雙肩沉重，不勝負擔。

『你的事業，剛剛開始，離「飛黃騰達」四個字還遠得很。你倒已經不可一世，輕狂得不得了，這叫我傷心；我指望了半輩子，不過是這麼個器小易盈的兒子！』說着，做母親的掉下兩滴淚來。

這讓李益慚愧得幾乎無地自容，『娘！』他想了半天，掙出一句話：『我，我聽妳的敎導。』

『這你算明白了！』李太夫人嘉許地點點頭：『我不知道替你打算過多少遍了。娘祇有你一個兒子，全副心血都在你身上。』

李益不響，祇以期待的眼光看着他母親。

『李家這幾年時運不濟，可是名望究竟在的；重振舊家聲，看來都要靠你了。』李太夫人住口不語；然後，突地發問：『你自己想過你的婚事沒有？』

這一問，問得李益心慌意亂；小玉的事，怎能在嚴峻的母親面前吐露隻字半語？『沒……沒有。』他囁嚅着回答。

"I know." Li Yi answered quickly.

"What do you know? I'm afraid you don't know how hard I've tried to keep the family going in this style."

How could he not know it? She did it simply for the sake of maintaining the reputation of the Li family in Longxi.

"I did it all for you!" Mrs Li said. "Since I have a son who isn't lacking in achievement, I have to save face for him. When your fame spreads in the future, I've made sure there will be no dirty marks left from your past. Otherwise, people will look down on you as a nouveau riche."

Only now could Li Yi appreciate all the painstaking effort she had made on his behalf, and he decided that this was the time for him to repay her. When he thought about it, he felt a weight on his shoulders that was too heavy for him to bear.

"You're just at the beginning of your career; you're still a long way from success. But you already feel you're on top of the world and have started to put on airs. I feel sorry for you. For all the efforts I made on your behalf over half a lifetime, all I've got is a son who is so narrowed-minded." Tear drops fell as she spoke.

This made Li Yi felt so ashamed that he wanted to hide. "Mum," he struggled to say after thinking hard, "I will follow your advice."

"I'm so glad that you understand me!" Mrs Li nodded approvingly. "I've thought everything out for you many times. You're my only son, and I pin all my hopes on you."

Li Yi remained silent and stared at his mother with hope in his eyes.

"Our family has fallen on hard time the last few years, but we still have our reputation. We're counting on you to regain our reputation. Mrs Li paused, and then she asked suddenly, "Have you thought about your marriage?"

This question put Li Yi totally off guard. How could he say anything about Xiaoyu to his stern mother? "No, no," he answered hesitantly.

『我可早就替你看中了。可是，也祇不過看中而已。』

母親的話費解，李益不由得追問：『是誰家的？』

『你想是誰家？你舅舅家的！』

『原來是表妹。』李益腦中，立刻浮現了一個滿頭珠翠，亭亭玉立的少女的影子；她，曾爲他愛慕過的，然而他已久絕妄念，聘錢百萬，從何而來？不絕此妄念，又待如何？

『怎麼？』李太夫人問道：『你自己的意思如何？總有句話吧？』

『我，叫我怎麼說？』李益遲疑地答道：『這聘禮——。』

『爲難的就是這一點。不然，我早就作主替你聘下了。』李太夫人說，『且先不管這些，明天再去看一看你舅父舅母再說。』

這是李益第二次來看他的舅父——范陽盧家，天下最有名的少數望族之一；李益的舅父很多，此刻在洛陽的，是李太夫人嫡堂的哥哥盧章，以戶部尚書致仕，定居東都；雖已優遊林下，但以盧家門生故舊遍天下，所以在仕途中仍有不可忽視的潛勢力。

拜見了舅父舅母，又請見表妹盧鬱香。她是個性格冷漠，不喜歡接近男性的女孩子；然而中表至親，情分不同，畢竟還是出來了。

『表妹好？』李益含笑相問。

"I picked out a girl for you a long time ago. But that's as far as I've gone."

His mother's words baffled him. He couldn't help asking, "Who is her father?"

"Who do you think? Your uncle!"

"Oh, so it's my cousin." Immediately, the image of a gorgeously bejewelled young woman appeared in his mind. He had adored this girl before, but stopped because he lacked the one-million cash betrothal gift. What could he do even if he fancied her?

"Well?" Mrs Li asked. "What do you think?" You've got to say something."

"What can I say?" Li Yi answered hesitantly. "The betrothal …"

"That's where we're stuck. Otherwise, I would have given her the betrothal presents long ago," said Mrs Li. "Let's leave this aside. Tomorrow, go and see your uncle and aunt and see what can be done."

 This was Li Yi's second visit to his uncle. The Lu family of Luoyang was one of the few great families in China. Li Yi had quite a few uncles. Lu Zhang, his mother's elder brother, settled here in the Eastern Capital in his official capacity as Minister of Finance. Although he was retired, his acquaintances and disciples were spread throughout the empire, so his influence could not be taken lightly.

Having greeted his uncle and aunt, Li Yi expressed his intention to meet his cousin Lu Yuxiang. Yuxiang was a rather cold and aloof young woman, who didn't enjoy the company of men. But since they were cousins, she agreed to come out to meet him.

"How do you do, cousin?" Li Yi greeted her with a smile.

『表哥好。』同樣的寒暄，但聲音中一點熱氣都沒有。

『表妹越發出落得天仙化人似地了！』李益向他舅母說。

『就是脾氣還不改。』盧太夫人皺着眉頭回答。

『表妹還做詩不？』李益準備了幾首舊作，抄在一個手卷上，籠在袖中，想找機會展露一下。

但是，答語讓他失望，『早不做了！』她說。

『那麼，也常讀詩？』

『也沒有。』

『然則，看些甚麼書？』

『佛經。』

李益抽了口冷氣，說不下去了。

盧太夫人倒有些過意不去，『鬱香！』她說：『妳也陪君虞到妳書房去看看。』

『不！媽。』盧鬱香不肯，卻又不說原因。

『中表至親怕甚麼？』盧章也慫恿着，『妳不是常說，家裏沒有一個人可以陪妳談談。連我，妳都說我話言無味。妳表哥可是好詞令——上月初，吏部郎中到洛陽公幹，特爲來看我，說妳表哥「書、判、身、言」，無一不佳；言詞便絡，更叫人激賞。這一來，妳可別再成天怨着無可與言了！』

盧鬱香還未有所表示，李益卻趕緊轉身拜謝：『舅父，太誇獎我了！』他轉眼看着盧鬱香又說：『表妹生具夙慧，精通禪理；祇怕我這鈍根人，不足與言。』

『聽見人家說的沒有？』盧章笑着對她女兒說：『拿話把妳拘

"How do you do?" she returned the greeting without the slightest trace of warmth in her voice.

"Cousin is becoming more and more attractive!" Li Yi said to his aunt.

"But her temper is still the same," Mrs Lu answered, knitting her brows.

"Do you still write poetry, cousin?" Li Yi had a few poems in his sleeve and wanted to get a chance to read them to her.

But her answer disappointed him. "I stopped writing poetry long time ago," she said.

"Well, do you often read poetry?"

"No."

"What do you read then?"

"Buddhist scriptures."

This remark caught him off guard and he didn't quite know what to say.

Mrs Lu, feeling a little uneasy now, said, "Yuxiang, why don't you take Junyu to your study?"

"No, mum." Lu Yuxiang gave no explanation.

"You two are cousins. Is there anything wrong?"

Lu Zhang also urged her. "Don't you always say that there's no one in the family you can chat with? You even tell me that I'm boring. Your cousin's a good conversationalist. Early last month, the Secretary of Civil Office was in Luoyang on official duties. After his trip, he came to see me and said that your cousin excels in calligraphy, legal judgments, physique and language. His eloquence is beyond praise. From now on, don't ever say that you have no one to talk to!"

Before Lu Yuxiang could reply, Li Yi turned round and thanked his uncle with clasped hands. "Uncle, you flatter me!" He then turned and looked at Lu Yuxiang, "Cousin is gifted and knows the Buddhist scriptures well. A stupid chap like me isn't good enough to chat with her."

"Did you hear what he said?" Lu Zhang said to his daughter,

住了。快去吧,去鬭鬭你們的機鋒;可別入了魔!鬱香,不是我說妳,』盧章皺着眉,看了李益一眼,『年輕輕的,學甚麼佛?』

李益會意了,報盧章以一個領悟的眼色;然後向盧鬱香微笑道:『表妹,能讓我瞻仰瞻仰妳的書齋嗎?』

『說甚麼「瞻仰」?』盧鬱香漸漸覺得她表哥不是那狂妄自大不識趣的人,於是便稍稍假以詞色:『跟着我來!』

李益站起身來,不慌不忙地朝上說道:『舅父、舅母,我先跟你告假!』

『去吧!』盧太夫人答道:『回頭來陪你舅父喝酒。』

『是!』李益恭恭敬敬地答應一聲,退後兩步,然後瀟洒地一轉身,追逐着餘香,出了迴廊。

盧鬱香的步伐很快、很穩;一折向北,南風撲面,她那紫羅衫子上薰染着的香味,散播愈烈,把走在下風的李益聞得心旌搖蕩,興起無數綺念。

滿院綠蔭,五楹精舍,那就是盧鬱香獨有的小天地。由右側雨廊踏上臺階,盧鬱香站住了腳,吩咐侍兒:『先去煎茶;用我自己喝的那一種。』

原來她是面冷心熱!李益心裏有數,等她跨進門檻時,趕緊代替了侍兒的職務,搶上去扶住她的撩住裙幅的手臂說:『表妹走好!』

這一扶,直到她的書房才放手。她坐在楊妃榻上,笑着:『你「瞻仰」吧!』

李益自然要細看。第一眼就看到牆上一幅絹本水墨的觀世音像;

smiling. "He's outwitting you now. Go and see which of you is sharper. But don't go too far! Yuxiang, I don't mean to criticize you …" Lu Zhang, his brows knitted, glanced at Li Yi and said to his daughter, "You are still young, what's the point of studying Buddhism?"

Li Yi knew what he was saying, and gave his uncle a wink. Smiling, he turned to Lu Yuxiang and said, "Cousin, would you allow me to pay a visit to your study?"

"Why be so formal and say 'pay a visit'?" Lu Yuxiang was beginning to realize that her cousin wasn't as bombastic and boring as she had thought. So she forced out an invitation, "Come with me!"

Li Yi rose and said to his aunt and uncle, "Allow me to take a short leave."

"Go!" Mrs Lu said, "Come back later and have a drink with your uncle."

"Certainly." Li Yi answered politely. He retreated a few steps, then quickly followed the lingering fragrance into the corridor.

Lu Yuxiang walked with quick yet firm steps. She turned north, and the southern breeze wafted past her, spreading wide the fragrance of her purple brocade dress, and arousing countless fantasies in the much infatuated Li Yi down-wind.

The Five-pillar Vihara in the shady courtyard was Lu Yuxiang's little world. On approaching the terrace from the right of the portico, Lu Yuxiang stopped and instructed the maids, "Brew some tea with my favourite leaves."

So cold on the outside yet so warm in her heart. Li Yi seemed to know her better now. As she was about to cross the threshold, Li Yi went up to her, took her arm and helped her with her skirt like a maid. "Take care, cousin."

He helped her all the way to her study. Seated on a Yang Guifei couch, she said with a smile, "Now you've 'visited' my study!"

Li Yi, needless to say, wanted to take a closer look at her study.

袒胸趺足，寶相莊嚴，但長眉星目、高鼻闊口，是男人的面貌。右下角題着一行正楷：『大歷六年佛誕日弟子盧鬱香敬造。』

『行筆細而不弱，深得楊庭光的遺意。』他點點頭，裝出內行的姿態批評。

『難得，你居然是個行家。』盧鬱香有着令人驚喜的知音之感；她的畫，正學的是與吳道子齊名的楊庭光。

『祇是這不像女菩薩。』

這話可外行了，『觀世音本是男身。』她冷冷地答說。

『面貌倒有些像我。』

盧鬱香笑了，『不害羞！你也配？』她指着佛像前的香案說：『配我朝夕頂禮？』

『那麼，表妹，妳再畫一張給我。畫上妳自己的玉貌；讓我掛在書房裏，朝夕頂禮！』

那半眞半假的語氣，似笑非笑的神情，耳目所及，陡覺心弦大震；盧鬱香趕緊定一定神，故意呵斥似地答道：『別胡說，褻瀆菩薩！』

『那裏還有菩薩？妳就是活菩薩！黃金鑄像，香花供養，我一個人的活菩薩！』

盧鬱香大笑，一面笑，一面喘着氣說：『越說越不成話了。』然後，忍住笑，作勢瞪眼：『你再胡說八道，我可要攆你！』但，話還沒有完，她自己到底又忍不住笑了。

The first thing that caught his attention was a painting in ink of the Goddess of Mercy. The goddess, wearing a decollete gown and seated with her legs crossed, looked quite majestic. But with her long eyebrows, starry eyes, high nose, and large mouth, her face resembled that of a man. A line in regular script was inscribed in the lower righthand corner: "Reverently drawn by Buddhist disciple Lu Yuxiang, on the Buddha's birthday in the sixth year of Dali."

"The brushwork is fine and forceful, modelled after Yang Tingguang," he said, nodding his head like an expert.

"It's hard to believe that you're an expert in painting." Lu Yuxiang was delighted that he was so knowledgeable. She had actually modelled her calligraphy on that of Yang Tingguang, a painter who ranked with the great Wu Daozi.

"But it doesn't look like a female buddha."

This remark exposed his superficial knowledge of Buddhism. "The Goddess of Mercy was actually a man," she said coldly.

"His face looks more or less like mine."

Lu Yuxiang laughed. "Shame on you. Do you think you deserve that?" She pointed at the altar in front of the painting and said, "Deserve to be served by me day and night?"

"Well, cousin, paint me a portrait of yourself that I can hang in my study and serve day and night!"

His expression, at once solemn and joking, struck a chord in her heart. She quickly composed herself and gently scolded him, "Don't talk nonsense. It's blasphemy."

"Where is the Buddha? You are the living buddha! I'll cast you in gold, serve you day and night, and make you my personal living buddha!"

Lu Yuxiang laughed out loud and said somewhat breathlessly, "You're getting more and more ridiculous all the time!" Then, suppressing her laughter, she glared at him and said, "If you go on talking nonsense like this, I'll kick you out!" But before she could finish, she burst into laughter again.

　　煎了茶來的侍兒，詫爲異事。匆匆奉茶已畢；趕着要到老主人面前去獻殷勤。

　　李益告辭了，盧鬱香也向父母道過晚安，回自己院子去了，盧家老夫婦卻還在燈下閒話。

　　『看來鬱香這孩子，跟她表兄倒有些緣份。』盧太夫人說。

　　『嗯。』盧章點點頭。

　　『姑太太有意無意提過好幾次了，門第相當，而且也中了進士選了官；親上加親，就成全了他們吧！』

　　『看一看再說。聽說君虞在長安的名聲不怎麼好！』

　　『那也不過年少風流。想你當年，比他還荒唐……。』

　　『得、得！』盧章最怕她提起往事，『夫人，妳別又扯上我。說君虞，妳得知道，他家是個空架子！』

　　『那怕甚麼？「百足之蟲，死而不僵」，放着姑臧李家的門第、君虞自己的才幹，怕將來沒有飛黃騰達的一天？』

　　『那是將來，眼前呢？眼前就不過日子了？』

　　『這更不要緊了，咱們多陪嫁些，還怕鬱香過苦日子？』

　　『我原有打算的，聘錢百萬，我再陪嫁百萬，都讓鬱香帶了過去。可是，妳說他家能張羅到這筆聘禮嗎？』

The maid who was serving them tea was taken aback. She served the tea in a hurry, for she wanted to please her master with what she had seen as soon as she could.

 After Li Yi left and Lu Yuxiang bid goodnight to her parents and retired to her room, the Lus were still chatting under the lamplight.

"It looks like Yuxiang and her cousin can make a good match," said Mrs Lu.

"Yes," Lu Zhang nodded.

"Your sister has mentioned the possibility of their marriage several times now. Our social status is more or less the same, and he is a *jinshi* and has just been assigned a post. This marriage could bring us even closer."

"We have to wait and see. I've heard that Junyu has a bad reputation in Chang'an."

"It's nothing more than a little adolescent fooling around. Just think how you behaved in those days. You were even worse ..."

"Cut it out." Lu Zhang didn't like to be reminded of his past. "My dear, let's not touch on that. As for Junyu, don't forget that his family is poor."

"So what? As the saying goes, 'Centipedes don't fall over, even when they're dead.' With his family's reputation and his own talent, Junyu is sure to go far."

"That's the future. How about the present? How can they get on now?"

"That's nothing. We can give her dowry big enough so we won't have to worry about her."

"In fact, I've already worked out a plan. His million cash betrothal gift and the million cash from us can belong to Yuxiang.

　　『這怕難！』盧太夫人輕輕地說，『爲了鬱香，咱們一切從權吧。』

　　『這，怎麼行！』盧章大搖其頭，『多少年、多少家高門望族定下來的規矩，萬不可壞！否則，傳了出去，人家不說咱們體恤乾宅，祇以爲鬱香做了甚麼見不得人的事，趕着要送出閣。這不但咱們盧家的面子丟不起，對君虞的名聲，也有妨礙。』

　　盧太夫人默然。

　　『姑太太再要提這事。妳就說，讓她送聘好了。空口說白話，可不管用！』

盧章的話，很快地傳到了李太夫人耳朵裏。以前祇是可進可退地試探口風，此刻卻等於得到了確定的答覆。她——像許多舊族中居孀的女主人一樣，家世、教養、以及從小磨鍊出來的那一份責任感和雄心，在此衰微及孤立的時候，最能發生作用；燈下千萬遍思量，再度確認了重振舊家聲的關鍵，即在聯此一門新姻；那百萬聘錢，不惜任何手段要把它籌借出來。

　　於是，她把李益找了來商量，『阿虞！』她問：『你說過，你聽娘的教導。這話可還算數？』

The problem is whether or not his family can manage to get up this sum of money?"

"That, I am afraid, might be a bit difficult for them." Mrs Lu said softly. "For Yuxiang's sake, let's make it a little flexible."

"No, not like this!" Lu Zhang shook his head vigorously. The rules laid down by countless prominent families and followed by them for so long cannot be changed. Otherwise, when people learn about the arrangement, rather than thinking that we're being kind to the groom's family, they'll say that our Yuxiang must have done something indecent so that a quick marriage was necessary. If we do this, not only will our family lose face, but Junyu's reputation will be ruined as well."

Mrs Lu remained silent.

"If your sister brings up the matter of marriage with you again, just tell that she can send over the betrothal gift. Empty verbal promises are of no use."

Mrs Li soon learned what Lu Zhang had to say. Before this, she had simply been testing the water; now she had a definite answer. Like so many widows in traditional clans, she had the responsibility for and an ambition of making the best use, in time of decline and isolation, of her up-bringing and the education she had acquired since childhood. She thought the matter over several times under the lamplight, and realized that all hope of regaining the family's reputation hinged on this marriage. By hook or by crook, she had to get the million cash.

So she called for Li Yi and discussed the matter with him.

"Yu," she asked, "you said that you'll follow my advice. Does that still hold?"

『怎麼不算數？我不聽娘的敎導，聽誰的？』

李太夫人緩慢地，但極滿意地點一點頭：『有你這話，我把所有的心血花在你身上也值。阿虞，你聽我告訴你，生死有命，富貴可並不在天，要靠自己。』

『娘，妳祇說，我該怎麼去做？』

『該怎麼做，一時那裏說得盡？仕途之中，翻雲覆雨，都靠自己能隨機應變，這先不提。眼前第一大事，要把你表妹娶了過來。你先說一句，你可喜歡你表妹？』

李益幾乎要脫口相答：『自然喜歡。』然而終於訥訥不能出口，一種無形的力量拉住了他那一句話──對小玉的誓言。

『怎麼？』李太夫人不悅了，『難道你表妹配不上你？』

『不是。』

『那麼，你不喜歡她？可怎麼又要拿她當「活菩薩」供養？』

李益大窘，一時忘情的戲謔，怎又會讓母親也知道了？看這情形，無可抵賴，祇好紅着臉：『娘既然連這話都知道，還問我喜歡不喜歡，幹甚麼？』

『你這孩子，倒真會哄人！』李太夫人笑着罵了一句，『你表妹是有名的「泥塑美人」，居然也讓你花言巧語哄得改了樣子。看來，你舅母的話不錯，你們有緣份！』

李益不響，但臉上有着掩抑不住的笑意；一顆心飛到了盧鬱香的書齋，鼻中所聞到的是馥郁的衣香，眼中所見到的是甜俏的臉龐，耳中所聽到的是嬌媚的甜笑……

"Of course! If I don't follow your advice, whose advice can I follow?"

Mrs Li nodded slowly with satisfaction. "In that case, I feel fully rewarded for all the time and money I spent on you. Yu, let me tell you: it's true that heaven has a hand in deciding our fate, but wealth has nothing to do with heaven; that depends on one's own efforts."

"Mum, just tell me what should I do."

"How can I tell you what you should do in a few words? The twists and turns of officialdom are a test of your ability to deal with different situations. But we'll leave this subject for now. The most important thing is for you to marry your cousin. First, tell me whether you like her or not?"

Li Yi was on the verge of saying "Of course I do", but in the end he didn't say it because an invisible force — his oath to Xiaoyu — held him back.

"So?" Mrs Li was displeased. "Is it that your cousin isn't a fair match?"

"No."

"Then, you don't like her? If so, why did you say you would serve her like a 'living buddha'?"

Li Yi was embarassed. How had his mother learned about the naughty things he had said at a moment when he was carried away? Since she knew about it already, he couldn't deny it, so with a reddened face he said, "Since you even know the things I said to her, mum, why ask me whether I like her or not?"

"My child, you're really good at coaxing people!" Mrs Li rebuked him gently with a smile. "Your cousin is known as a 'clay beauty', though she was moved by your sweet words. It seems that your aunt is right in saying that you two make a perfect match!"

Li Yi didn't reply, but a smile emerged on his face. Suddenly, his heart was transported to Lu Yuxiang's study. His nose detected the fragrance of her dress, his eyes discerned her pretty face, and

『你先別高興。』李太夫人打斷了他的思緒，『這聘錢百萬，從何而來？』

這句話就如當頭棒喝，震醒了李益的美夢，迷惘而慌張地望着他母親，半晌說不出話來。

而他母親的神態是沉着的，『到底你的閱歷還淺！』她略顯得意地說：『一遇到難題，就沉不住氣了。』

聽這話，李益知道母親胸有成竹，稍稍放寬了心，強笑道：『所以說，要娘教導啊！』

『我自然有主意。祇是要你自己去做。趁這半年假期，別在家裏閒着白耽誤了功夫，趕快到江淮去走一遭，找你叔叔想辦法。』

『叔叔會有甚麼辦法？他流落江淮，自顧不暇；而且又不是親的叔叔。』

『你懂得甚麼？六親同運，盧、李都是宰相世家，李家式微，盧家還十分煊赫，如說這兩家又聯了姻，大家對你叔叔，也會另眼相看。』李太夫人說到這裏，歇一口氣，又接着侃侃而談：『至於說你叔叔自顧不暇，那是指做官而言；張羅些錢，江淮之間，有的是他當宰相時提拔過的人，多少有些交情，集腋成裘，便是一筆整數——若非如此，你叔叔一家數十口，難道喝西北風不成？』

李益不能不佩服他母親的分析，『但是，百萬錢，數目到底太大了！』

『不要緊，他湊得出來的。見了你叔叔，祇說我說的：先跟叔叔暫借百萬。早則半年，遲則一年，決定如數奉還。』

his ears picked up her sweet soft laughter.

"Don't get too excited yet," Mrs Li cut in while he was sub-merged in thought. "Where can we get a million cash for the betrothal gift?"

This question came like a blow on his head, shattering his sweet dream. He glanced at his mother in confusion, and remained dumbfounded for a number of minutes.

But his mother remained calm. "You haven't seen much of the world," she said confidently. "You can't take things in stride when you have a problem."

Li Yi now knew that his mother had a plan in mind. He felt relieved and forced a smile. "That is why I say I always need your guidance!"

"I have a plan. But you have to execute it yourself. Don't stay at home and waste your time. Make the best use of this six-month leave. Go to Jianghuai as soon as possible, and pay a visit to your uncle to ask him for help."

"Do you think uncle will help? He's in excile there and can't even look after his own affairs. Also, he isn't related to us."

"How ignorant you are! The six closest relations are all related in fortune. The Lus and the Lis have produced prime ministers for generations. While the Lis have declined, the Lus are still thriving. If the two families were affiliated by marriage, people would certainly treat your uncle differently."

Mrs Li paused for a breath and went on. "Officially, it is true that your uncle is down and out. But financially speaking, it's quite a different story. Jianghuai is full of officials who received favours from him when he was prime minister. The contributions from his former subordinates add up to a tidy sum. Otherwise, how could he maintain his big family?"

Li Yi admired his mother's insight. "But a million cash is still a lot of money!"

"Don't worry, he'll manage it when you see him. Tell him exactly what I've told you: borrow a million cash from him, and

『娘！』李益提醒她說：『到那時候拿甚麼來還？』

『儍孩子！』李太夫人放低了聲音：『新婦有兩百萬陪嫁在手裏——祗要你們小夫婦感情好，她能不拿出來替你還債？』

『啊——！』李益恍然大悟。

『不但還債，』李太夫人的聲音越來越低了，『以後的排場、交遊，都不必發愁。你祗要巴結上進，不出十年，可入臺閣。到那時候，你才佩服娘替你所作的打算。』

於是，三天以後，李益便又離家。臨行之前，在盧章家盤桓了一整天，除了依禮辭行以外，大部份時間逗留在盧鬱香的書齋中，現賣一段離愁，又預售了別後的相思，把他那尊『活菩薩』擾得大動凡心，背人拭淚。

在家住不到十天，李益就讓他母親催逼着又踏上征途，自河南取道山東，遠涉江淮。

六月底七月初，爍金流火的天氣，跨馬長行，可眞是一大苦事。回想到跟小玉在一起的日子，此時竹簟涼床，浮瓜沉李，那簡直是神仙的生活；不想出仕做官，反來受此苦楚！這一轉念，他的內心有着無限的委屈和難以宣洩的抑鬱。

say that we'll pay him back in six months, or a year at most."

"Mum!" Li Yi reminded her, "how can we pay him back in six months?"

"My son," Mrs Li lowered her voice, "your newly-wed wife has a dowry of two million cash in hand — if the two of you love each other, won't she let you have one million cash to settle your debt?"

"Ah …!" Li Yi suddenly understood.

"Not only will the debt be settled," Mrs Li lowered her voice even further, "in the days to come, you'll have a good life with nothing to worry about. If you manage to please your superiors, you'll be a minister in ten years' time. By then, you'll appreciate all the things I've done for you."

Three days later, Li Yi was on his way again. Before he left, however, he spent a day at Lu Zhang's house. Apart from bidding farewell to him, he spent most of the time in Lu Yuxiang's study. He turned the sorrow of parting and the lovesickness he would feel in future to good account, touching his "living buddha" so deeply that she even shed tears.

12 Li Yi remained at home for nearly ten days. Urged on by his mother, he set out from Jiangnan, headed south, and arrived at Jianghuai via Shandong.

The long ride on horseback in the smeltering heat of late June and early July was testing. He recalled the days he spent with Xiaoyu at this time of the year, lying on a bamboo couch all summer long like an immortal. He never expected he would have to endure such suffering to obtain a post. Thinking about this, he felt a load of grievances and disgruntlement that were hard to vent.

　　然而他沒有一絲一毫想再回到小玉那裏去的意思。少年浪跡四方，以他的詩篇、詞令、丰儀，歆動教坊娼家，也結交了不少豪貴子弟；但他終於發現，他的這一切並沒有得到最好的報酬，貴族豪門自有其天地，他始終未能闖了進去。

　　這使他不能甘心——起初是隱隱約約、不甚分明的意識，從乞假歸省以後，這份潛在的意識，極快地浮現、擴大，使他清楚得幾乎可以觸摸到了。當然，這主要是由於他的嚴毅的母親的教誨啓迪，其次是他親見舅家的富貴而生的羨慕和感觸。家世的懷念和現實的刺激，逼出他一片雄心，要把『姑臧李』，這個姓氏的光輝，從他手裏恢復過來。

　　於是，他自我製造了一份莊嚴的責任感——對姑臧李家的祖先和活着的族人，他覺得自己是個承先啓後的大人物；他不能爲了小玉放棄他的這份責任。他倔強地否認命運中的好的東西，必須伴隨着壞的東西一起接受；他要選擇，不受任何約束的自由選擇。

　　但畢竟也有不容他選擇的東西；眼前就是！江淮之行，非他所願，卻不能不走這一遭。他發誓，類此就食四方，告幫求援的行動，這是最後一次！

　　以吃得苦中苦的心情，自我磨鍊着志氣，他自然不會再去想到小玉家那些溫馨得足以消沉壯志的生活；沒有回顧，祇有前瞻，他所想到的是：那頭稍覺高攀的好婚姻，由這頭婚姻替他帶來的新的社會地位、政治奧援、裙帶關係以及盧鬱香的那份豐盛的嫁粧——包含兩百萬錢現款在內。

But he had absolutely no intentions of returning to Xiaoyu's place. A young man should travel widely. His ability to write poetry, his eloquence, and his appearance made a deep impression on all the courtesans he encountered and won him many friends among the scions of the rich and powerful. But eventually he realized that all his efforts were in vain. The prominent families and clans lived in a world of their own, a world beyond his reach.

But he wouldn't give up. At first, he was only vaguely conscious of his discontent. When he took his leave to visit his mother, this unconscious feeling loomed larger, so much so that it was almost tangible to him. This, so course, was a result of the lesson he had learned from his strong-willed mother. It also arose from his envy of his uncle's wealth. Spurred on by nostalgia and harsh reality, he resolved to restore with his own hands the glory of the Li family of Guzang.

In so doing, he took on a self-made mission. He felt like a great hero in whom both his dead and living clansmen placed their hopes to carry on the glorious tradition. He couldn't give up his mission merely for the sake of Xiaoyu.

He adamantly refused to accept the fact that one must take the bad things as well as the good in life. He wanted choices, choices he could make without constraint.

Nevertheless, there were some things where there was no free choice. A case in point was his present trip to Jianghuai, something he simply didn't want to do. He swore to himself he would never engage in this kind of mendicant endeavour again.

Knowing full well that there would be no sweet without sweat, and obsessed with an ambition to further himself, Li Yi would never think of luxuriating in the comfort of Xiaoyu's house and thus be prevented from realizing his lofty aspirations. He would only look ahead, never turning back. The only thing on his mind was the upward marriage that would raise his social status, improve his political influence and connections, and confer upon him the enormous dowry from the Lu family, including two mil-

　　而這一切，需要他用一百萬錢去交換。『百萬錢，那裏去找這百萬錢？』他常常在夢中這樣喊着。

　　『那裏去找這百萬錢？』李揆聽他斷斷續續地說明了來意，啞然失笑地說：『你們母子都把事情看得太容易了！』

　　李益原有很好的口才，但到底年輕臉皮薄，遇到求人的場合，便變得笨嘴拙舌了，『母親的意思，』他囁嚅着說：『千萬要求叔父成全。』

　　『我你叔姪，若可爲力，那有不成全你的道理？無奈，做叔叔的自顧不暇。』李揆拈着花白短髭，容顏慘淡地說：『這光景我不說，你也看得出來，流寓江淮，欲歸不得，上下大小幾十口，都張着嘴等，全靠我賣老面子，找門生故舊接濟度日，你想想，過的是這種日子，可那裏替你去找出百萬錢來？』

　　李益看着那雜木的几椅、粗糙的食具，以及他叔父身上那襲褪了色的舊羅衫，再也無法想像從前那鐘鳴鼎食的宰相家風！一寒至此，還提甚麼百萬鉅款？李益連開口再往下談談的勇氣都失去了。

　　誰知李揆卻又不是拒人於千里之外，『也罷！』他以安慰的語氣說：『且先過了節，再作商量。』

lion cash.

But he needed a million cash to acquire all of this. "One million cash. Where can I get a million cash?" He even shouted this question in his dreams.

 "Where am I going to get a million cash?" When he heard Li Yi stammering out the purpose of his visit, Li Kiu replied with a dry smile, "You and your mother have handled things too casually!"

Even Li Yi, who was by nature quick-witted, found himself tongue-tied. He was, after all, too young and thin-skinned to ask others for assistance. So he spoke haltingly, "My mother hopes uncle can help me to realize my ambitions."

"You are my cousin. If I can, there is no reason why I shouldn't help you. The question is: I have my own problems." Li Kui pulled on his short grey whiskers and said, "There is no need for me to tell you about the situation I am in. You can see with your own eyes. I am now living in exile. I am not allowed to return to my native place. There are a few dozen mouths to feed in my family. I live on donations from my disciples and acquaintances. Living a life like this, where can I get a million cash for you?"

Li Yi looked at the cheap wooden table and chairs, the crude eating utensils and his uncle's worn-out gown, and found it hard to imagine the pomp and ceremony that Li Kui must have enjoyed when he served as prime minister. Since Li Kui was so poor, how could Li Yi have the cheek to mention the one million cash? He no longer had the courage to go on.

Surprisingly, Li Kui didn't shut the door on him. "Well!" he comforted him, "Let's wait till after the Festival and discuss the matter then."

『過節？』李益猛然一震，慌亂地說。

李揆不明白他何以有此神情？祇提醒他說：『今兒十三，後天就是中秋。』

『是，後天中秋。』他定一定神，附和着說。

怎麼一下子就到了中秋？他如夢方醒似地茫然自問，覺得耳邊有一句話顛來倒去，不斷地在響着，好久，他才能清清楚楚地辨出那是他自己的一句話：『中秋，天上人間一齊團圓。』

於是，以這句話爲線索，抖出一連串的往事，那晚，他對小玉的激動，以及在激動中對小玉所作的誓言，彷彿如在眼前。『該死！』他搥着自己的腦袋在罵：『豈非鬼迷了頭？跟她說那些話幹甚麼？』

那頭高攀的好婚姻將成泡影，小玉給他的回憶，倒是眞實的存在。不管怎樣，那總算也是個退步之處。可是，中秋之約，已成虛願，負心之罪已不可逃。如果——。

如果，一直音信不絕，那麼，即令中秋不能踐迎來團圓之約，還可找個託詞搪塞。壞就壞在自離長安，便把小玉置之腦後，從無片紙隻字寄去，這，這不是存心騙她的鐵證？

想透了這一層，他才知道，所當痛悔的還不是隨便對小玉許下誓言；而是一時大意，因循自誤，竟造成了無可轉圜辯解的局面；忘恩負義，已是鐵案如山的了！

悔恨如一條毒蛇樣咬嚙着他的心。他幾次衝動，想利用多餘的假期，遄程趕回長安——他知道，此刻還不算太晚，祇要他回到小

"The Festival?" Li Yi was both surprised and confused.

Li Kui didn't understand why Li Yi was so disconcerted, and simply reminded him, "Today is the thirteenth. The day after tomorrow is the Mid-Autumn Festival."

"Ah! The day after tomorrow is the Mid-Autumn Festival." He composed himself and repeated his uncle's words.

"How can it be the Mid-Autumn Festival already?" He asked himself absent-mindedly, as if just waking from a dream. Some words kept ringing in his ears. It was only after several minutes that he realized this was his own promise. "The Mid-Autumn Festival is the time of union for both heaven and man." This promise led him to recall a series of past events: his feeling towards Xiaoyu that evening, and the oath he made to her later — it all seemed to float before his eyes. "Damn it!" He cursed himself, "Was I bewitched? Why said those things to her?"

Though the marriage that would raise his status now seemed quite impossible, his happy memories of Xiaoyu were real. Whatever happened, Xiaoyu was someone to fall back on. But now the Mid-Autumn appointment could not be kept and evitably he was guilty of being heartless. If ...

If he had kept in touch with Xiaoyu, then even though he failed to meet her at the Mid-Autumn Festival, he could still find an excuse. But the worst thing was that ever since he left Chang'an, he had put her totally out of his mind, and did not send her a note at all. Wasn't this a conclusive evidence of his intentional deceit?

Having straightened out his thinking, he knew that what he should have remorsed was not only the casual oath he made to Xiaoyu, but also his oversight and procrastination which had ended him up in this irreversible situation. His ingratitude was undeniable.

Remorse bit into his heart like a venomous snake. Several times, he had the impulse to make use of the rest of his leave and hurry back to Chang'an, and he knew it wasn't too late to do it. If

玉身邊，隨便他怎樣飾詞解釋，她都會相信他的。

　　然而，他始終下不了那個決心；因爲李揆那句『且先過了節，再作商量』的話，如游絲一線，拴住了他的腿。

　　中秋，很快地過去了。他知道，每多過一天，他向小玉解釋的機會便減弱一分；那就像坐視一艘翻覆的船，一寸一寸往水中沉去而不能有所作爲一樣，急得人要發瘋。

　　就這時，李揆把他找了去，給他一封信，叫他到蘇州去拜訪劉刺史，『這劉刺史算是我最得意的一個門生。』李揆說，『等閒我不去找他。因爲，我自知大限將至，一旦倒了下來，少不得要他來料理我的後事。此刻，說不得了，旣然你的婚姻，關乎一族的榮枯，那就先去賣了這個情吧！這劉刺史宦囊頗豐，必能如你所望。但盼你好自爲之，我這幾年衰病侵尋，怕看不見你騰踔雲路了！』說着，黯然地搖一搖頭。

　　聽他說得那樣悽慘，李益無法不掉兩點眼淚，但心裏是興奮輕快的。希望重生，煩惱解除——小玉不再是他心頭的一重負擔，『算了！』他豁出去了，『負心就負心，形勢所迫，身不由己，隨人家怎麼去說好了！』他這樣在心中自語。

　　於是，離開江淮重鎮的徐州，來到人文薈萃、財賦雄區的姑蘇。整肅衣冠，到刺史衙門投帖請見。

　　『老弟來得不巧，』劉刺史看完了李揆的信說：『昨天剛接到京裏的「除書」，奉調嶺南瓊州，萬里之行，這筆資斧如何籌措？不瞞老弟說，正在煞費躊躇！』

Xiaoyu were at his side, he could get her to believe in any excuse he would make up.

However, he couldn't make up his mind to do it. Li Kui's words — "Let's wait till after the Festival and discuss the matter then" — were like a thread of floating gossamer binding his feet.

In no time, the Mid-Autumn Festival had passed. He knew that as the days went by, his chance of explaining the situation to Xiaoyu grew dimmer. This was like watching an overturned boat sinking slowly into the water and being unable to do anything to save it. He was nearly driven to madness by the situation.

Just at that juncture, Li Kui called him to his side, gave him a letter and asked him to pay a visit to Governor Liu in Suzhou. "Governor Liu was my favourite disciple," said Li Kui, "I wouldn't trouble him unless it was something important. I know that my life is drawing to a close. When I die, I need somebody to handle my funeral and other matters. Well, I can't bother myself with this now. As your marriage will affect the prosperity of our entire clan, I must ask him to do me a favour now. Governor Liu is quite well-off; he will surely give you what you want. I hope that you'll make good use of it. For the last few years, I have been terribly ill. I'm afraid I won't live long enough to see you rise high in your career!" As he spoke he shook his head sadly.

Hearing this, Li Yi couldn't help shedding a few tears, but secretly he was relieved. Here was a ray of hope to take his troubles away — Xiaoyu was no longer a burden to him. "Well, it's settled!" He muttered to himself, " Let her call me heartless. Given the situation, there's not much I can do. Let people say what they like!"

Thus he left Xuzhou and went to Suzhou, where culture and wealth abounded. Having dressed up properly, he headed off for the Governor's office to see Liu.

"My friend, you have come at the wrong time," Governor Liu said after reading Li Kui's letter. "I have just received an appointment letter from the capital: I've been transferred to Qiongzhou in

　　由繁華富庶的蘇州，調至炎方瘴癘的瓊州，明明是貶謫；別人在仕途中栽了大跟斗，怎麼還好意思說甚麼？李益咬一咬牙，說了幾句安慰的話，立即站起身來告辭。

　　『老弟請稍待。』劉刺史拉住他說：『千里遠來，又是恩師所命，自然沒有讓你空手而回之理。等我通盤籌劃一下，好歹總有個交待，老弟先請回旅舍息一息，必當有以報命！』

　　到晚來，劉刺史派人送來五十萬錢。這在李益已是大喜過望了。然而還差一半，別無可以告貸的人，並且假期將滿，也不容他再去奔走了；盤算了一會，覺得唯有先帶着這五十萬錢回家再說。

　　十月裏回洛陽，十一月初重到鄭縣；一轉眼，他那主簿做了快兩年了，一直在任上，沒有離開過一步。

　　一口氣談到這裏，體弱多病的崔允明，已累得必須要歇一歇了。

　　浣沙滿臉脹得通紅，一股既怒且怨的突兀不平之氣，在胸中橫衝直撞，找不着發洩的地方。祇有大口大口地

distant Lingnan, and will need to spend a tremendous amount on moving expenses. To tell you the truth, I am still worried about these expenses!"

A transfer from the bustling town of Suzhou to hot and disease-ridden Qiongzhou was clearly a demotion. While Liu was having difficulties in his official career, how could Li Yi have the nerve to ask for help? Li gritted his teeth, said a few words to comfort him, and then rose to leave.

"My friend, please wait a moment." Governor Liu held his hand and said, "You've come a long way with the instructions of my respected teacher, so naturally I can't let you go away empty-handed. Let me work something out and let you know later. Go back to your lodgings and rest now, I promise to do what I can."

In the evening, Governor Liu had five hundred thousand cash delivered to Li Yi. This was more than he had expected. But he was still five hundred thousand cash short, and had no one to ask for a loan. As his leave would soon be over, he had little opportunity to run round seeking help. After some calculation, he decided to take the five hundred thousand cash first and work out something later.

He returned to Luoyang in the tenth month, and arrived in Zhengxian early in the eleventh. Before he knew it, he had served as Registrar for nearly two years. He had remained at his post throughout and hadn't left the county once.

Cui Yunming, who was weak and ill, stopped telling his story here. He was so tired that he had to take a rest.

Huansha was livid. A strong feeling of indignation, fired by anger and resentment, reeled about in her chest, and she had no way to vent it. All she could do was mutter, "And

喘着氣；『以後呢？』她明知道得讓崔允明緩緩氣再說，但畢竟忍耐不住，要問的話，脫口而出：『那傢伙到底娶了他表妹沒有？』

『沒有。』上半句話還好，下半句又叫人生氣，『但也快了！』

『呃！』浣沙也好恨那嘴裏唸經、心裏動情的盧鬱香，『聘禮就祇五十萬錢？五姓望族的名媛，身價跌了一半？』

『就爲的要湊齊那百萬錢的聘禮，才耽誤了下來。現在，說是快行聘了。』

一聽這話，浣沙更怒，咬一咬牙冷笑道：『可那裏又找來的這五十萬錢？是偷還是搶？』

『不偷不搶；可是——。』

『說嘛！』浣沙沒好氣地催促着。

『雖不偷不搶，可也跟又偷又搶差不多。』

『呃！』浣沙極注意地追問：『這話怎麼說？』

『我也是耳食之言，其事眞假，猶待求證……。』

『唷，你倒是怎麼啦？別跟我酸溜溜地儘說廢話！』

『浣沙，妳性子好急！』

『不錯，我性子急！』浣沙的聲音慢了，從眼中看出來，她在回憶：『從前，大家都說我最有耐性；兩年的工夫，變得這樣子！那是叫人家把我的耐性磨掉了。兩年，這兩年過的甚麼日子？祇有我自己知道。那忘恩負義的東西，有朝一日讓我遇見了，我眞能咬他一塊肉下來！』

聽浣沙是這樣要食肉寢皮而甘心的態度，崔允明不能不有所顧忌，越發遲疑着不肯出口。

浣沙十分機警，知道自己說錯了話，趕緊又苦笑道：『其實我

then?" Though she knew that she should let Cui Yunming rest, she couldn't wait and the question slipped out, "Has that fellow married his cousin or not?"

"Not yet." This half-answer was comforting, perhaps, but what followed was irritating: "But he'll do it soon!"

"Ah!" Huansha felt sorry for Lu Yuxiang, who recited the scriptures with her mouth but loved Li Yi in her heart. "With only five hundred thousand cash? So the betrothal gift for the daughter of one of the five prominent families has been reduced by a half?"

"It was because of the difficulty of collecting enough money to make up the betrothal gift of a million cash that the marriage has been postponed. Now I hear that it is going to take place soon."

This made Huansha even more furious. She gritted her teeth and sneered, "So how did he manage to get the five hundred thousand cash? Did he steal it?"

"No, he didn't steal it, but ..."

"Come on, tell me!" Huansha pressed him.

"Though he didn't steal it, his methods were in fact quite similar."

"Oh!" Huansha asked attentively, "How is that?"

"I heard some rumours, the truth of which needs to be verified ..."

"Hey, what's with you? Don't talk nonsense to me!"

"Huansha, you are very impatient!"

"Yes, I'm very impatient!" Huansha said slowly. One could see in her eyes that she was recollecting. "In the past, people used to say that I was very patient. In the last two years, I've changed! My patience has been worn thin. Only I know what sort of life we've been living the last two years. If I ever run into that heartless fellow, I'll bite off a mouthful of his flesh!"

Huansha's vow to eat Li Yi's flesh had Cui Yunming so worried that he was reluctant to speak.

Huansha was clever enough to know that she had said something wrong, and immediately corrected herself, "I'm just bluffing.

也是說說而已。已變了心的人,你宰了他也沒用。我祇是在想,怎麼樣想個辦法,能使得我家小娘子死了那條心,大澈大悟,重新做人?崔郎,你可是位又講理、又講情的君子人,我家小娘子全靠你救她一救了』

『當然,當然。』

『那麼,你就接往講吧,如何叫做「跟又偷又搶差不多」?』

『聽說是這樣,』崔允明放低了聲音說:『君虞的上司——鄭縣縣令是撈錢的一把好手;縣衙門裏,六曹參軍,各司其事,唯有主簿,朝夕不離縣令左右,一應文書,先替縣令過目。這樣子,如果不聽縣令指使,便幹不下去;聽了縣令的指使,少不得有所分潤。妳懂了吧?』

『原來狠狠為奸!』浣沙冷笑道:『無情無義的漢子,原就是做貪官的材料。祇是拿這骯髒錢行聘,不羞辱了他的表妹?』

崔允明默然。心想,浣沙真好利口;少不得將來有遇見李益的日子,那時候倒要看他怎麼受得了浣沙的痛責?

『閒話少說。』浣沙回到正題:『崔郎,趁今日天色還早,你就勞駕一趟,對我家小娘子實話實說,好叫她別再朝思暮想了。』

『這怕不妥。』崔允明比較持重,『小玉一聽這消息,萬念俱灰,怕逼出別的變故來,那就大失妳我的本心了。』

『不礙。』浣沙答道:『我想過了,至多一時暈厥,大哭一場——哭去了心中的痞塊,慢慢調養,她的病才有痊癒的希望。』

It's pointless to kill someone who's no longer faithful. I'm just trying to think up a way to make my lady lose heart, come down to earth and start a new life for herself. Mr Cui, you're a reasonable man. I'm pinning all my hopes on you to save my lady!"

"Certainly, certainly."

"Well, tell me what you mean by 'quite similar'."

Cui Yunming lowered his voice and said, "I've heard that Li's superior, the magistrate of Zhengxian, is a first-class money-grubber. In the magistry, all officials perform their duties respectively except the Registrar, who is with the magistrate all the time, and who handles every document before the magistrate go over it. In such a situation, if he doesn't do what the magistrate tells him to do, he's finished. But if he does, he can share the spoils. Do you follow?"

"It's a conspiracy!" Huansha said with a sneer. "Heartless men make greedy officials. Isn't it a shame for his cousin to accept a betrothal gift of dirty money?"

Cui Yunming remained silent. He thought to himself: Huansha really has a sharp tongue. The day would come when she would meet Li Yi. He wondered how Li Yi would endure her tongue-lashing.

"Enough of this." Huansha said. "Mr Cui, since it is still early, would you mind calling upon my lady and telling her the truth so she can stop yearning for him day and night?"

"That might not be a good idea." Cui Yunming was more cautious. "When Xiaoyu learns of this, all her hopes will be dashed, and she might be driven to do something foolish. This would go against our original intentions."

"That doesn't matter." Huansha answered. "I've thought it over. At worst, she might faint and cry her heart out. Once she cries away the pain in her heart, she will be able to regain her health gradually. But only if she does that is there any hope of a full recovery."

Cui Yunming remained silent for a long while, and then,

崔允明躊躇久久，狠一狠心說：『好，長痛不如短痛。』

果然不出浣沙所料，聽到一半，小玉一慟而絕。崔允明和浣沙，雖已預見及此，但親見小玉面如金紙，剩下心頭一絲微溫，不由得也慌了手腳，搯人中、灌薑湯，拚命呼喊，才把她弄得悠悠醒轉

然而，第二步浣沙卻沒有料到，小玉並未大哭，瞑目如死，祇眼角微微滲出淚水。

『小玉！』崔允明勸她說：『有句話說得好；「提慧劍斬斷情絲」，我那表弟，負心漢是做定了。妳在割捨不得他，豈非太傻？』

小玉不響，好久，睜開眼來，在枕上擺一擺頭說：『崔郎，我不信！』

浣沙一聽這話火氣就大了，『難道我跟崔郎串通了來騙妳不成？』

『傳聞失實也是有的。』小玉平靜地說。

浣沙氣得張口結舌，好半天說不出話來。

『小玉！』崔允明覺得她癡得可憐，便又問道：『要怎樣妳才相信？』

『我得親口問一問他。唉──！』小玉長嘆一聲：『祇恨我離不得這張床！崔郎，』她忽然淚流滿面，哀懇着說：『我求求你，好歹叫「那人」跟我見一面。』

making up his mind, said, "All right, a short suffering is better than a prolonged one."

Just as Huansha had predicted, Xiaoyu fainted in despair half-way through the story. Although both Cui Yunming and Huansha knew this would happen, they were nevertheless shocked when Xiaoyu's complexion turned a ghastly pale colour, and her only vital sign was a thread of warm breath. They only managed to bring her around by massaging the acupuncture point between her nose and upper lip, giving her ginger soup, and shouting into her ear.

But what followed Huansha hardly expected. Xiaoyu didn't cry, but rather closed her eyes tightly like a corpse, while tears oozed out from the corners of her eyes.

"Xiaoyu!" Cui Yunming comforted her. "There's an old saying: 'Use the sword of wisdom to sever the threads of love.' It's now quite certain that my cousin is going to desert you. Isn't it foolish of you not to give up hope on him?"

Xiaoyu didn't reply. After a while, she opened her eyes and shook her head on the pillow, "Mr Cui, I don't believe you!"

This made Huansha furious. "Would Mr Cui and I conspire to cheat you?"

"Sometimes rumours can be misleading," Xiaoyu said calmly.

Huansha clucked her tongue in anger, and couldn't say anything for a while.

"Xiaoyu!" Cui Yunming, seeing that she was still infatuated, asked, "How can I convince you then?"

"I have to ask him in person. Oh ...!" Xiaoyu heaved a long sigh. "What a pity I can't get out of bed!" Suddenly tears started rolling down her cheeks as she pleaded with him, "Mr Cui, I beg of

　　『我盡力去辦！』崔允明慨然許諾。

　　但事後他卻大爲懊悔。執迷不悟的小玉，一見了李益的面，證實了他的負心，絕望化爲怨毒，這後果必是不測的、可怕的！

　　因此，他悄悄地又跟浣沙去商量，『還是騙騙她吧，就是君虞來了，我也不敢引他來見——看這光景，一見了面，兩個人總有一個人死，「怨毒之於人，甚矣哉！」……。』

　　『別跟我掉書袋，』浣沙冷冷地答道：『你答應了她，就不能騙她。祇要她動了疑心，催問個沒有完，那可不是叫我受罪？』

　　『唉！』崔允明深深失悔，『我太輕率了！』

　　看他那樣深自痛責，浣沙倒有些不忍，安慰他說：『反正你祇寫封信給你表弟就行了，來不來是人家的事，用不着你擔責任。』

　　『妳有所不知。我那表弟——，』崔允明吃力地說：『明年春天會來。』

　　『你怎麼知道？他來幹甚麼？』

　　『來迎娶。』

　　『不說盧家住在洛陽？到長安又迎娶的是誰？』

　　『盧家移居長安了。他家在洛陽的第宅鬧鬼，成了兇宅，住不得了。』

　　『這可奇怪，怎麼忽然又鬧鬼？』

　　『這裏面一言難盡，今天沒功夫談。總之，吵着要搬，還是盧鬱香的主意。今年春天搬來的；洛陽的消息，我那表弟年內行聘，來年春暖花開，便是佳期。』

　　『哼！佳期！但願他是死期！』

you, find a way for him to meet me!"

"I'll try my best!" Cui Yunming promised on impulse.

But he immediately regretted what he had said. When Xiaoyu, knowing his heartlessness, met Li Yi, her despair would turn to resentment, and the result could be terrible and unpredictable.

Thus he calmly discussed the matter with Huansha. "It would be better to deceive her for the time being. Even if Junyu comes, I don't dare arrange for him to meet her — the way things stand, when they meet, one of them is bound to die. 'How deeply resentment rankles in men's hearts!'..."

"Stop showing off your knowledge of the classics," Huansha said coldly. "Since you've promised her, you shouldn't fool her. If she starts getting suspicious and persists in asking about it, it'll make things very difficult for me!"

Cui Yunming now regretted his hasty promise. "I spoke too rashly!"

Sensing this, Huansha was moved and comforted him, "In any case, you only have to write a letter to your cousin. Whether he comes or not is up to him, not you!"

"You don't know the whole truth," Cui Yunming spoke with effort. "My cousin will come here next spring."

"How do you know? What for?"

"To get married."

"Didn't you say that the Lu family is in Luoyang? Who's he marrying in Chang'an?"

"The Lus have moved to Chang'an. The family's house in Luoyang is haunted and they had to move."

"That's strange! Why are ghosts after them all of a sudden?"

"It's a long story, we have no time to talk about it today. In brief, it was Lu Yuxiang who kept saying that they have to move, so they moved here in the spring. The news spread in Luoyang that my cousin was going to present the dowry this year, and next spring, when the flowers are in blossom, they'll get married."

"Ah, get married! He ought to go out and get himself killed!"

　　『這，』崔允明說：『浣沙，連妳都是這樣，我可更不敢把他帶來了。』

　　『隨便你！』浣沙咬着牙說；心裏在打主意；祇要李益到了長安，打聽到了住處，她就要去哭求延先公主主持公道，狠狠懲治這個負心人。

　　浣沙的話一點不錯，自此以後，小玉便心心念念專指望着崔允明，三天兩頭打發浣沙去催問消息。

　　起先倒還容易敷衍，祇說已寫信給李益了，請他務必到長安來一趟；想來覆信快到，勸她耐心等待。小玉想想也是，道路艱難，總得有些日子，才有好音傳來，所以催問歸催問，心裏卻還不太急。

　　轉眼大雪紛飛，殘年將盡，算算託了崔允明快三個月了，再麻煩的事也該辦出個結果來；小玉可真忍不得了，這天早晨，掙扎着要起床，叫浣沙和桂子來幫她梳洗。

　　動一動、喘一喘，那一把支離的瘦骨，看去彷彿一碰便要散了似地，『算了吧，』浣沙勸她，『妳還是躺着，倒舒服些。』

　　『睡久了，骨頭疼，我想出去走走。』

　　『又不是有好太陽的日子，不妨出去走走散散心。妳看！』浣沙指着窗外彤雲密佈的鐵灰的天色，『又快下雪了。』

　　『真的，小娘子！』桂子也幫着勸：『天冷，風又大；咳嗽剛好些，不宜受寒。』

　　『不！』小玉固執地說，『我定要出門，有大事要辦。』

To this Cui Yunming replied, "Huansha, if you behave like this, I don't dare bring him here."

"That's up to you," Huansha said, grinding her teeth. She promised herself: when Li Yi comes to Chang'an and I find out where he is living, I'll plead with Princess Yanxian to have him severely punished.

Huansha was right. From then on, Xiaoyu pinned all her hopes on Cui Yunming. Every two or three days, she would send Huansha over to ask him for the news of Li Yi.

At first, it was easy to cover up the truth. He would say that he had written to Li Yi, telling him that he should come to Chang'an at once; the reply was soon to come, and she had to wait with patience. Xiaoyu believed that this was the case. The journey was long and hard. It would be some time before the good news came. So although she never ceased her enquiries, she was still not overly impatient.

Soon, heavy snow was falling and the year drew to a close. It was almost three months since she had first asked Cui Yunming to write to Li Yi, even a more complex matter could have been solved in so much time. Xiaoyu couldn't bear it any longer. One morning, she struggled to get up and asked Huansha and Guizi to help her comb and wash.

Every movement of hers was accompanied by panting. Her emaciated body seemed as if it would fall apart at a finger's touch. "Take it easy." Huansha admonished. "Better you should stay in bed."

"Lying in bed too long hurts my bones. I want to take a walk."

"On a fine day, there'd be no harm in that. But look at the weather!" Huansha pointed at the cloudy iron-grey sky. "It is going to snow soon."

"That's right," Guizi also advised her. "It's windy and chilly outside. You've been coughing less the last few days. Better you don't catch cold."

"No," Xiaoyu said adamantly. "I've to go out. I've got some-

『是何大事？』浣沙問。

『噯！』小玉苦笑道：『妳好傻！不想想，我還有甚麼大事？我要親自去看崔郎，問個明白。』

『這也容易得緊，我再去一趟就是了。』

小玉閉上眼搖搖頭，有氣無力地說：『不用妳去！妳去了，還不仍舊是那幾句話？』

浣沙臉一紅，拍胸擔保：『小娘子，妳看着，今天無論如何有句確實話給妳。若是我辦不到，妳再去。那時別說下雪，就天上下刀子，我也不攔妳。』

良久，小玉頷首同意：『也罷！妳既如此說，我就依妳，快去快回；替我給崔郎問好。』

離了家，浣沙祇在東市打轉。她不必老遠地到崔允明家去；去也無用——一本帳都在她肚子裏，崔允明跟她早算計好了，祇等李益來年春暖花開，入都迎娶，便死活不管，把他拉了來跟小玉見一面；此時卻不必先寫信跟他打交道，因為料定了決無覆信，反倒打草驚蛇，叫那負心漢有了防備。

然而，現在看來是搪塞不過去了！浣沙不斷的在尋思，想些甚

thing important to do."

"And what important thing might that be?" Huansha asked.

Smiling bitterly, Xiaoyu said, "How stupid you are! Just think what important thing I have to do? I've got to talk to Mr Cui and get an answer from him."

"That's easy enough. I'll go there for you."

Xiaoyu closed her eyes, shook her head, and said weakly, "You don't have to go! Every time you go, you come back with the same answer."

Huansha blushed, but struck her bosom and made a promise. "Lady, you just wait and see. Today I'll get a definite answer for you. If I don't, then you can go. Even if it is snowing or falling knives from the sky, I won't stop you from going."

Xiaoyu finally nodded in approval. "All right, then. I'll take you on your word. Go now and return as soon as you can. Also, send my regards to Mr Cui."

 After leaving the house, Huansha lingered about the East Market. She didn't have to go all the way to Cui Yunming's house; and there was no use going there in the first place. She had it all worked out in her mind. She and Cui Yunming had laid the groundwork. They would wait until spring when the flowers were in bloom — the time when Li Yi would come to the capital, and they would simply get him to see Xiaoyu. At present, they didn't have to write him because they figured he wouldn't reply. Writing letters would only alert this heartless fellow to what was taking place and assist him in taking precautions.

But it seemed they couldn't procrastinate any longer. Huansha kept making up excuses that could keep Xiaoyu in the dark, and

麼話來騙她一騙？好歹先把她的心定一定再說。

　　那就實話實說吧！『不管用！』她自語着搖搖頭，已跟她說過了，她不相信李益會攀上了盧家的親事；此刻自然也不會相信他明年春天要到長安成親。

　　然而，明年春天能見得着面，那總是事實；信不信祇好由她了。

　　這算是想停當了。看看逛逛，消磨到東市快將收歇，回家覆命。

　　『說也正巧！』浣沙擺一擺沁汗的鬢腳，裝得喜孜孜地說道：『一到崔家，崔郎剛要出門；說是來看小娘子有話說。小娘子，妳道是甚麼話？』

　　『莫非十郎的消息？』

　　『一猜就着。』浣沙故意拿蹻，坐了下來，抬起腿拿手捏一捏半舊的線鞵，自語似地說了兩個字：『好累！』

　　那小玉急在心裏，卻不便催，弄得有些手足無措，看浣沙慢條斯理地捏了這隻腳，又捏那隻腳，她可真是等不得了，『好妹妹，妳快說給我聽聽，消息如何？』

　　『妳也容我喘口氣嘛！是好消息總是好消息，急甚麼？』

　　一聽是好消息，小玉頓時眉眼舒展，臉上平空閃出一層光采，笑嘻嘻地答道：『祇「好消息」三字就夠了，我不急。』她把她自己喝的茶推向浣沙，『妳喝了茶，息一息，慢慢兒說給我聽。』

　　『也沒有多少話。』浣沙不敢把假話說得太樂觀，『祇說開春要到長安，一切面談。』

let her feel relieved for the time being.

Tell her the truth then! "That's useless," she said to herself, shaking her head. She had told her the truth before, but Xiaoyu refused to believe that Li Yi would marry the daughter of the Lu family. So she had no reason to believe that Li Yi would come to Chang'an to marry next spring.

Nevertheless, it was a fact that they would meet next spring. It was up to her whether to believe it or not.

This settled it. Huansha spent the day wandering about the East Market and returned home to report to her lady when the market was about to close.

"What a coincidence!" Huansha arranged the sweaty locks of hair on her temples, feigning excitement. "When I got to Mr Cui's house, he was just about to go out. He said he was going to tell you something. Lady, can you guess what?"

"Something to do with Shilang?"

"You're right," Huansha sat down, crossed her legs, and then raised one leg and started picking at her half-worn cotton shoes. She murmured to herself, "I'm very tired."

Xiaoyu was very impatient, but felt it improper to push her, so she didn't know what to do. Watching Huansha slowly picking at one shoe and then the other, she couldn't hold back any longer. "My good sister, please tell me the news now?"

"Let me catch my breath, no? If it's good news, then it's good news all right. There is no point in getting impatient."

On hearing that it was a good news, Xiaoyu felt immediate relief and her face lit up with hope. She said with a smile, "Just 'good news' is enough. I'm in no hurry to know." She handed the tea she was drinking to Huansha. "Drink some tea and rest. Take your time and tell me the news when you're ready."

"There isn't much to tell you anyway." Huansha didn't dare paint too bright a picture. "He only said that Shilang will come to Chang'an next spring, then everything can be sorted out face to face."

小玉微感失望，問道：『是跟我？』

『不是跟妳小娘子面談，難道是跟我浣沙？』

『嗯！』小玉怔怔地沉思着，漸漸地，神情轉爲平靜恬適，『對的，對的。』她點點頭說，聲音也清清朗朗，非復斷斷續續，上氣不接下氣的樣子了。『日子不過兩年有餘，事情有多多少少？信裏那說得盡？想來十郎定有無數委曲，母老家貧，他又是個孝順的；做個八、九品前程的小官，先顧了老娘，自然就顧不得我了。事出無奈，該當體諒他的。浣沙，妳說是不是？』

浣沙怎麼說呢？祇好唯唯稱是。

『好了！』小玉忽然精神十足地說：『天大的事，過了年再說。去年，前年，過得可眞不是味兒；今年咱們好好過一過。』

說也奇怪，小玉的病勢，原已藥石無靈；自這天以後，居然大爲好轉，臉上慢慢有了血色，秋後敗草樣的枯黃頭髮，也逐漸有了光澤，這使得醫生都驚奇得不得了，背着人把浣沙找來問淸了原因。

『怪不得！我原說妳家小娘子是心病。心病有了心藥，自然好得快。不過，』醫生神情突趨嚴肅：『她的病根未去，再要犯啦，可就仙丹都救不了命！妳當心點兒，不能讓她受驚嚇、受刺激；但能笑口常開，便可帶病延年，切記，切記！』

這是非同小可的事，浣沙不能不找桂子商量一下。

『事情再明白不過，』桂子說：『世間若有催命判官，便是那喪良心的李十郎！』

Xiaoyu was slightly disappointed. "Sort things out with me?"

"If not with you, can it be with me then?"

Xiaoyu mused anxiously. Gradually, she became calm. "Yes, yes," she said nodding. Her voice was loud and clear, quite a contrast to the confused and breathless way she used to speak. "It's been more than two years; so many things have happened. How can he say everything in letters? Shilang must have endured many disappointments. His mother is old and his family poor. And he is a filial son. Serving as an official of the eighth or ninth rank, he can only earn enough to take care of his mother, so he can't take care of me. Since there's nothing he can do about it, we should be sympathetic towards him. Isn't it right, Huansha?"

What could Huansha say? She could only reply in the affirmative.

In high spirits, Xiaoyu said, "Everything can be discussed after the Lunar New Year. Last year and the year before last, we spent the New Year in misery. This year, let's celebrate."

Strangely enough, Xiaoyu's illness, seemingly incurable, made a turn for the better. And since the day she learned the news, there was an obvious improvement. Her complexion became healthy and her dry, yellow hair, which resembled autumn hay, look more and more lustrous. This surprised her physician, who secretly fetched Huansha to ask about the reason.

"Now I understand. All along, I've been saying that your lady's illness has something to do with her broken heart. Once her heartbreak is cured, she will surely recover quickly." The physician became serious. "The root of her illness remains. If she has a relapse, even the elixir of life won't cure her. You must take great care that she suffers no emotional shocks. As long as she remains happy, she can live a long life. Keep this in mind."

Since this was a matter of great importance, Huansha had to discuss it with Guizi.

"It's simple." Guizi said. "If there is one life-shortening official in this world, it's the heartless Li Shilang!"

『那姓李的，明年春天一定會來；死拖活拉，見上一面，我倒是有把握的。』

『照我看，不見也罷；見了面會更傷小娘子的心。』

『對啊！』浣沙憬然有悟，『若是話不投機，不如不見。不見，小娘子可又怎麼肯依？這不難煞了人？』

『姊姊！』桂子忽然興奮地說：『我倒有個主意了——。』

『喔，有客在這裏！』驀地裏掀開棉門簾，闖了進去的浣沙，自覺莽撞，趕緊又退了出來，在門外叫道：『侯伯伯，你請出來，我有話說。』

話未完，侯景先已掀簾招呼：『來吧，浣沙，怕甚麼？』

『有生客，怕不便。』

『不礙！』侯景先說：『是好朋友。』

於是，浣沙怯怯地進了櫃房。首先看到那穿黃衫的生客，約摸三十歲年紀，長眉入鬢，一雙明亮的眼，灼灼地跟着浣沙轉；她讓他看得很不好意思，微微點一點頭，便疾趨到靠裏陰暗的一角，垂頭坐下。

『今天好冷。』侯景先說：『我拿熱茶妳喝！』說着便出了櫃房。

『坐這裏來吧！這裏暖和。』

浣沙聞聲抬起眼來。這下才看清楚，那黃衫客高踞胡床，一面

"Li is certain to come here next spring. I am quite sure that I can pressure him into seeing her."

"It seems to me it would be better if they don't meet. It'll harm her even more."

"That's right!" Huansha seemed to get the message. "If they don't get along, it would be better if they don't meet. But would she agree to it? What are we going to do?"

"Sister!" Suddenly, Guizi was elated, "I have an idea ..."

 "Oh, sorry, I didn't know you had a guest!" Huansha, who had lifted up the cotton door curtain and rushed into the room, realized she was being rude, so she immediately withdrew and shouted from outside, "Uncle Hou, please come out, I want to talk to you."

But before she had finished speaking, Hou Jingxian had already lifted up the curtain and greeted her. "Come in, Huansha, it doesn't matter."

"You have a guest. It's not convenient."

"It doesn't matter," said Hou Jingxian. "He's a good friend."

So Huansha slipped into the room. The first thing she noticed was that stranger clad in yellow, who looked like he was in his thirties. His long brows stretched in his temples, his bright eyes followed every one of Huansha's movements. She felt shy being stared at in that manner, so she nodded to him and made her way to a secluded corner of the room, sat down and lowered her head.

"It's cold out," said Hou Jingxian. "Let me get you a cup of hot tea." He went into the next room.

"Come and sit here, it's warmer."

Upon hearing his voice, Huansha looked up. She could now see clearly that the man in yellow was sitting on a folding bed.

放着把雪亮的劍；一面放着一大盤炙肉，一大海碗白酒；面前一個大火盆，他正拿着根肉骨頭，在撥弄着快熄下去的木炭。

屋中別無他人，他的話自然是對她說的，『謝謝！』她說，『這裏也很暖和。』

黃衫客看了她一眼，不響，咕咚一聲扔掉骨頭，用兩隻手指捏起海碗，大口喝酒。放下酒碗，撈起衣襟拂拭他那把原已點塵不染的劍；然後，倒捏劍身，用劍把叩擊着銅火盆的邊緣朗聲高吟：

> 邯鄲城南遊俠子，
> 自矜生長邯鄲裏。
> 千場縱博家仍富，
> 幾處報仇身不死。
> 宅中歌笑日紛紛，
> 門外車馬常如雲，
> 未知肝膽問誰是？
> 令人卻憶平原君！
> 君不見今人交態薄，
> 黃金用盡還疎索？……。

浣沙也是能彈善唱的，起先還聽不清他吟的甚麼？自第三句起，就聽懂了，『千場縱博家仍富』，好狂的口氣，心想，這也是個浮滑少年，便懶得再去偷覷他。

然而她無法聽而不聞，他的嗓音很寬，衷氣更足，聲音振得那間密不通風的櫃房，嗡嗡作響，聽來十分舒暢；因此她情不自禁地

Beside him was a glittering sword, a plate of roast pork and a large bowl of wine. In front of him was a huge brazier. He was holding a bone and poking the charcoal in the brazier.

As there was no one else in the room, naturally he was addressing her. "Thank you!" she said. "It's warm over here too."

The man in yellow looked at her and said nothing. He tossed the bone onto the floor, picked up the bowl with two fingers and gurgled down the wine. Then he put down the bowl and start to polish the spotless sword with his sleeve. He then plucked the blade of the sword and started singing a song, striking the edge of the brazier with his sword as accompaniment:

> A wandering swordsman from the south of Handan
> Proudly claims that he was born in Handan.
> After a thousand losses in gambling, he is still rich;
> After taking several revenges on others' behalf,
>   he still survives.
> Day after day, his house is filled with music and laughter,
> Carts and horses thick as clouds wait before his door.
> Those who don't know him ask his name?
> He reminds one of Prince Pingyuan.
> Can't you see that men of today are devoid of loyalty?
> Once you've spent all your money,
>   you are left alone; nowhere to turn.

Huansha was also skilled in music and singing. At first, she couldn't make out what he was singing. But she began to understand it after the third line. "After a thousand losses in gambling, he is still rich." How bombastic that man in the poem is! She thought to herself: the man in yellow is also a boastful type, so she didn't bother to look at him any more.

But she couldn't turn a deaf ear to his song. His tenor was so forceful that it shook the stuffy little room and set it buzzing, which made it very pleasant to listen to. So without thinking she began to follow the lyrics. When she heard the lines —

循聲尋字，按拍細聽，聽到『君不見今人交態薄，黃金用盡還疏索』這兩句，陡然憶起小玉這兩年貧病交迫，卻又癡心不改的境況，眼眶一酸，隨即模糊了。

　　黃衫客的吟聲，悠然而止；接着是侯景先的聲音：『好詩，好詩！除非是你，第二個人也不配。可是你自己作的？』

　　『我沒那麼好的才情。』

　　『那麼是誰呢？』

　　『誰知道是誰作的？那天聽南曲王家的采兒在唱，我就記下來了。』黃衫客接着又說，『好了，你別嚕嘛了！招呼你的客人去吧！』

　　浣沙可是老早就拭去了淚痕在等了。侯景先把一盞熱茶湯遞了給她，伸手說道：『拿來！』

　　浣沙愕然，『拿甚麼？』她低聲問。

　　『不是過不了年，又找出甚麼東西託我來賣？』

　　『喔！』原來如此，浣沙微微笑道：『就不作興來看看你老，非有事，才上門？』

　　『唷、唷！』侯景先高興地笑了，『幾時，妳的嘴變得這麼甜了？』略停一下，他又湊過去說：『其實倒是可惜了，我那朋友昨夜在平康坊三曲擲骰子，贏了二十萬錢；若有東西變賣，恰是個好主顧。』

　　『可惜沒有。』

　　『這樣吧，』侯景先越發發低了聲音：『把妳的耳環摘下來，我包妳賣得個意想不到的好價錢——我那朋友，錢不當錢，花他幾個在他毫不在乎；妳跟妳家小娘子這個年可就過得很舒服了。』

Can't you see that men of today are devoid of loyalty?
Once you've spent all your money,
    You are left alone; nowhere to turn.

— it reminded her of Xiaoyu: she had remained loyal to Li Yi during the last two years, though she was stricken by poverty and illness. Her eyes turned red and became blurred.

The man's song finally came to an end. Then Hou Jingxian spoke. "Excellent poetry, excellent! Only you can fit that description. Is it your own work?"

"How could I have such talent?"

"Who wrote it then?"

"Who knows? The other day, I heard Cai'er of the Wang family in Nanqu sing it, so I copied it. All right, enough of that! Take care of your guest!"

Huansha had already wiped her tears away and was waiting for him. Hou Jingxian handed her a cup of hot tea and stretched out his hand to her. "Give it to me!"

Huansha was astonished. "What are you talking about?" she asked, lowering her voice.

"I thought maybe you don't have enough money for the New Year Festival and have brought me something to sell?"

"Oh, I see!" Huansha smiled, "Can't I just come to see you sometimes? Do I have to come on business?"

Hou Jingxian smiled back. "Since when did you become so mealy-mouthed?" He paused, moved closer to her and said, "What a great pity! My friend here won two hundred thousand cash playing dice at Sanqu in Pingkang Square last night. If you've got anything to sell, he'd be a good buyer."

"But I've got nothing to sell."

Hou Jingxian lowered his voice even further, "you take off your earrings and I guarantee that you'll get a good price. This friend of mine is easy with money, and doesn't mind spending a few more cash. In this way you and your lady can enjoy yourselves during the New Year Festival."

『多謝侯伯伯想得週全。』浣沙平靜地答道：『不過這哄騙的勾當，還是不做它吧！』

『好！』侯景先一翹拇指說：『浣沙，妳身份不高，品行尊貴，我眞服了妳！』

『好說、好說。侯伯伯，說實話，倒是有件大事來跟你商議。』浣沙悄悄地把小玉病勢好轉，以及醫生的鄭重的告誡，都說了給侯景先聽。

『這可眞是意想不到的。』侯景先說：『怕祇怕，來年春天見不着姓李的那傢伙的影子，可不又把妳家小娘子急出病來！』

『是的。』浣沙說，『我跟桂子商議過；小娘子一顆心，癡得再不回頭了，索性騙得她死心塌地吧！』

『那也要姓李的肯騙她才行。』

『就是這話囉！桂子的話也有道理，李十郎到底是讀書人，總不能一點不念香火之情；眼看小娘子已到了這步田地，他不能見死不救。咱們不指望進他李家的門，祇請他別再那樣子不理不睬；祇當小娘子是他一個外室，有錢也罷，無錢也罷，反正不叫他爲難。若是放了外任，儘管帶了他的正室夫人去；就別忘了三兩個月捎封書信來，哄哄小娘子就行了。侯伯伯你想，照這樣子，既不會害他夫婦失和，又不會妨害他的前程，他若是還有點人心，能不答應嗎？』

『妳跟桂子想倒是想得入情入理。祇是妳問過妳家小娘子，她肯這樣委屈嗎？』

『用不着問！一定肯，千肯萬肯！』浣沙答道，『侯伯伯，你還不知道，小娘子才眞叫能體諒人呢！你道她說甚麼？』

『說甚麼？』

"Uncle Hou, thank you very much for being so considerate." Huansha answered calmly, "but I don't think we should be dishonest!"

"Good!" Hou Jingxian raised his thumb and said, "Huansha, though your position is low, you have a sense of dignity, and that is what I admire most."

"Thank you, Uncle Hou. To tell the truth, I have come to discuss a matter of great importance." Huansha then told Hou Jingxian about Xiaoyu's recovery and her physician's advice.

"This is rather unexpected!" said Hou Jingxian. "My only worry is that if Li actually shows up next spring, your lady's condition will worsen!"

"Indeed." Huansha said, "I've already discussed this matter with Guizi. My lady is so infatuated with him that she can't see the truth. It'd be best to keep her completely in the dark!"

"That depends on Li's willingness to comply."

"That's the crux of the matter. What Guizi said makes good sense. After all, Li Shilang is a man of letters, and he's bound to uphold the promise he made. Now that my lady is in such a plight, he can't just stand there and let her die. We don't expect her to become a member of the Li family, but rather hope that he won't ignore her completely. He can simply treat my lady as a concubine, with or without an allowance, and we'll be satisfied. If he's assigned to a frontier region, he can take his wife with him as he wishes, but he shouldn't forget to send my lady a letter once every few months to maintain the illusion. Uncle Hou, if this works out, he can have a harmonious marriage as well as a successful career. If he has any conscience at all, don't you think he'll agree to this?"

"You and Guizi have done an excellent job. But the point is: have you asked your lady whether or not if she is willing to be a concubine?"

"We don't have to ask her! She will certainly agree to it," Huansha answered. "Uncle Hou, do you know what she said?"

"What?"

　　浣沙學着小玉的姿態說：『「想來十郎定有無數委曲。母老家貧，他又是個孝順的；做個八、九品前程的小官，先顧了老娘，自然就顧不得我了。事出無奈，該當體諒他的。」』她又好笑又好氣地補了一句：『還問我，「是不是？」侯伯伯，你看看，這種人，拿她有甚麼辦法？』

　　『唉！』侯景先嘆口氣說：『女人真是好欺侮！』

　　『是呀！』浣沙立即接口，『連我，原來打算着出口惡氣的；現在反倒要求他了。侯伯伯，我在想，這番意思，該先透露給他才好。』

　　『那妳找他表兄。』

　　『去過了。』浣沙答道，『剛才我就從崔家來。崔明經說，他的話不管用，得找個有面子的人給李十郎寫封信。我想到個人，侯伯伯你看行不行？』

　　『誰？』

　　『延先公主。』

　　『這面子倒是夠了。不過，』侯景先沉思良久，徐徐說道：『第一，老何不在長安，讓淮南節度使請去雕琢玉器去了，要過了年才能回來，眼下無人引見；第二，這些話，信裏寫不明白。照我看，既然姓李的開春要來，不如等他來了，再求延先公主把他找了去，當面開導明白，豈不是既省事，又切實？』

　　『是，是！』浣沙覺得侯景先的打算，確比崔允明又來得高明，便欣然同意，告辭而去。

　　等浣沙一走，黃衫客問道：『你們咕咕噥噥談些甚麼？』

　　『談個天下第一等的負心漢。』侯景先約略說了些李益和小玉的故事。

Imitating Xiaoyu's manner of speaking, Huansha said, "'Shilang must have endured many disappointments. His mother is old and his family poor. And he is a filial son. Serving as an official of the eighth or ninth rank, he can only earn enough to take care of his mother, so he can't take care of me. Since there's nothing he can do about it, we should be sympathetic towards him.'" Huansha, half jokingly and half angrily, added, "She also asked me 'Am I right?' Uncle Hou, come to think of it, what can I do with her?"

Hou Jingxian sighed. "Women are so easily deceived!"

"Indeed!" Huansha replied, "Including myself. At first I planned to lash him, but now I'm about to plea to him. Uncle Hou, I was wondering if the message should be conveyed to him first."

"Why don't you go see his cousin first."

"I did." Huansha answered. "I've just been to the Cui's house. Cui said that his words carry no weight and that we have to find someone influential who can write a letter to Li Shilang. Uncle Hou, I have one person in mind and wonder if you think she is all right?"

"Who's that?"

"Princess Yanxian."

"She is certainly influential enough," Hou Jingxian mused for a while and said, "but the first problem is: Old He is out of town now. He's been invited by the Huainan Commander to carve some jade pieces and won't be back until after the New Year Festival. So there is no one here now who can introduce us to her. The second problem is that these things can't be stated in a letter. The way I see it, if Li comes next spring, why not wait until then and ask Princess Yanxian to convince him face to face? Isn't that more practical?"

"You're right!" Huansha agreed that Hou's plan was better than Cui's. She gave her consent and took her leave.

Once Huansha had gone, the man in yellow asked, "What have you two been murmuring about?"

"We were talking about the most heartless fellow in the

　　黃衫客聽完，冷笑着用劍挑起一塊紅炭，拋向空中，然後使劍一揮，把那段炭斬成兩截，火星濺舞，把侯景先嚇了一跳。

　　『此輩不情不義的小丈夫，就該吃我一劍！』黃衫客恨恨地說。

　　『噯、噯！』侯景先趕緊搖着手說：『你可千萬魯莽不得！你要知道，你這一劍是兩條命！』

　　『還饒上誰的一條？』

　　『霍小玉呀！』侯景先說：『她就等着見他一面，治她的相思病。姓李的死了，霍小玉可也就完蛋了！』

　　黃衫客嘿然無語。然後，微微一笑，跳下胡床，提着他的劍，瀟瀟灑灑地走了。

楊柳青遍了灞橋和咸陽渡口，青遍了曲江池畔，也青遍了思婦樓頭。

　　春天來了，而李益的蹤跡杳然。

　　自過了燈節，小玉便打算着李益隨時會來，每天一早起身，督促浣沙和桂子，掃地焚香，把屋子收拾得乾乾淨淨；她自己呢，薰香更衣，盛粧而坐，就像命婦等候着覲見皇帝似地。到晚來，看看這一天沒有指望了，才悄然閉門，卸妝上床，可又希冀着先從夢中相會。

　　九十春光過半，小玉又有懨懨成病的樣子，浣沙看在眼裏，不

world." Hou Jingxian told him about the story of Li Yi and Huo Xiaoyu.

Having heard the story, the man in yellow make a sneer, picked up a piece of glowing charcoal with his sword, tossed it into the air, and sliced it into two pieces, with sparks flying in every direction. Hou Jingxian was startled.

"This sort of heartless scoundrel deserves a taste of my sword!" the man in yellow said in disgust.

"Oh, no!" Hou Jingxian waved his hands and said, "Don't act rashly! Don't you know, your actions might cost two lives!"

"Whose is the other life?"

"Huo Xiaoyu's!" said Hou Jingxian. "She is waiting to see him to cure her lovesickness. If Li dies, Xiaoyu's life will be at stake!"

The man in yellow said nothing. Then, with a smile, he jumped off the bed, picked up his sword, and strode out of the room.

 The willows turned the Ba Bridge and the Xianyang ferry crossing green. They also turned green the banks of the Qu River, and the tower of the yearning woman. Spring came, but there was no sign of Li Yi.

Ever since the Lantern Festival, Xiaoyu had been expecting Li Yi. Every morning when she got up, she instructed Huansha and Guizi to sweep the floor clean, burn incense and tidy up the house. She herself put on perfume, dressed up in anticipation of his arrival. She was like an imperial lady waiting for an audience with the emperor. When evening came and there was little hope of seeing him that day, she closed her door silently, undressed and went to bed, hoping that she would meet him in her dreams.

Spring was nearly over, and Xiaoyu seemed to be getting ill

但焦急，而且有着無比的疚歉；因爲李益開春一定會來的話，是從她口中說出去的，那喪盡了良心的薄倖人眞個不來，變得她無法交待了。

『三月三日天氣新，』長安千門萬戶，十室九空——都已湧向曲江，『小娘子！』浣沙勸她也去逛一逛，『今天皇帝賜宴百官，曲江熱鬧得很，去踏一踏青，也散一散心；別眞個在家裏悶出病來。』

『妳跟桂子去吧！』小玉答道：『我在家守着，十郎說不定今天會來。』

反正就是離不了『十郎』二字，浣沙想了下說：『也罷，待我再到崔家問一問信息。』

『這倒使得。』又說：『要去就去！』

崔允明一看見浣沙，不用她開口，便已知道她的來意，搔着蕭疏的短鬢，以不勝惶惑歉疚的語氣說：『眞奇怪！到現在還沒有消息。』

『崔郎，你倒是去打聽過沒有？是眞的沒有來，還是已經來了而你不知道？』

『無從打聽。』

『盧家呢？你們不也算親戚？嬌客來了，盧家萬無不知之理。』

崔允明苦笑着搖搖頭：『轉彎抹角的表親，與路人無異。盧家

again. Huansha noticed this and felt both anxious and regretful: it was she who had told Xiaoyu that Li Yi would come in the spring. If the heartless fellow really didn't turn up, she would be at a loss to explain.

"On the third day of the third month, the weather turns fine." Nearly the entire population of Chang'an went to the Qu River on this day to enjoy themselves. "My lady!" Huansha admonished her to go out, "today the emperor will hold an imperial banquet for his officials. The banks of the Qu River will be very crowded. You should go for a walk in the country and relax a little; staying cooped up in your room like this isn't good for your health."

"You go with Guizi!" Xiaoyu answered. "I'll wait here. Perhaps Shilang will come today."

It was always the same: "Shilang". Huansha thought for a while and said, "All right, I'll go to the Cui's house and ask about him again."

"Good idea," Xiaoyu said. "Go right now."

The moment Cui Yunming saw Huansha, he knew why she had come. He scratched his wispy sideburns and said apologetically, "It's really strange! I haven't heard a thing from him."

"Mr Cui, have you asked round? Perhaps he hasn't come, but perhaps he has and you don't know about it?"

"There is no way to know."

"How about the Lu family? Aren't you related to them? If their future son-in-law is in Chang'an, there's no way they won't know."

Cui Yunming shook his head and smiled bitterly. "A remote cousin isn't much different from a stranger in the street. The Lu

聲勢煊赫，豪奴成羣；浣沙，妳看我這寒酸樣子，如何上門？』

『不是說來迎娶嗎？』浣沙又說：『想這高門大戶辦喜事，少不得大大地舖張一番，豈有個打聽不出來的道理？』

『妳的話不錯，我也想到了，而且打聽過了，盧家尚無動靜；一說，婚禮要延到初夏。』

『是何緣故？』

『這可不知道了。』

『若是令表弟來了，』浣沙問道：『可是一定要來看你？』

『過去，每一次來，定會來看我。不過，這一次就難說了！』

『祇是爲了我家小娘子的緣故？』浣沙冷笑道：『爲了有個人不敢見，連中表至親都不敢往來了？』

崔允明默然點頭，緊皺着眉，表情顯得相當痛苦似地。

浣沙想了好一會，突然問道：『崔郎近日境況如何？』

這是甚麼意思呢？且不管它，照實回答：『還不錯。上個月受人之託，做了兩篇墓誌銘，諛墓之金，足夠半年澆裹。』

『好極！』浣沙欣然說道：『旣然如此，我有個不情之請，請崔郎可憐我家小娘子，發個慈悲，去一趟洛陽，打聽個確實消息回來，可使得？』

『使得、使得。妳家小娘子相待甚厚，理當效勞。』崔允明點點頭又說：『妳的辦法好！他不來，我就去找他，看他還躲得了不？』

『多謝崔郎雪中送炭的恩德。』浣沙裣袵爲禮，『半月之後，來聽好音。』

family is powerful and has numerous servants. Huansha, you know very well that they won't let me in their door the way I look."

"Isn't the purpose of his visit to get married?" Huansha went on. "When prominent families celebrate happy occasions, they make a big fanfare out of it. How is it that you haven't heard anything about it?"

"That's right. I've thought about it and asked around. There is nothing going on at the Lu's mansion. Rumour has it that the wedding ceremony will be postponed to early summer."

"Why?"

"I don't know."

"If your cousin comes," Huansha asked, "doesn't he always come to see you?"

"In the past, when he was in Chang'an, he would come to see me. But this time it's hard to say."

"Is this because of my lady?" Huansha sneered. "Is he unwilling to visit a close relative like you just because he's afraid to see her?"

Cui Yunming nodded. He frowned uncomfortably.

Huansha asked, "How have you been lately?"

What did she mean by this? In any case, he told the truth. "I'm all right. Last month I was commissioned to write two epitaphs. The remuneration I received is enough to keep me going for half a year."

"That's marvellous!" Huansha said. "If that is the case, I have a request to make. I hope you will have pity on my lady and show her some compassion. Will you go to Luoyang once and get some news?"

"Certainly, I will. Your lady has been good to me, so I ought to render service to her." Cui Yunming nodded and said, "It's a good idea. If he doesn't come, I'll go see him and find out how long he plans to stay away."

"Mr Cui, thank you for your kindness." Huansha said, bowing

一騎瘦驢，東出灞橋，不期交臂錯過；崔允明出都之日，恰是李益進京之期。

果然如崔允明所預料的，李益知道他跟小玉接近，有心躲避，在近南城的靖安坊，賃了一所房子住下；開出門來，便是安善坊的大教弩場，除了威遠軍一月三次較射的日子以外，等閒人跡不到，十分僻靜。

這次重到長安，自然與當年進京赴試不同，鮮衣怒馬，盡洗寒酸。然而他不敢招搖，怕有風聲傳到小玉耳朵裏，會找上門來；因此，除了盧家以外，甚麼地方也不去。

婚期選定了：四月十五；還有一個多月的日子。盧章囑咐他，該趁這餘暇，大事交遊，廣通聲氣，對於將來在仕途中上進，可獲極大的幫助。這層道理，李益自然懂得，祇是別有苦衷，不敢明說，祇好唯唯稱是。

但這一來，為了要假裝聽從盧章的話，日事交際，就不便天天到盧家去了。在家看了兩天書，覺得氣悶得很，便問他的書僮：『附近可有甚麼能走走的地方？』

to him. "I'll come in a fortnight to hear the good news."

20 Riding a frail donkey, Cui Yunming headed eastward across the Ba Bridge, unaware that he had just missed Li Yi. For the day of his departure from the capital was the very day of Li Yi's arrival.

As Cui Yunming had predicted, Li Yi dodged him deliberately because of his connection with Xiaoyu. Li Yi rented a house in the Jing'an Lane at South End and stayed there. In front of the house was the Anshan district archery field. Except for the archery practice by the imperial guards three sessions a month, very few people came to the neighbourhood. It was a perfectly secluded spot.

Li Yi's return to Chang'an this time was quite different from his last visit when he had taken the civil service examination. He dressed stylishly and rode on horseback; there was no trace of his former poverty. But he avoided public appearances, for fear that Xiaoyu might get wind of it and come to look for him. Thus he confined his visits to the Lu mansion.

The marriage was set for the fifteenth of the fourth month, a little more than a month away. Lu Zhang kept reminding Li Yi that he should use his leisure time to make social contacts which would help him in his future career. Li Yi, of course, knew this, but had his own difficulties which he was reluctant to mention. All he could do was to nod in agreement.

But in order to create the impression that he was following Lu Zhang's advice, he found it inconvenient to go to the Lu house everyday. After spending two days reading at home, he became bored, and asked his attendant, "Is there anywhere nearby worth visiting?"

『怎麼沒有？宅西崇敬寺的牡丹，全長安數一數二；這兩天開得正盛。』

『好吧，上崇敬寺看牡丹去。』

由於路途不遠，李益一個人安步當車，慢慢地走了去。那崇敬寺建於前朝開皇年間，一度廢圮；本朝龍朔二年，高宗把它賜給高安長公主，因而變成了尼寺。那裏的比丘尼，戒律甚嚴，祇憑施主看花，並不接待遊客，加以地址偏僻，所以遠不及另一處也是以牡丹負盛名的慈恩寺元果院，那種『三條九陌花時節，萬里千車看牡丹』的盛況。

對李益來說，正中下懷，他不願意到人多的地方去，怕遇見熟人。誰知道偏偏遇見了！那也是個高門華胄，武后朝名相韋安石的後人韋夏卿，世居長安城南韋曲。

韋夏卿字雲客，出身貴族，卻無膏粱子弟的習氣，衣飾樸素，起居節約；聲色犬馬，一無所好，祇愛聊天，所以朋友極多，李益是他談詩的朋友。

『幸會，幸會！』既然躲避不了，李益便索性裝得親熱些，『你是本地人，怎麼避至今日，才來看牡丹？』

『這已是第五度來訪艷了。』韋夏卿問道：『你呢？那一天到的長安？何以未聽人說起你來？』

"Well. The peonies in the Chongjing Temple to the west of this house are the best in Chang'an. They're in full bloom now."

"All right, then, I'll go to the Chongjing Temple and have a look."

As the place was close by, Li Yi went to the temple on foot. The Chongjing Temple had been built during the Kaihuang period of Sui but had subsequently gone to ruins. In the second year of the Longsuo reign of the present dynasty, Emperor Gaozong gave it to Princess Gao'an who turned it into a nunnery. The nunnery had strict rules and regulations. Visitors were allowed to admire the flowers; they were not permitted to lodge there. Situated in a remote place, this nunnery was less famous as the Yuanguo Court of the Ci'en Temple, also known for its peonies which has been described as follows: "When the flowers are in bloom, the three roads and nine lanes are crowded with countless horses and carriages bearing admirers of the fine peonies."

This was exactly to Li Yi's taste. He didn't want to go to crowded places for fear of being seen. How did he know that he would run into a familiar face? This particular person was also the scion of a prominent family. His name was Wei Xiaqing; he was a descendent of Wei Anshi, a famous premier during the reign of Empress Wu. He had lived in Wei Lane of the South End of Chang'an for years.

Though Wei Xiaqing, styled Yunke, was born in a noble family, he had none of the vices of the sons of the rich and powerful. He dressed simply and led a modest life. He didn't indulge in sex or gambling, but rather led an active social life. He had many friends; Li Yi was one with whom he could discuss poetry.

"How nice to see you!" Li Yi said. As he could hardly avoid him, Li Yi feigned intimacy with the man. "You live here all year round. Why wait so long to see the peonies?"

"This is the fifth time I've been here." Wei Xiaqing replied. "How about you? When did you arrive in Chang'an? Why hasn't anybody mentioned that you were here?"

『剛來不多幾天，還沒有來得及去拜訪親友。』

『下榻何處？』

李益不肯透露住處，支吾其詞地說：『暫住舍親家。』

『噢。』韋夏卿說：『聽說你在鄭縣，頗有能名。簿書之暇，詩興如何？』

李益這兩年忙着撈錢，那有功夫作詩？所以聽了韋夏卿的話，臉一紅，略微有些窘地笑道：『風塵俗吏，奔走差使。詩，可眞是少作了！』

韋夏卿點點頭，又問：『此行爲公爲私？』

這是李益早就想好了的：『奉上官差遣，來查一件案子。』

『喔。』韋夏卿笑道：『這樣說，怕仍舊是沒有功夫做詩了？』

『這倒不然。客中消遣，莫如忙裏偸閒，覓句寄興；今天或有拙作，可以請敎。』

『好極了！面對國色，不能無詩。』韋夏卿手指西廊：『你看，那方雪白的粉壁，恰像是爲你留着的。崇敬寺的牡丹，得你「姑臧李益」的品題，身價更自不同。你等等，我找這裏的小尼姑去借副筆硯來！』

李益心想，題壁留名，不等於自己招供了行蹤？此事大大不妥，想要阻止，韋夏卿卻已走得遠了。

"I've only been here a couple of days. I haven't even had time to visit my relatives."

"Where are you staying?"

Li Yi was reluctant to disclose his address, so he muttered, "I'm staying at a relative's home for the time being."

"Oh!" Wei Xiaqing said, "I've heard that you've made quite a reputation for yourself in Zhengxian. Do you still write poetry after work?"

For the last two years, Li Yi had been involved with the business of getting together enough money for his marriage; how could he find time to write poetry? So what Wei Xiaqing said embarassed him somewhat, "I am a vulgar functionary dealing with trivial matters. I really haven't written much poetry," he said, blushing.

Wei Xiaqing nodded and asked again, "Are you here on business or is this a private visit?"

Li Yi had contrived a ready answer for this kind of question, "I've been instructed by my superior to come here to investigate a case."

"Oh!" Wei Xiaqing said with a smile. "In this case, I'm afraid you won't have much time to write poetry."

"You never know. One way to relax is to jot down a few lines to vent one's feelings, if one has a spare moment or two. Perhaps I can write something today and submit it for your approval."

"Excellent! Such beautiful scenery cries out for poetry!" Wei Xiaqing pointed to the Western Corridor. "Look over there. That snow-white wall seems to have been reserved for your poem. The fame of the peonies of the Chongjing Temple will spread far and wide once we have an inscription signed 'Li Yi of Guzang'. Wait here a few moments. I'll have a nun here to get you some brushes and ink!"

Li Yi thought to himself: writing a wall poem and signing it would be a way of revealing his whereabouts, something highly undesirable. But before he could stop Wei, he had gone.

憑欄沉思的李益，想不出個推辭的好辦法，心中好不煩惱。就這時候，聽見身後有人在問：『足下可是姑臧李十？』

李益微微一驚，回身去看，祇見一個三十左右，身着黃羅袷衫的英俊男子，含笑而立；身後跟着個剪短了頭髮的小胡奴，手中抱着一張琴，身上揹了把彈弓，稚態可掬地也仰望着他。

李益愛惜聲名，不肯否認，點頭，反問道：『足下何人？』

『敝處山東。』黃衫客答道：『下走麤魯不文，祇懂走馬放鷹，鬥雞打毬，然而雖乏文藻，亦知敬愛高賢。足下聲華，久已仰慕，剛才聽令友提及大名，豈可失之交臂？所以不揣冒昧，想奉約到蝸居一聚；妖姬八九、駿馬十數，或可盡一日之歡。千祈足下，不恥下交。』

李益看他那儀表談吐，估量着必是山東大族的子弟，走向遊俠一路；這些人萬金贈人，千里報仇，不當回事，若能結納，是個極有用的朋友。又想到正可借此機會，辭卻了題壁那件惱人的事。於是欣然答道：『萍水相逢，一見如故。我，從命！』

『還有令友，自然一起去盤桓。』

李益正要回答，看到韋夏卿興匆匆捧了筆硯走來，便先迎了上去，約略說了根由，韋夏卿面現怏怏之色：『這可不行，我還約了別的朋友，在此相會。』

Musing by a railing, Li Yi could think of no way out, and became vexed. At that moment, he heard someone behind him asking, "Are you Li Yi of Guzang?"

Li Yi was somewhat astonished. He turned round and saw a handsome man, about thirty years old, clad in yellow silk, smiling at him. Behind him stood a Tartar servant with his hair cut short, holding a stringed-instrument and with a bow and arrows on his back, gazing up at him like a child.

Li Yi valued his reputation too much to hide his identity, so he nodded and asked, "May I know who you are?"

"I am from Shandong," the man in yellow answered. "I am uncultivated and uncultured. My principal occupations are riding, hunting with falcons, cockfighting and football. Though I lack literary ability, I have deep respect for men of learning. I learned of your reputation long ago. When I heard your friend mention your name, I knew this was a rare opportunity to meet you. I therefore take the liberty of inviting you to my humble home. I have several maids and some fine horses; they could enable us to have an enjoyable time together. I hope that you won't mind condescending to make friends with me."

Li Yi judged from his appearance and manner that he was the son of one of the prominent families in Shandong who had chosen to live as a wandering swordsman. Men of this type could give away ten thousand cash or travel great distances to take revenge on someone's behalf without expecting any rewards. If he could make friends with him, it might be very useful. He also wanted to take this opportunity to get out of the business of writing a wall poem. So he said, "Though we have met by chance, I feel as though we've been friends for years. I accept your invitation."

"And naturally your friend should join us."

Li Yi was about to reply when he noticed Wei Xiaqing coming back with a brush and inkslab in his hands. He went up to him and told him about his new plans. Wei Xiaqing was obviously disappointed. "This won't do. I have asked another friend of mine to

李益也不再代爲堅邀，祇說：『那麼，再圖良晤吧！我的詩，等作好了再請敎。』

『就這樣說了。你請！』

李益跟黃衫客一起走了。韋夏卿目送着他們的背影，無緣無故地笑了起來。

 那些馬好駿！眞正的大宛純種，跑得又快又穩；主客僕從，一行五人，向北而去，轉眼間便到了皇城大街。

黃衫客在前引路，由安上門前，一折向東，往崇仁坊與平康坊之間奔了下去。李益忽然想到，再過去，便是東市以北，興慶宮之西的勝業坊，小玉住在那裏，遇見了便逃不脫，太危險了！

因此，他猛然勒住了馬，大聲叫道：『黃衫尊兄請稍待！』

黃衫客聽見聲音，圈馬回來，問道：『有何吩咐？』

『忽然想起一個約會，不便失信。祇好改日再來拜訪了。今天有負盛情，抱歉之至。』

『喔！』黃衫客答道：『蝸居馬上快到了。就是改天再聚，且先認一認門戶，以後也容易尋找。』

meet me here."

Li Yi immediately dropped the idea of inviting him, and said, "In that case, let's find another time to meet. Once I write the poem, I'll ask for your opinion."

"That's a deal. Farewell!"

Li Yi left with the man in yellow. Wei Xiaqing watched them as they retreated, chuckling to himself.

 The horses they rode were truly fine! Thorough bred Dawans, they were both fast and steady. The host, his guest and his servants made up a team of five. They headed northward, and arrived at Main Street in the capital in no time.

The man in yellow led the way. After passing through Anshang Gate, they turned eastward and headed for the Chongren and Pingkang districts. It suddenly occurred to Li Yi that they were riding in the direction of the Shenye Lane, located to the north of the East Market and to the west of the Xingqing Palace. This is where Xiaoyu lived. If he happened to meet up with her, there was no way out for him. It was simply too risky.

Reining in his horse, he said loudly, "Please wait a moment, my friend in yellow!"

His host turned his horse around and asked, "Is there anything I can do for you?"

"I suddenly remember that I have an appointment now. So I have to come some other day to pay you a visit. I'm terribly sorry that I can't accept your kindness."

The man in yellow replied, "But my house is just around the corner. Even if you come some other time, take a look at my front gate so that it will be easier for you to find your way back here the

　　話說得極有道理，李益無法推辭，心想，總也不致於那麼巧，偏偏這一刻就撞見了熟人，好歹看一看他的住處，便即離了這是非之地，料也無妨。

　　於是，重又放馬前行。這一次黃衫客不在前面了，由他所帶的兩名健僕，在前引路，他自己跟在李益馬後，再後便是那小胡奴；人小，卻也是騎的高頭大馬。

　　一路風馳電掣，出崇仁、平康兩坊之間，往北進了勝業坊，不但進了勝業坊，那道路而且越來越熟悉，竟是走到小玉所住的那條街上來了。

　　心亂如麻，轉而為神思恍惚的李益，偶然轉臉，看到黃衫客臉上的詭秘微笑，一下子完全明白了！來不及轉第二個念頭，便直覺地猛揮一鞭，手裏一扯韁繩，那匹棗紅大馬如離弦之箭般往橫路裏躥了下去。

　　『使弓！』黃衫客吩咐小胡奴，『別太傷了馬！』

　　『不會！』那小胡奴的手腳真俐落，一縮脖子，退下彈弓，右手從口袋中拈取一粒泥丸；祇聽弓弦輕響，那粒泥丸在棗紅馬的屁股上砸得粉碎。

　　馬一護疼，唏咻咻一聲長嘶，前蹄往上一掀，把李益顛下馬來；兩名健僕，飛也似地趕到，一個搶住了脫韁的馬，一個俯下身去，一伸手便撈住了李益，略停得一停，那匹馬掉轉身來，亮開四蹄，一陣風似地捲了回去。

　　半昏迷中，李益聽得黃衫客大叫：『李十郎來也！』然後，他

next time."

This seemed reasonable, and thus Li Yi found it hard to decline. He thought to himself: only by the greatest coincidence would he run into someone he knew right now. In any case, it would do him no harm to take a look at his residence before leaving this inauspicious place.

So he let his horse continue on. This time, the man in yellow did not take the lead. Instead, his two muscular servants led the way while he rode behind Li Yi, followed by the young Tartar servant. This servant, though small in stature, rode a full-sized horse.

Running like the wind, they passed through the Chongren and Pingkang districts and entered Shenye. This neighbourhood was very familiar to Li Yi, and much to his surprise, they stopped in the very lane where Xiaoyu lived.

Perplexed and lost in reverie, Li Yi turned around and observed a mysterious smile on the man's face. Everything fell into place now. Without a second's hesitation, he whipped his horse and let fly the reins, whereupon his ruddy horse shot through the lanes like an arrow.

"Shot him down!" The man in yellow instructed his servant, "but don't injure the horse too badly."

"Don't worry!" The skilful servant bent down, prepared his bow and took out a clay bullet from his pocket. With a "twang" from the bow, the clay bullet struck the belly of the horse and burst into pieces.

The horse gave a long neigh and kicked up its front hooves, tossing Li Yi to the ground. The two muscular servants rushed forward. One got hold of the horse and the other bent down and pinned Li Yi to the ground. Moments later, the horse spun around and fled like a blast of wind.

Semi-conscious, Li Yi heard the man in yellow shout, "Li Shilang is here!" Li Yi was then hauled off the back of the horse, and he heard the man in yellow say, "Lock the door of the cart!

被放下馬來，又聽得黃衫客吩咐：『把車門鎖上！留個人在這裏看着！』

這一陣喧嚷，自然驚了小玉，她身體虛弱，嚇得冷汗淋漓，『快看看去！出了甚麼亂子？』她的聲音都是發抖的。

浣沙和桂子結伴走了出來，一看庭中男子的背影，桂子眼尖，疑惑地說：『像是李十郎！』

『見鬼！啊──，』浣沙改口了，『怕真是的！』她試着高喊一聲：『十郎！』

李益一驚，定定神回過身來，看見浣沙和桂子，勉強點一點頭，『是我！妳家小娘子呢？』

『多虧你還記得小娘子……。』

性情平和的桂子，搶着打斷了她的話：『浣沙，妳快去告訴小娘子。我來接待十郎！』

浣沙也會意了，想一想，好不容易喜從天降，且讓他們先見了面再說。有多少委屈，反正以後總有跟他的算帳的日子，不必忙在一時。

『小娘子，妳猜是誰來了？』

『誰？』小玉細看了看浣沙的臉色，忽然雙眼睜得極大，又驚又喜地問：『是十郎？』

『可不是！』浣沙如釋重負似地說：『我的老天爺！朝思暮想，可總算盼着了！』

小玉再顧不得跟浣沙說話，匆匆出了臥房，三腳併作兩步，往前廳走去。但走不了幾步，便氣喘心跳，不能不停下來。

One of you should stay here and keep watch on him."

These sounds were naturally distracting to Xiaoyu, who was very weak. Thoroughly frightened, she said to her maids, "Go and see what happened! Something terrible has happened!"

Huansha and Guizi went out together. When the sharp-eyed Guizi saw there was a middle-aged man in the courtyard, she said, "That looks like Li Shilang!"

"You must be kidding! Oh, no ...," Huansha said, "Why, yes, it's him!" She raised her voice and shouted, "Shilang!"

Though thoroughly shaken, Li Yi composed himself and turned to see who it was. When he saw Huansha and Guizi, he nodded, "Yes, it's me all right! Where's your lady?"

"So you haven't forgotten my lady ..."

Gentle-tempered Guizi cut in, "Huansha, go tell our lady that Shilang is here. I'll take care of him."

Huansha got the message and thought to herself: it had taken a great deal of effort to get Shilang here, let the two lovers be alone for a while now. No matter how many accounts remained unsettled, there was plenty of time for this in the future, and no need to sort them all out at once.

"Lady, guess who's here?"

"Who?" Xiaoyu noted Huansha's expression, and suddenly opened her eyes wide and asked, "Is it Shilang?"

"Yes, it's him!" Huansha said, greatly relieved. "Good heavens! You've been thinking of him day and night and now he's here at last!"

Xiaoyu paid no further attention to Huansha, rushed out of the bedroom and quickly made her way to the front hall. But after taking just a few steps, she started to pant and had to stop to catch

　　浣沙趕到她身邊，一看她這神氣，自然有所警惕；心裏深深懊悔，不該忙着通報，該先跟李益把話說明白了，才比較妥當。此刻卻是來不及了，祇好先把她的癡心，點一點破，讓她心理上有個準備，才不會發生意外。

　　於是，她以低沉而認眞的聲音說道：『小娘子，十郎今非昔比了。今日之來，意不可測，小娘子須作最壞的打算。』

　　『如何叫做「最壞的打算」？』

　　『須防他，翻臉無情。』

　　『不會的。』小玉停了停，緩過氣來又說：『既然今日肯來，自然還念舊情。』

　　說完，她又往前走了。將出廳門，忽然畏縮；幾近三年的刻骨相思，到底會落得怎麼樣的一個收緣結果？這以性命作孤注的一場賭博，到了揭曉謎底的一刻，她卻不敢看了。

　　『怎麼？小娘子？』

　　『我怕！』小玉撫着胸口說。

　　『怕？』浣沙心想，越是這樣，越容易讓李益欺負，便即答道：『別怕，可也別生氣！妳祇看他怎麼說。』

　　他會怎麼說呢？自然是解釋、致歉、以及向她商量今後的日子。三年的日子，隻字全無，定然另有一番她所意料不到的苦衷，倒眞要聽聽他怎麼說？

　　就這樣想着，冷不防裏面桂子已打起了門簾；第一眼就看到穿

her breath.

Huansha quickly went to her side and was naturally alarmed at the state of her health. She regretted having notified Xiaoyu so brashly. It would have been more proper to tell Li Yi about her condition before they met. Now it was too late; all she could do was to try to diffuse her infatuation somewhat, and prepare her mentally for anything untoward.

So in a solemn voice, she said, "My lady, Shilang isn't his same old self, and it's anybody's guess why he has come. My lady, you should prepare for the worst."

"What do you mean by 'prepare for the worst'?"

"You should be prepared for anything. He might turn a cold shoulder to you."

"No, he wouldn't do that." Xiaoyu paused, caught her breath and continued, "The fact that he came here today means that he still loves me as before."

When she finished speaking, she headed for the front door. But just as she was about to leave the sitting room, she suddenly stopped in her track. How would things turn out after a three-year-long bout of lovesickness? At this moment, she couldn't bear to confront the outcome of her gamble with her own life.

"What's the matter, my lady?"

"I'm scared." Xiaoyu rubbed her chest nervously.

"Scared?" Huansha thought to herself: the more Xiaoyu behaves like this, the easier it will be for Li Yi to gain the upper hand. So she said, "Don't be scared, and by all means don't get angry. Wait and see what he says to you."

What would he say to her? Naturally, there would be plenty of excuses, apologies, and questions about their future life together. For three whole years, she had not heard from him once. He must have suffered in ways she could hardly imagine. She really had to hear what he had to say to her.

At this moment, Guizi suddenly raised the door curtain. Xiaoyu's eyes fell instantly upon Li Yi, clad in brand-new spring

着簇新春服的李益，四目相視，渾疑夢中；他那較別時來得豐腴的臉上，是她想像得到的愧歉之色，祇有十分之三；是她想像不到的慍怒怨厭的神情，卻有十分之七。

盼望了多少日子，一見面所看到的竟是這樣一張臉！小玉透骨一陣冰涼，兩眼發黑，幾乎支持不住。

『小玉，妳，妳好？』李益勉強說了這一句，站起身來，退在一邊。

這好像是禮貌，其實是疏遠了。小玉明白，浣沙和桂子也明白。

『你好，十郎！』小玉扶着門框，吃力地說，『想來你是真好。比從前胖了！』她不自覺抬手摸着自己的臉，稜稜角角，盡是骨頭；相形之下，把壓抑已久的哀怨，一下子都挑了起來，『我———，』她強忍着眼淚，但改不去話中的哭音：『我可是瘦了。你看我，瘦得這樣子。』

李益木然無語。他知道她是為他瘦損的，但他也知道承認了這個事實，便有責任，便有麻煩——做了兩年撈過大把的錢的官，他已學會了緊要關頭狠一狠心，挺了過去的秘訣；『哼！』他在心裏冷笑：『你們弄這詭計，把我騙了來；打量我會聽你們的擺佈？那叫做夢！』於是，他微微仰臉，冷漠的視線，落向小玉的上方。

冷眼傍觀的浣沙，簡直把肺都要氣炸了！然而為來為去為的是小玉，今日之下，無論如何要把局面挽救過來，第一步要把它由冷變熱，這便得學一學鮑十一娘的手段了。

『唷！』她作個打趣的姿態，『三年不見，倒真像是生疏了！來，來，小娘子，妳先坐了，聽十郎慢慢兒說。』她扶了小玉坐下，

gown. When their eyes met, it was like a dream. His face, which was fuller than when they had last met, had only a small portion of the resentment she expected to see there, while the rest was anger and contempt.

After so much longing, an angry face! Xiaoyu felt a wave of chill in her bones. She began to lose consciousness and nearly blacked out.

"Xiaoyu, how … how are you?" Li Yi greeted her with some reluctance, stood up and stepped to one side.

His politeness was in fact simply estrangement. Xiaoyu sensed it, as did Huansha and Guizi.

"And how are you, Shilang?" Supporting herself against the doorway, Xiaoyu spoke with an effort. "You look fine. You've put on weight!"

She subconsciously raised her hand and touched her bony face. The contrast aroused her long-suppressed grievances. "I …," she held back her tears but couldn't conceal the sorrow in her voice. "I've lost weight. Just look how thin I am."

Li Yi said nothing. He knew that she had grown thin because of him. But he also knew that if he admitted this, he would have to bear the responsibility for it. During his two years of office when he had amassed a great fortune, he had learned to stand firm at critical moments. "So," he said to himself, "you want to trap me and get me to do what you want. You're daydreaming!" He looked up and cast a cold and indifferent glance at the empty space above Xiaoyu.

Huansha, who had been looking on indifferently, grew so furious at this moment that her lungs felt they were about to burst. But for Xiaoyu's sake, she had to keep the situation under control. The first step was to create a more cordial atmosphere, following the example of Eleventh Lady Bao.

Huansha made a teasing gesture and said, "Your three-year separation seems to have estranged both of you. Come, come, my lady, sit down and listen to what Shilang has to tell you." She

又去拉李益的手，『十郎，你也請坐。不忙，有的是從容細談的功夫；三年間，多少事，一時不知從何說起。是不是？十郎，你請放心！小娘子知道你有不得已的苦衷，做了官，又有白髮老娘在堂，自然身不由主；這些，小娘子無不體諒的。往後若有難處，既是同枕共衾的人，都可以商量；十郎，你祇想一想，小娘子一片心都在你身上──。』說到這裏，有些接不下去了，她便使個眼色，呶一呶嘴，暗示他去陪個笑臉，說幾句好話，而猶恐他不明白，特別再補了一句：『十郎，你是絕頂聰明的人，女兒家的心，摸得最熟，不必我再廢話了。』

默默聽着的小玉，覺得浣沙的話，句句打入心坎，越發覺得心血如沸；同時又想到她平時祇提起李益，便橫眉瞪眼，從無好臉嘴，而眞的見了他，卻是綢繆宛轉，曲盡衛護，可知她是爲別人受了多大的委屈？這對於浣沙的感激，加上她自己的委屈，併作一副翻江倒海的眼淚，嗚咽不止。

而李益卻又是一種想法，『眞好做作！』他在心裏說；同時又想：這盤帳不能細算了，算起來還不清。且讓她開個價，再作計較。

於是，他說：『事與願違，就如妳所說的，「一時不知從何說起？」既然妳家小娘子完全體諒，自然最好。別的也不用說了，祇說，要我怎麼樣吧？』

一聽這話，小玉哭得更厲害，浣沙卻是火氣直冒，忍了又忍，

helped Xiaoyu to her seat and, grasping Li Yi's hand, she said, "Shilang, you be seated too. There's no hurry. We've got plenty of time to talk. So many things have happened the last three years that I don't know where to begin. Isn't that so? Shilang, don't worry! My lady knows that you have been through hard times. You're an official now and with your mother to look after, you naturally can't do whatever you please. My lady understands all of this. From now on, if you have any difficulties, you can sort them out with her like a husband and wife. Shilang, just think about it, my lady is totally devoted to you ..." At this point, she found it hard to go on, so she winked at Li Yi and pouted her lips, indicating to him to smile at Xiaoyu or say something to please her. Somewhat worried that he might not get the message, she added, "Shilang, you're a clever man. You know only too well what a lady likes. There's no need for me to beat around the bush."

Xiaoyu, who had listened to all of this in silence, felt every one of Huansha's words cut deeply into her heart, and she was overwhelmed. At the same time, she could appreciate the way that Huansha, who would curse and shout at the mere mention of Li Yi, was now tactfully dealing with the situation in order to protect her; Huansha had buried her grudge against him for her own sake. Her gratitude towards Huansha and the sufferings she herself had experienced brought tears to her eyes and she sobbed without restraint.

But Li Yi saw the entire matter in a different light. "How pretentious!" he said to himself. Settling accounts now would be difficult, and only make things more complicated. Let her make an offer first and see.

So he said, "Things have gone contrary to my wishes. Just as you said, 'I don't know where to begin.' Since your lady fully understands the situation, then nothing more needs to be said. Simply tell me what you want from me."

These words made Xiaoyu cry even harder. Huansha was very angry. She tried to control herself but she was so enraged that

還是氣得說不出話，倒是平靜的桂子，答了句很着力的話：『弄到這步田地，該十郎拿句話來。怎麼倒問起別人要怎麼樣呢？』

『是啊！』情緒略略平定了的浣沙接口也說，『你總有了個計較，才會來此。不然，你來幹甚麼？』

『並不是我自己要來的。』李益脫口相答。

此話一出，連小玉都駭異地住了哭聲：『這話倒要說清楚。』她轉臉問浣沙：『是妳託崔郎把他硬請了來的？』

『沒有啊！崔郎不是到洛陽去了？』

『那麼……。』

一句話沒有完，祇聽車門『呀』地一聲打開，人聲喧嘩；小玉禁不得一點嚇，頓時停住，慌張地望着窗外。

窗外車門邊站着個不相識的男子；門外正有四名壯漢，抬着兩個大食盒進來；殿後的是個小胡奴，手捧一具粉定窰的大花瓶，瓶中插一叢初放的牡丹，魏紫姚黃，艷麗非凡；長安買牡丹，論朵計值，這一叢約摸三十朵，論時價，可抵得三、五戶中人之家的賦稅。

浣沙不明白是怎麼回事，搶先迎了出去，大聲問道：『喂，喂！怎的亂闖？』

抬食盒的壯漢遲疑地止了步，看着那小胡奴；而那十一、二歲的醜孩子，卻是出奇地老練：『沒有錯兒！』他大模大樣地吩咐那四個壯漢，『抬進去，擺出來！』

食盒抬到廳上，極其精緻的四乾果、八酒餚，又是八大盤蒸膾燒炙的飯菜，外加一大壺京城名酒『蝦蟆陵』和一籠白麵蒸餅，擺滿了几案。

words failed her. And so it was the calm Guizi who confronted him boldly, "At this point, it's you who should have something to say."

"Indeed!" Huansha, having calmed herself down somewhat, cut in, "You must have had something on your mind before coming here. Otherwise, why did you come?"

"I never want to come here in the first place," Li Yi answered off-handedly.

Xiaoyu was so shaken by this that she stopped crying and said, "You better make this absolutely clear." Then she turned to Huansha, "Was it you who got Li Yi here with Mr Cui's help?"

"No, I didn't! Didn't Mr Cui go to Luoyang?"

"Then …"

Before she could finish speaking, they heard the sound of a cart door opening, and a lot of bustling. Frightened, Xiaoyu looked out the window.

She saw a stranger standing beside the door of a cart, and four husky men carrying food containers. To the rear was a Tartar servant carrying a large white Ding-ware vase containing a bouquet of half-opened peonies. The purple and yellow flowers were dazzling. Peonies in Chang'an were sold by the bud. This bouquet consisted of about thirty bunches, the total cost of which was equal to the annual taxes paid by three to five average households.

Huansha didn't know what was happening. She ran outside and shouted, "Hey, who says you can come in without asking?"

The men carrying the food containers hesitated and glanced at the Tartar servant. But that ugly eleven-year-old boy was extremely tactful. "Everything's all right!" He then instructed the four men with a swagger, "Carry them inside and set them out!"

The food containers were carried into the sitting room and spread out on all the tables. There were four kinds of exquisite dried fruit, eight appetizers, eight main courses, a jug of "Frog Hill", a famous wine from the capital, and a steamer full of wheat buns.

　　最後，那小胡奴把一瓶牡丹也放了下來，朝上作個揖，有板有眼地說道：『我家主人，虔祝李十郎和霍小娘子，重修舊好，白首同心。祇是薄酒粗餚，不成敬意，請十郎和小娘子寬飲一杯！』

　　那李益嘿嘿冷笑，小玉和桂子茫然不知所措，祇有浣沙問道：『你家主人尊姓？』

　　小胡奴翻一翻眼，答非所問地說：『妳可就是浣沙？』

　　『是啊。』

　　『是浣沙就該知道我家主人。』

　　『小郎！』浣沙越發困惑了，『你的話說得叫人不懂！』

　　『妳不懂，我可懂。何苦做作不休？』李益冷冷插言，又轉臉對小胡奴說：『你回去告訴那穿黃衣服的，他的手段我領教了。』

　　一提『穿黃衣服的』，浣沙陡然記起去年年底在侯景先寄附舖櫃房中所見的黃衫客；再回想李益進門之前的那一陣喧嚷，恍然大悟！心中稱快，臉上便有了笑意，『小郎！』她親熱地執着小胡奴的手說：『請你回去，說我浣沙拜上黃衫大爺：若是蒼天有眼，改日李十郎和我家小娘子，雙雙來叩謝黃衫大爺成全的恩德。』說完，又叫桂子取一貫錢作腳力，把那抬食盒的壯漢，一起打發走了。

　　面對着一席盛饌，在小玉卻是觸目成愁；事有蹊蹺，不問可知。但不管如何，祇看李益那如凝寒霜的臉色，把她那顆不知碎了多少次的心，凍結得無復一絲熱氣生趣。原來她是靠回憶，靠強自編織的美夢支持下去的，而此刻，回憶和美夢都消失了。腦中空空地，祇覺得天旋地轉，此身無主；眼前的一切皆不甚分明，唯一能把握

Finally, the Tartar servant put down the vase of peonies, bowed to heaven and said in a measured voice, "My master sincerely celebrates the reunion of Li Shilang and Miss Huo, and wishes them a happy marriage. He offers this coarse wine and food as a token of his esteem. Shilang and Miss Huo, please raise your glasses!"

Li Yi laughed grimly. Xiaoyu and Guizi didn't know what to do. Only Huansha was able to say anything, "What's your master's name?"

The Tartar servant rolled his eyes and asked, "Are you Huansha?"

"Yes, I am."

"If so, then you should know my master."

"Young man, I don't follow!"

"If you don't follow, I certainly do. Why keep on pretending?" Li Yi interrupted her rudely, and then turned to the Tartar servant, "Go tell the man in yellow that I've enough of his tricks."

Huansha suddenly recalled meeting this "man in yellow" at Hou Jingxian's inn at the end of the previous year. And when she thought about the bustling noise they had heard before Li Yi came in, she suddenly realized what had happened, and a smile began to emerge on her face. "Young man," she said, grasping the Tartar's hands, "tell your master that Huansha bows to him in respect. If there is justice from heaven, Li Shilang and my lady will thank him for his kindness some day." She then asked Guizi to give a string of cash to the men who had brought in the food containers and dismissed them.

Though a banquet of rich dishes was spread out before her, Xiaoyu was miserable. It need not be said that something odd had taken place. But in any case, Li Yi's chilly expression froze her heart, a heart that had been broken many times before. In the past, she had survived on reminiscences and self-made dreams. Now, these were no more. Her mind was a blank, everything seemed topsy-turvy, and she felt totally helpless. Her vision suddenly

得住的，祇是一個意念：要弄一弄明白，他心裏究竟是怎麼想來的？

『桂子！』浣沙卻越發沉着了，平靜地囑咐：『妳把小娘子先扶進去息一息，我跟十郎有話說。』

小玉確也支持不住了，讓桂子扶着往後而去。但到了廳後，她忽又不甘於就此退避，隱在屏門後面，不肯再走；桂子無奈，祇好搬一張小榻，讓她靠着休息。

廳上，浣沙和李益的交談，清晰可聞。

『十郎，今天不是你自己願意來的？』

『何必明知故問？』李益氣咻咻地答說。

『你以爲是我請那黃衫客，把你騙了來的？不是！』浣沙搖搖頭，『照我想，祇是他愛打不平，出手管這閒事而已。』

『他——黃衫客，又何以知道這段閒事？』

『那定是聽寄附舖掌櫃侯景先所說。』

『侯景先又從何得知？』

『哼！』浣沙冷笑道：『「若要人不知，除非己莫爲！」』

李益的臉色鐵靑，聲音卻出奇地冷靜：『想來是妳跟侯景先說的？』

『要拜託人家典賣釵環衣飾、治病服藥；要託人家打聽消息，盼你十郎回心轉意，自然少不得細說根由。』

『就在那寄附舖中？』

『不在那裏，又在何處？』

『恨煞我也！』李益猛然擊案，瞪着浣沙：『妳就在那人來人往的寄附舖中，信口雌黃，壞我的名聲？』

blurred, all that mattered boiled down to one thing: what was on Li Yi's mind.

"Guizi!" Huansha called to her calmly, "Take lady inside and let her take a rest. I have something to discuss with Shilang."

Xiaoyu could hardly support herself so she let Guizi help her back to her room. But when they got to the sitting room, she decided she didn't want to miss out on anything, so she hid behind a screen and refused to move. Guizi brought her a small bamboo couch and let her rest on it.

They could hear the conversation between Huansha and Li Yi in the sitting room clearly.

"Shilang, you really didn't want to come here today?"

"Why ask such a question when the answer is so obvious to you?" Li Yi replied testily.

"Do you really think that I asked the man in yellow to bring you here? Well, the answer is no." Huansha shook her head. "I imagine he stuck his nose into this matter because he likes to right injustices."

"How did ... the man in yellow learn about this matter?"

"From Hou Jingxian, the inn-keeper."

"How did Hou Jingxian find out about it then?"

"Huh!" Huansha sneered. "As the saying goes, 'If you don't want people to know what you do, don't do it!'"

Li Yi paled, but his voice remained calm, "I believe it was you who told Hou Jingxian about it."

"We needed help to sell some jewellry in order to pay the doctor and buy medicine, and we had to ask people to find out about you in the hope that you would change your mind and come back to my lady, so naturally the whole story got out."

"At the inn?"

"Where else?"

"You are impossible!" Li Yi banged the table and glared at Huansha, "So it's you who have been ruining my reputation by talking sheer nonsense at that inn where everyone and his uncle

『如何叫做信口雌黃？信誓旦旦，說八月中秋，天上人間一齊團圓，可曾團圓？將近三年，隻字全無，可是事實？』

『即有其事，又何足爲外人道？』

『好個「何足爲外人道」！十郎，這一說，你可是我家的親人囉！』

『誰是妳家的親人？』李益大聲地說，『妳那樣可惡，便是我的仇人！』

『奇了！就許你負心，別人說一說都不許？』

李益被駁得瞠目結舌，越發惱羞成怒，霍地站了起來：『妳說我負心，就負心。再無可談的了！祇是我警告妳，』他放下臉來，以縣令坐堂的聲口說：『若再捏造事實，信口誹謗；妳可記着，京兆府的戶曹參軍，是我族姪！』

浣沙大怒，正要反唇相譏，拿延先公主的名頭壓他一下；驟聽得身後急促的步履聲，回頭一看，臉色慘白得如一張紙的小玉，腳步跟蹌地正奔了出來！

『李十郎！你好猙獰的面目！』小玉捉住李益的手臂，頓足哭道：『你逼得我們一口氣不出，可是要我今天就死在你面前？可是？』小玉突變爲猙厲的神色，舉起案上的一杯酒，酹在地上，仰天喊道：『過往神靈，請聽李益的誓約！』然後斷斷續續，淒淒慘慘地，背那定情之夕，李益親筆所寫的誓約。

背不到一半，突然一陣抽搐，整個臉都歪曲了，浣沙和桂子大驚，李益更是慌張得手足發抖。就這一轉眼間，小玉的頭一歪，倒

goes?"

"What do you mean 'talking sheer nonsense'? You swore that by the Mid-Autumn Festival, you would come back to join my lady. Did you do it? Isn't it also true that for nearly three years, you didn't write to us?"

"Even so, why spread it among strangers?"

"'Spread it among strangers?' Shilang, do you mean you're one of us now?"

"Who's one of you?" Li Yi shouted. "You're disgusting. I'll settle with you someday!"

"How ridiculous! No matter how heartless you are, no one is allowed to say anything about you?"

Li Yi was so infuriated he couldn't say a word. He suddenly rose and said, "If you think I'm heartless, so be it. There's nothing more to say." He pulled a long face and spoke like a magistrate giving an order, "I want to give you a warning. If you ever tell such lies again and slander me by talking nonsense, remember that my cousin is the commander of the capital garrison!"

Huansha was about to retaliate by mentioning Princess Yanxian's name to snub him, when she heard the sound of footsteps behind her. She turned and saw Xiaoyu, her face as pale as paper, stumbled her way in.

"Shilang, how cruel can you be!"

Xiaoyu grabbed his arm and cried, stamping her feet, "You've forced me to a point where I can hardly breathe, do you want to watch me die before you today? Do you?"

Xiaoyu's face was a ghastly pale. She picked up a cup of wine from the table, poured it onto the floor and shouted to the sky, "You the gods of the past: listen to Li Yi's oath!" Then, haltingly, Xiaoyu recited the oath that Li Yi had written to her on the eve of their engagement.

Half way through, she had a sudden convulsion, which distorted her entire face. Huansha and Guizi were shocked, and Li Yi was so terrified that his hands and feet began to shake. Then

在李益胸前，雙手垂落，嗆啷一聲，酒杯掉在地上，打得粉碎。

『小娘子，小娘子！』桂子一面喊，一面放聲大哭。

『別哭！』浣沙惡狠狠地叱斥着；上前扶住小玉的屍體，對李益說道：『你走吧！我們不罵你、不打你；你有你白絹黑字寫下的誓約，如果變心，「神人共棄，爲厲鬼擊腦而死！」喏，』她指着小玉的可怕的臉說：『厲鬼在這裏！』

李益猛然打了個寒噤，抖動着雙腿，逃出了小玉家。

不久，李益娶了盧鬱香；但馬上傳出駭人聽聞的消息，說洞房花燭之夜，李益便拿一張漢朝的古琴，打他的新婦；原因是，他在新婦懷中搜得異性所贈的一枚斑犀鈿花盒子，裏面盛着兩粒寄相思的紅豆，和少許媚藥，而新婦果非完璧；一說，那張男相的觀世音像中，藏着一段曖昧——自然，那是莫可究詰的；但李益與岳家涉訟公庭，終於出妻，卻是事實。

又不久，李益路過二分明月的揚州，納名姬營十一娘爲妾，卻又怕她不貞，居然想出一個異想天開的防範辦法，每次出門以前，

Xiaoyu's head dropped and she fell into Li Yi's arms, her hands falling to her sides. With a crash, the wine cup fell to the floor and broke into pieces.

"Lady, lady!" Guizi shouted.

"Stop crying!" Huansha howled. She stepped forward and took Xiaoyu in her arms. "Go away!" she said to Li Yi. "We won't curse you or beat you. We have the oath you wrote on a white silk handkerchief, in which you said that if you are unfaithful to Xiaoyu, 'you'll be deserted by gods and men, and die by being struck on the head by fierce ghosts!'" She pointed at Xiaoyu's face and said, "Look, the fierce ghost is right here!"

Cold shivers ran up and down Li Yi's spine. He fled from Xiaoyu's house, his legs still trembling.

 Not long after, Li Yi married Lu Yuxiang. But then some shocking news leaked out. One story had it that on the very night of the wedding, Li Yi struck his wife with an antique zither from the Han dynasty. The reason was that he had found in the folds of her gown a rhinoceros horn box containing a pair of symbolic red beans and a small quantity of aphrodisiac powder that must have been given to her by a former lover; and he discovered as well that she was not a virgin. Another story had it that a rather dubious affair was somehow related to the painting of the Goddess of Mercy with a male face, but the source of this tale was beyond investigation. One fact was certain: Li Yi and his parents-in-law were involved in a lawsuit which ended up in divorce.

Shortly afterwards, Li Yi passed through Yangzhou, and took Eleventh Lady Ying, a famous courtesan, to be his concubine. To prevent her from being unfaithful to him, he devised a rather

把營十一娘用澡盆覆扣在床上，外加封識；回家以後，要細細檢點了才放她出來。營十一娘不堪這樣的虐待，終於引劍自殺。

從此，李益的妬名，大於他的詩名。每到一處，人人以異樣的眼光看着他；這叫他十分頭痛——厲鬼擊腦了！他常常這樣在疑惑。

怕眞的是霍小玉化作厲鬼擊過他的腦；因爲他的行爲，證明他的頭腦是有毛病的！

bizarre method. Whenever he left town on business, he would put her on the bed, cover her with a bathtub, and seal the edges with paper stripes. When he returned, he would check the stripes carefully before releasing her. Unable to bear such torture, she committed suicide with a sword.

From then on, Li Yi was better known more for his jealousy than for his poetic talents. Wherever he went, people would give him strange looks, which he found most disturbing. That wicked ghost is attacking my brain! — he was always under this suspicion.

Perhaps Xiaoyu had actually turned into a wicked ghost, and was indeed attacking his brain, for everything he did only goes to prove that he was truly insane.